Praise for

DEATH OF A GARDEN PEST

"Gardening and murder make a fascinating combination in *Death of a Garden Pest.* Gardener sleuth Louise Eldridge offers an enchanting view of gardens while facing down dauntingly evil opponents."
—Carolyn G. Hart

"A good lighthearted diversion from summer weeding and deadheading."
—*The Plain Dealer,* Cleveland

"Ripley tells her gripping tale in engaging, down-to-earth prose, interjecting bits of gardening advice."
—*Publishers Weekly*

"Informative and fun."
—*Kirkus Reviews*

"Ripley's follow-up to *Mulch* will tempt gardening buffs seeking a mystery enhanced by plenty of tantalizing garden details. . . . Readers drawn in by the 'green' story line will not be disappointed as intrigue surrounding the murderer's identity unravels."
—*Booklist*

"This hybrid of traditional whodunit and up-to-the-minute gardening guide is certain to appeal to mystery readers with a green thumb."
—*The Denver Post*

Other Gardening Mysteries
by Ann Ripley

DEATH OF A GARDEN PEST

and coming soon in hardcover
DEATH OF A POLITICAL PLANT

Mulch

Ann Ripley

BANTAM BOOKS
NEW YORK • TORONTO • LONDON • SYDNEY • AUCKLAND

MULCH

A Bantam Book / Published by arrangement with the author.

PUBLISHING HISTORY

St. Martin's Press edition published June 1994

Bantam revised paperback edition / January 1998

Interior art by Joanna Roy.

ISBN 0-553-57734-4

Published simultaneously in the United States and Canada

Bantam Books are published by Bantam Books, a division of Bantam Doubleday Dell Publishing Group, Inc. Its trademark, consisting of the words "Bantam Books" and the portrayal of a rooster, is Registered in U.S. Patent and Trademark Office and in other countries. Marca Registrada. Bantam Books, 1540 Broadway, New York, New York 10036.

PRINTED IN THE UNITED STATES OF AMERICA

OPM 10 9 8 7 6 5 4 3 2 1

TO TONY AND THE GIRLS

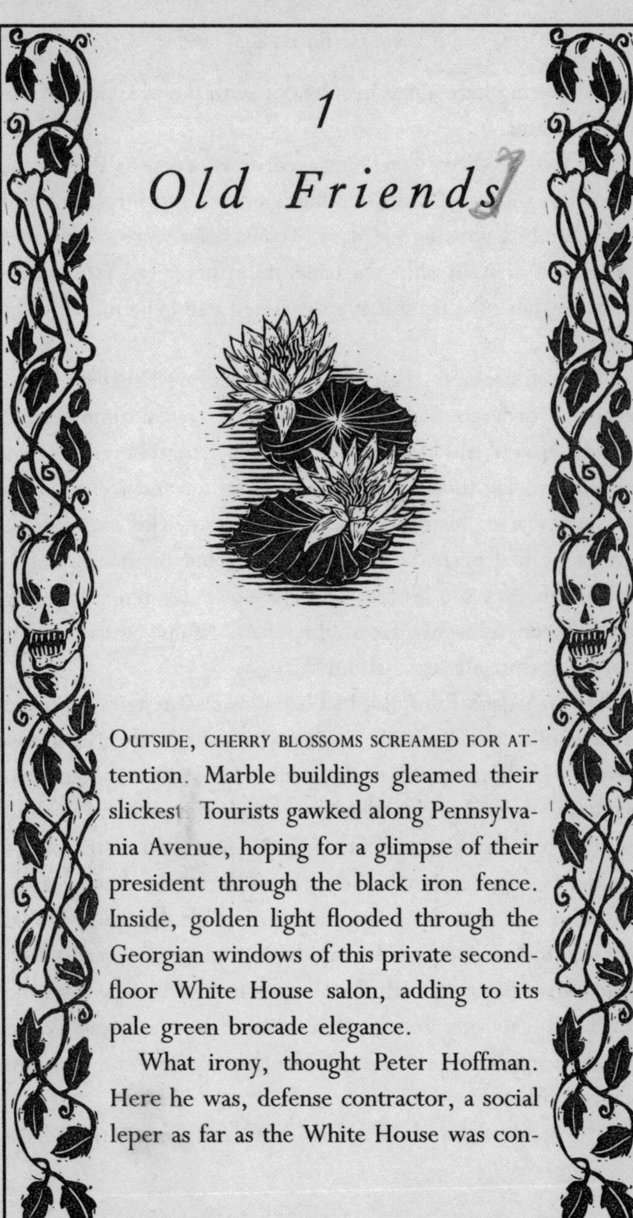

1
Old Friends

OUTSIDE, CHERRY BLOSSOMS SCREAMED FOR ATtention. Marble buildings gleamed their slickest. Tourists gawked along Pennsylvania Avenue, hoping for a glimpse of their president through the black iron fence. Inside, golden light flooded through the Georgian windows of this private second-floor White House salon, adding to its pale green brocade elegance.

What irony, thought Peter Hoffman. Here he was, defense contractor, a social leper as far as the White House was concerned, sitting here alone in splendor with the president of the United States.

The two of them were hunkered down deep in the room, out of the sphere of those terrific windows and into the thrall of the fire in a glowing fireplace. Their chairs were situated on either side of it. A slim tea table stood between. Obviously, this was where the president entertained guests he didn't want seen.

To his amusement, Peter had just discovered that the chief executive ordered the fire to be lighted both summer and winter. Nixon had done that, too, he remembered. Not a good omen. He took a sip of coffee from a translucent teacup and peered over his glasses at the president. The man was as trim as he had been thirty years before, but his hair was too tan and his eyes too blue to be believed. Peter bullied his big fingers through his own faded blond hair. *He'd* aged too, but at least he wasn't afraid to admit it.

This man, Jack Fairchild, had been his classmate at MIT and a fellow officer in Vietnam. A guy who was always a little too in love with himself and at the same time a little too anxious to please—by today's standards, *born* to be president. Fairchild had ignored Peter's existence for the first two years of his presidency—pretended he didn't know about the damage control Peter had done long ago, the dirty work that had enabled Fairchild to become president in the first place. Peter could do his lucrative business with the Department of Defense, but he didn't rate socially for anything more than a large White House reception where the president shook his hand and two hundred others.

But President Fairchild needed him now. Peter tipped his

head back and chuckled. It was a raucous noise but muffled by the thick orientals.

The president gave him a curious look. Then he decided to smile. "I know why you're laughing."

"You do? Why? I don't even know myself."

"You think it's incredible that the guy you did time with in 'Nam is sitting in the White House, running the country. . . ."

Peter grinned. "Neatest trick is that nobody has discovered exactly what you *did* in the service."

The president waved his hand airily. "That's all been hashed over endlessly. 'Army intelligence.' The voting public accepts that, just like they accept any military record; Kennedy and his story, George Bush and the way he was shot down . . . no one questions it any more . . . it's part of history." His optically enhanced blue eyes were guileless as he looked straight at Peter.

"Ah, but who do you think tidied up our little part of that history—"

The president put his hands up like a barrier, as if the words were fatal germs he might catch. "Just don't tell me, Peter. I know we closed off normal human sympathy back then, so that we could do the most appalling things. Kill, so casually, with a piece of piano wire, or a quick thrust of a blade. In the years since, I've regretted it, but that was for our *country,* for God's sake. You and your extracurricular activities—I don't want to know about them."

"The records all cleansed—" continued Peter in his penetrating voice.

"No, I can't listen. Don't make me regret bringing you

here." Fairchild stared at him, his lips pursed into a stubborn line.

Peter leaned back and put his hands up in a gesture of surrender. "Okay, let's forget all that. It's only sensible for a man in your place—'Hear no evil' and 'see no evil,' at the very least." He cast a glance around the elegant room. "You have a lot to lose. It's very, very nice here, Jack. Just take this parlor by itself—I've heard it's the best fuckin' room in the whole fuckin' White House."

The president, unsettled by the references to the old days, brightened immediately when Peter broke the code of politeness and inserted crude language into the conversation. He had seen it before with Army vets, Pentagon types, and tight-ass politicians. They could hardly get the doors closed fast enough before they made every other word a profanity.

"It's partly the light—it transforms the place." He leaned toward Peter. "But I don't give a goddamn about the trappings, Pete. We just live here. It's interesting for my wife and children. But unreal—people always listenin' and lookin' in at your lives—not a fuckin' thing you can do that someone isn't lookin' at, writin' about, and then blattin' about on the evening news."

Peter leaned his large frame farther back in the Louis Quinze chair and crossed his long legs at the ankle, his heels anchored comfortably in the silk oriental. He was beginning to feel at home. The president was happy he was here; he was sliding right back into the vernacular of the boys.

Peter took his middle finger and shoved his gradient density bifocals up to their proper place on his hawk nose. "Okay now,'' he said, ''let's have it; you want something from me. What do you want?''

The president sighed deeply. ''Well, we're already your chief customer for your latest weapons. And what weapons they are . . . that new artillery piece. Cheap. Easy to manufacture. Deadly. And now the laser stuff; it's exactly the kind of thing we've needed, in this world filled with little wars.''

''I can say without bragging that it takes a special mind to invent weapons like that.''

The president straightened, his cup perched on his knee, and his voice grew serious. ''Pete, I need more than weapons from you, I'm in a delicate political situation.'' He waved as if batting away a large insect with the back of his hand. ''It's not bad enough that the world is unstable; forces in this country are clashing like armies in the night. It's scary. We don't know who'll go down. What do I want from you? I want you on my team. Specifically, I want you in Defense. You're on the cutting edge in weapons. And you're convincing as hell. I *need* you in there to stanch the bloodletting by the secretary of defense.''

Peter said in a level tone, ''You want me to keep the fucker straight.''

The president nodded. ''That's it, exactly. As you know, he's too dovish. He's causing me a shitload of trouble: constant public undermining of what *I* and every other reasonable man think our defense posture should be. For Chrissake, pretty soon we won't be able to take *Grenada* if it gives us trouble. Problem is, the focus groups split on this—actually, sometimes even tip *his* way.'' His voice rose querulously. ''Tell me, from what you know, am I right or aren't I?''

Peter nodded. "Not what the country needs right now. Why don't you can his ass?"

"Can't." The president frowned and scratched his thick, carefully dyed hair. "Too many negatives right now . . . those scandals in the EPA. A president can't have too much turmoil at one time." His voice lowered several notes. "Hell, it could even affect my getting nominated next year." He shook his head slowly. "There's dogs in the manger, Pete. Y'never know how many until you enter public office."

Peter's gaze unfastened from the president and he stared into space. He had a sudden flashback to thirty years before and remembered that this man—as a young officer—was apt to swing from good humor to bad within minutes. He hadn't changed. Except now he was in charge of the whole damned country.

Now the president's voice was rising with optimism. "But you give me new hope, Pete. I'm turning to you because you can do just about anything. You can be the key to maintaining our defense in the right posture. *These* days it should be full-court press." He put up a cautionary hand. "But there's a couple of things. One is a given: You turn over your arms business to others to run and put your assets in a blind trust." He waved the matter off: "Standard procedure for everybody. The only other thing is . . ." Peter was beginning to fidget in his French chair. His back was stiff from slouching. Yet he deliberately maintained his sprawling pose. He knew what was coming, and he wasn't going to sit there like a remorseful schoolboy and take it.

"You have reservations about me."

"Pete, we went through a lot together in 'Nam."

He narrowed his eyes and looked at his old friend. "I remember every minute of it, Jack."

"Well, that was then, and this is now. But . . ." Again he looked as if he'd rather walk on hot coals than to say what he was going to say. "We have to be careful. That girl, a few years ago . . ."

"Girl. What girl?"

"The girl who drowned on that Rhine River trip. There was talk. I hope someone doesn't come across it before the confirmation hearings." He adjusted himself in the French chair. "But even if they do, the matter could be explained. What really bothers me is the here and now. We keep hearing things about . . . women. I can't emphasize it too much, Pete: We have to assure there's nothing current that might cast a shadow on your nomination. The religious right, you know."

"The religious right? Jesus! Are people still worrying about the religious right? What do they have to do with your choice of a deputy secretary of defense?"

The president looked incredulously at him. "I forgot. You're totally apolitical. You haven't changed a bit."

"Well, not entirely," said Peter with a smile.

"You mean you watch the TV news, and read the *Times* and *Post.* 'Fraid that doesn't cut it, Pete. Let me explain."

Casting a wary eye about the chamber as if searching out hidden listeners, the president said in a low voice, "The fuckin' religious right has half the small towns in America by the balls . . . don't you realize that?" With a clatter he set his cup into its saucer. His voice was still low.

"Pete, goddamn it, they're drivin' me from the right *and*

the left, just like they're driving every other politician. It's crazy—there's no middle any more! And there's no money. But worst of all, there's no fuckin' *middle*!'' He looked at Peter, who looked back without expression.

''Don't worry about things so much, Jack. To answer your concerns, the woman on that Rhine River trip died accidentally; there was even a formal investigation by the German police.'' He reached over to the table and grabbed a cookie and took a large bite. Buttery crumbs spilled on his brown Harris tweed as he munched. ''As for the here and now, didn't you know that I'm a proper married man?'' He waved the fragment of undevoured cookie at President Fairchild. ''Married for three years, no children, big designer house near Alexandria in a funky little subdivision called Sylvan Valley. It's real normal for Washington: filled with bureaucrats workin' late and intellectuals workin' early.'' Using the cookie fragment as a pointer, he indicated a tan folder lying on the tea table. ''You know all that: It's all in there. Above reproach. Not a thing on me.'' He gobbled the rest of the cookie.

''Forgive me, Pete, I didn't even want to bring it up,'' said the president, his voice swollen with apology. ''I need you. I want you confirmed. Together, we'll bust his balls.''

''The secretary's.''

''Yeah,'' said the president.

''Hey,'' said Peter, casually, ''we'll do it.''

The men rose, Peter standing in close and, at six feet four, looking down on the commander in chief. President Fairchild said, ''There's no friend like an old friend. And you and I go way back. We saved each other's lives.''

''We saved each other's asses, too, as I recall.''

The president chose to ignore the remark. His savoir faire had returned. His voice had resumed its strong, velvety pitch. "We're going to make a great team. We're going to show 'em how a country can be strong *and* solvent at the same time." He extended an enthusiastic hand toward Peter.

Peter took the hand in a viselike grip and said, "We'll cut your defense secretary off at the knees." Jack Fairchild's eyes glistened with admiration.

Then Peter released the pressure on the president's hand and looked at his watch. A woman was waiting for him in Georgetown. At the thought he felt a pull through his body that only took a millisecond to focus in his groin. There were all those goddamn cherry blossoms out there, too. It was ridiculous for a man like himself, but he almost felt like he was in love.

2
Moving In

"YOU MEAN WE'RE LOST?" JANIE ASKED.

Louise clutched the steering wheel as if it were a life buoy. "I could have sworn it was *this* cul-de-sac. But it's not. Darn! Why did I leave that neighborhood map at the motel?"

"Map, my foot, why did you leave *Dad* in the motel? I bet he knows—"

"Look," Louise snapped at the fifteen-year-old beside her, "he couldn't help it; he had a meeting with his new boss in Washington. You heard him say that."

"Okay, Ma, sorry. Don't freak out—we can find it. Too bad your air-conditioning doesn't work."

"Isn't it," muttered Louise. As if for verification she fiddled again with the unresponsive controls on the dashboard of her seven-year-old Honda station wagon. She could feel the sweat in the armpits of her dress, a dress she picked up from the young people's department sales rack meant for Janie or Martha. When they both rejected it, Louise decided to keep it for herself. It was her color: French blue. Now the dress was riding up stiffly in folds like a Roman shade, so that her bare thighs felt as if they were glued to the vinyl seat cover. In contrast, Janie slouched comfortably, her long legs in faded cutoffs waggling steadily like an accordion.

She was lost. Couldn't even find her new house. This must be what they called hitting the bottom. How many times had they moved? Overseas twice. Back twice. From one foreign post to another, twice. From one domestic post to another, once. So here she was, forty-two, attractive, jobless, having masterminded another move to another town—the third time to this one—having sent Martha, her firstborn, to Chicago to start college, having said good-bye to friends, to her garden club, to her minister. Having stopped the phone, gas, electricity, papers in the house in New York, and ordered them up in the new home in Fairfax County. Having filled out scores of postcards telling people their change of address. Each process cutting a little at the roots they had established in their old town, until all the roots were severed. But now not having enough brains to find her new house! That was because Bill had done all the driving on their two visits to the house when they bought it back in May.

That in itself was strange: making one of life's biggest purchases after one or two quick looks. But at least they owned a house. For years they lived in government housing overseas or rented places in the States.

Bill had navigated while oblivious to street signs and landmarks, she had just sat and gushed over the scenery—excited as a child about living in the Virginia woods.

Tears sprang to Louise's eyes. She felt like stopping the car and having a good cry. Instead, she stiffened her spine against the seat, whipped the wheel around, and sped out of the nameless cul-de-sac.

"All riiight," said Janie, admiring the move. Her long blond hair blew in the unaccustomed breeze. After a moment she said, "Y'know, Ma, these woods make the roads seem like canyons, just like Milton said."

"Milton who?" asked Louise absentmindedly as she drove.

"Really, Ma. 'In this dark canyon of our souls,' something, something, something. I had it last fall in English."

"They do look like dark canyons, don't they? But Sylvan Valley is a wonderful place—modular homes with lots of glass, and the developers, for a change, didn't cut down the trees. Interesting people are supposed to live here, too. I bet you'll like it. And it's not too far from Bethesda, where you still have friends."

Janie agreed grudgingly. "Maybe it's not that bad. Just creepy and ominous, that's all. And the street signs are hidden behind trees." She waved a thin arm out the window as tribute to the greenery and declaimed in a ponderous Carl Sagan voice, "Billions and billions of trees." Then, in her normal voice: "And all those weird buzzing sounds . . ."

''Cicadas. You'll get used to them.''

''But I still think Dad should be here when we move into our seventh house.''

Louise smiled faintly. ''Seventh house. That's right, I guess.''

Despite the smile, she felt sad. Moving represented advancement for Bill: the next challenge as a deep-cover CIA agent. But so ironic. No one could share those glory moments with them, because he was a spy. The overseas posts, interspersed with assignments to the NSC, the UN, and now the State Department: Each was another step up the ladder. Someday, she thought wistfully, he might climb up into the light.

For Louise, moving was like having a tooth pulled without novocaine: the sharp loss of familiar people and familiar places. Not that she didn't bring it off gracefully. As a foreign service wife, it was expected of her.

Janie was warming to her subject. ''And you bought a new house and you can't find it. You know the moving truck is there by now. Boy, I can see it all now. They'll be big guys—they're always big guys with sweaty armpits.'' She was waving her arms now, her knees still waggling. ''I can see them all standing around, and really mad at us because we aren't there to tell them what to do with the stuff. And they're just standing there.'' She looked over at her mother to see what effect she was having. ''*Probably* in the sun, and the temperature is about two hundred—and all they really want is booze. They're living for the end of the day, when Dad'll give them those beers you bought, and maybe some of the whiskey that you packed—because you guys will be so grateful they didn't break any of your little knickknacks . . . your little glass menageries of things.'' Janie darted another glance at her mother. Their eyes met.

The sweat now dripped down Louise's cheek, the one that faced the 95-degree Virginia morning. She said, ''Janie, I have a great reservoir of affection for you, built up over the years. Let's not tamper with it. I feel foolish enough without you railing at me.'' Her voice had edged up several tones. ''Now help me find the damned *house*!'' She backed viciously into a driveway and returned the way they had come down the first dark canyon. Even in their confused passage she noted that the neighborhood had a road at the crest of a high hill named after their older daughter—Martha's Lane. It gave Louise another little twinge of loss; her first baby, gone to college.

Janie had fallen silent, as children do when they know they have gone too far. Her knees were still. ''Ma, I'm sorry I gave you a hard time. I'll help you find the house. But first, let's make a deal. We're in a new place; call me Jane, not Janie. In case you hadn't noticed, I'm not a little girl any more.'' She turned plaintive blue eyes at her mother.

''Oh, sweetheart, I'm sorry.'' Louise reached over and patted her daughter's bare leg. ''I will remember. I will call you Jane. And forgive me. You know it's not easy to move again, not for any of us.''

The girl said, ''Plus it's always harder because we move when it's hot.'' She cocked her head. '' 'Course, I ought to be used to it by now. My father gets transferred and I just tag along like the caboose on a train.'' She sighed and dropped her thin shoulders. ''Martha was smart. She unbuckled her car from the train before she had to move.''

''She unbuckled her car? You mean uncoupled her car?''

"Okay," said Janie. "Uncoupled." She turned in her seat toward her mother. "Oh well, that's enough of that. So, Ma, how're we going to find the place?" She wrinkled her nose. "Dogwood Court: what a weird-sounding address. Could you have picked it just because the street's named after a tree?"

"Of course not."

"Just speculating, because I know you and *gardens*. The first thing you're going to do after you move in is rip up the entire yard and make it all over your way."

Louise sighed. "Right now, the point's moot, since we can't find the house. I would ask somebody, but it's so humiliating. If everything in this neighborhood didn't look the same, we wouldn't be having this trouble. Our house is tan stain with white trim. It's one story, just like that one." She pointed to a flat-roofed house barely showing through the trees. "As opposed to that two-story type there that is like a house of glass. Isn't it pretty? And it's somewhere right near that big hill we're just coming to again."

"How about trees?" Janie asked slyly. "Does it have any distinguishing trees?"

"Oh, how *smart* of you—that's it! On the corner is a house with a gnarled old tree, a dogwood, I think. I noticed it because it needs a good feeding and pruning. That's where we turn!"

"There," said Janie, pointing ahead. "Is that what you call a gnarled old tree?"

"Yes, yes, yes, oh God, *yes*!" cried Louise.

As they approached they could see a giant blue van tucked into the shady reaches of the cul-de-sac. Four big men sat casually on the ramp near its open doors. Louise coasted in alongside its long, steel expanse and parked in front of it. The van. The van with their beds. Their chairs. Their antique loveseats. Their excess of books. Their files. Their fossil rocks. Their family photos. All the appendages that had safely crossed state and international borders, oceans, seas. Ready to be set up again in a new place by the resident homemaker.

Janie had the car door half open when she turned to Louise. "Mother. One more thing." She only called her Mother when she wished to clothe one of her overarching criticisms with respect. "I don't mean to be rude or anything, but Dad would never have got us lost like that."

Louise removed the key from the ignition and turned to look squarely at her daughter. The youthful dress had given up the fight and submissively turned with her. Louise reflected what a beautiful girl Janie was. Expressive eyes large and blue like her father's, but with dark lashes and eyebrows like Louise's. Long, tawny hair. A figure just ready to bud. So why did she feel like giving her a good slap in the face?

Janie leaned over and kissed Louise on the cheek, resting a gentle arm around her mother's neck like a softly placed garland. "On the other hand, Ma, you're fun to be with, and don't forget that. Some mothers are really boring." She was gone from the car and sauntering over to the movers. "Hi, guys," she said as if they were old friends. "Been here long?"

Louise sat quietly in the car, head bowed. Then she slowly got out and closed the door and leaned against it. She took a good look. Her eye traveled from the top of the hundred-foot forest trees down to the understory of dogwood and shrubs, lit from above with dappled sunlight. The only clues to a house in there were the glints of sun slanting off the panes of large glass windows. Forgetting the heat and aggravation of the trip here, she stepped under the canopy of the trees for a more intimate look.

Once her eyes adjusted to dim light, she could see the rangy house—even lower-slung because of the placement of the studio addition close by the front door. A pergola of weathered gray twelve-by-two timbers connected the two buildings and formed a handsome overhang for the front path. She couldn't believe this was all theirs.

As she came closer, her imagination went to work and began filling in the empty spots in the landscape.

The pergola was bare of plantings. A pleasant picture of an Italianate walkway with hanging clusters of grapes invaded her mind. She would put Concord grapes upon it, once she tested with Bill's light meter to see if there was enough sun to grow them.

Her gaze traveled to the front of the studio. It cried out for something. Almost instantly, she knew: A group of native rhododendrons, with their delicate, clawlike pink flowers, belonged there. Then, she would place a small grove of amelanchiers—their silvery bark echoing the color of the pergola—on the other side for balance.

She took in a deep breath. The air was moist and aromatic, redolent of gently rotting leaves. She smiled, enthralled with the place, and continued her way toward the trellised path, not noticing a stubby azalea bush in her way. When she tripped and fell, she found the forest floor quite soft, and for a millisecond longed to just lie there and take a rest. Instead she rose, absently brushed off her wrinkled blue dress, and ambled on until she reached the stone walk.

It was the kind of walk she had dreamed of as a child. A wet spring and summer had caused green moss to grow on the edges of each flagstone, making it into a path straight out of Hansel and Gretel. She could just picture it edged with groupings of narcissus, dog-toothed violets, parasol-shaped mayapples, and maybe a jack-in-the-pulpit or two.

But an uncomfortable feeling was beginning to creep into her consciousness: The price tab on her imaginary gardening improvements was growing. With a twinge of guilt, she promised herself at least she could cut costs by forgoing expensive bulbs. Instead, she would buy them in those big bags. With just one exception. She just had to have some of the rarer Hawera narcissus, with their distinctive yellow trumpets.

She gratefully sank down upon a tree stump, for it was hot here in her forest. The possibilities stretched on and on. Down a bit from the amelanchiers—they were now permanently placed in her mental blueprint—and not too far from the path, she would create another peaceful oasis. This one would have plantings of witch hazel, hellebores, and snowdrops, to delight passersby with their flowers in the last days of winter. And when fall came, the same area would be carpeted with the blue flowers and wine-colored leaves of plumbago. . . .

"Ma!"

At first, Janie's call didn't quite register. Then the girl found her, sitting on her stump. She reached down and grasped her mother's arm as if she were a prisoner who might try to escape. "Now, Ma"—her daughter's voice was softer now, as if talking to someone on another planet—"the men have been waiting to talk to you out at the truck before they start unloading." The teenager was flushed with heat and her eyes were wide with embarrassment. ''What're you doing, anyway? You look like you're in a trance.''

''Sorry, darling,'' said Louise, brushing her long hair away from her face. ''I was just dreaming.'' She waved her arm to encompass the woods around them as they walked toward the moving van. ''Just look at this place.''

''Yeah, like I said, billions and billions of trees, but knowing you, you'll plant more.'' The girl turned and faced her mother, hands on her hips. ''Just remember, don't dip into my college funds to pay for them.'' Then she danced away ahead of Louise, throwing back, ''Just kidding, of course!''

The leggy teenager ran forward and bestowed a big smile on the moving men. They had been waiting in the hot sun of the cul-de-sac for nearly an hour. Now they were stirring impatiently around the truck, like a bunch of hornets around a nest. ''Here she comes,'' called Janie, ''all ready to answer your questions.''

To Louise, it sounded as if the girl were doing a selling job on her, the message being, ''This person isn't really the dingbat she appears to be.'' That's what it was, all right. For Janie continued: ''And don't you worry a bit: You'll find she's really a very efficient woman.''

When Louise first entered the house, it was like another world. Silent. Bare. Beautiful, but bare. A strange house—all windows and wood floors. Not much substance. Could they really *live* here?

Janie was ecstatic.

''Wow, what a fireplace! What a great brick wall!'' she

cried, giving it an affectionate pat. She loped around the living room, then made a quick circuit of the house, returning quickly to her mother.

"I love it!" she cried, and gave Louise a big hug. "And to think it's ours forever. It's so *totally* modern, but my room even has a *nook*. You and Dad did real good."

"I'm glad you like it, dear."

The movers had formed a procession outside the front door, each carrying a dining room chair. Joe, the foreman, a giant of a man, introduced the three helpers. One was a young man. Two were older men with nicotine-stained fingers and stringy muscles who looked as bone-weary as old camels. One was limping a little, she noticed.

As they brought each piece, Louise and Janie told them where to place it. They followed a plan of the house that identified where everything was to go. Louise had made it to scale and photocopied it so that she, Bill, and Janie each had a copy. She noticed Janie was timing it so she could direct the young man with whatever he was carrying.

In less than an hour Bill arrived. He looked handsome in his business clothes, clean-shaven, crisp, every blond hair in place. He was carrying a paper bag of sandwiches and drinks for their lunch.

"Good, you're home," said Louise. Her smile was tight. "We missed you on the ride here."

He took off his suit jacket and placed it on the counter, then kissed her lightly on the forehead. "What's the matter . . . couldn't you find it or something?"

Louise crossed her arms over her chest. "As a matter of fact, we did have a little trouble. Is that so strange?"

He came over and held her by her elbows. "Honey, don't get mad at me. It's moving day; we can't afford to spend any energy on emotions." The blue eyes twinkled. He gave her a little peck on the lips and moved his body so it touched hers. "I'm getting inside your iron cordon," he warned, grinning.

"Don't try to co-opt me, Bill Eldridge. A person and their emotions are not easily separated." But she smiled and hugged him. "Honey, I love the house, and the woods—the woods are magical. Thank you so much."

At that he kissed her lingeringly on the mouth, until she wished time could telescope and they could just forget the next six hours or so. Finally, he broke away. "And now to our favorite task—moving in." He rolled up the sleeves of his white dress shirt and pitched in beside her and Janie, putting things in place as fast as the movers could bring them in.

By early afternoon, the job was well on its way. She and Bill were tiring but holding up; Janie had taken off somewhere. Louise was beginning to feel better. She found it exciting to see how well their antique furniture looked, juxtaposed against the modern lines of the house. "I'm beginning to like it," she told Bill, her eyes shining.

"Wait until we hang a few pictures. It will be as if we never moved."

She passed by the recreation room and saw the youngest of the moving crew working there on his own. Tall, muscular, but hardly more than a boy. He was pounding together the Charleston bed that doubled as a couch. Out of the fatigue that had already settled in on her she still noticed an inescapable fact: The young man was beautiful. Brown, wavy hair and brown eyes. Why on earth was he in the moving business?

She stood tentatively near the door. "Earl. It's Earl, isn't it? I just was curious. . . . How did you happen to get into this, uh, moving profession?"

He looked up at her from his kneeling position, and the dark handsomeness of his face startled her. The knowing eyes, the shadows behind his high cheekbones—a little American Indian in his past? "It's hardly what you'd call a profession, now, is it?"

"Well, maybe not." Louise looked down at her white tennis shoes, then back at the handsome young man. "You just seem so young, so . . ."

Earl set the hammer on the floor, rested his forearm on his knee, and looked up at her. Softly, he said, "Something happened. Last year, when I was seventeen. My dad died after an accident. Fell off a ladder. I was going to go to college, but I'm doing this instead for a while. Money's good." He grinned. "I just hope I don't strain my back. I discovered right away this business makes cripples out of good men."

Louise crouched down on her haunches, and her blue skirt puffed out around her. She was on eye level with him. "I bet it does . . . all this heavy old furniture. But couldn't you piece together something . . . there are all sorts of tuition grants and work-study programs. Then you could start school with your friends."

"Well, ma'am, you've heard of families running out of health insurance, and racking up great big bills at the hospital? We're one of those families. We owe 'em about a hundred and fifty grand for taking care of my dad when he was dying." He looked down. He gracefully picked up his hammer. "Didn't save him from dying, but sure was expensive. My mom is the type who takes bills seriously.''

Louise rose up slowly. ''That's such a shame. . . .'' She heard the other movers approaching. ''I know you want to get back to your work. Nice to talk to you.'' She smiled at him. He had an odd expression on his face. Then she forgot Earl and went to find Bill, to see what the next task was on this moving day.

Joe, the foreman, big, bald, sweaty, and satisfied, sat at the dining room table with Louise and Bill, his giant forearms cuddled protectively around a cold Michelob, a swath of papers in front of him. Around them stood large, opened boxes spewing wrapping paper. It was the time for settling up. Joe, however, was in no hurry.

He leaned back and took a pack of unfiltered cigarettes from the limp pocket of his shirt. Then, thinking better of it, he put them back. He regarded Louise and Bill with a challenging look. ''There's one thing about you guys I wanna know,'' he said. ''I wanna know how you guys learned how to move so good. You're like professionals.''

Bill smiled ruefully. ''That's because we've had so much practice.'' He looked at Louise. ''Right, honey?'' She nodded agreement.

Joe's assistants, Earl and the two older men, lounged in the kitchen doorway, drinking their beers but eyeing an open bottle of Weller's bourbon glowing dark amber on the antique pine table.

Noting this, Bill asked, ''Would you like a shot? It's mighty smooth stuff.''

The offering, thought Louise, just like in church. She uncrossed her long legs and got up stiffly. ''I've got some paper cups somewhere in the kitchen we can use.'' The men stepped aside deferentially as she passed.

''Thanks, ma'am,'' said Joe. He poured himself a shot of whiskey and then passed it to the others. Louise could smell their sweat as they hovered over her to reach for the cups. She didn't want to guess the last time they had showered. She pulled her own wilted skirt down a little. Bill, who came through life's dirtiest experiences looking clean, had emerged immaculate, from his blond, disheveled hair to his white shirt and tan pants.

Joe quickly threw back the shot, then heaved a sigh of satisfaction. Then he said, ''Another thing is, you guys got good taste.'' At this he cast an experienced eye at the furniture. ''I like this old stuff. You knew right where you wanted it. Not crowded either. Betcha threw out a lotta stuff.''

''We had to,'' said Louise. ''There's less storage space here.'' She wondered how long this ceremony was going to take.

''You got that little hut out there.'' He pointed his massive arm toward the front door. This was the arm that guided Louise's precious piano to safety, so how could she be impatient? ''You coulda put lotsa stuff out there.''

Bill looked at Louise and then at Joe. ''That addition, or hut, as you call it, is going to be Louise's studio. This is the first time she's had a place of her own. There's no way she'll let anyone store things out there.''

Louise saw one of the movers, flushed now from the straight bourbon, whisper to the others. She caught the tail end: "pussy-whipped." They all chuckled, even Earl. Louise was a little disappointed in the beautiful young man. She had thought him more refined than the others.

"Yeah, now," allowed Joe. "It's a nice hut, with that nice little woodstove and them big windows. And this is a real house in the woods. I like it." With that they all stared out through the tall windows into the darkening woods beyond. This is our silent communion, thought Louise; might as well get into it. She sat back and found herself relaxing for the first time all day. Suddenly there washed over her the sense of camaraderie that comes after working with others. She found herself beaming at her friends the movers, who only hours ago were strangers and who would be strangers again within minutes.

Then, abruptly, the ceremony was over. "Well, that's it for peace and quiet," said Joe, hefting his large frame up straight in the chair. "Mr. Eldridge, why dontcha sign these papers—you gotta sign each one—and we'll get outta your way."

He handed Bill the papers. While he was signing them, the mover pointed his Herculean arm again, this time toward the woods. "Little lady, you got a swamp way out there, depending on where your property ends. There's a low spot and standing water near that clump of—what is it anyway?"

Louise walked over to the window. "Bamboo," she said. "Yes . . . it looks like an invasion, doesn't it? I know for sure the little pond is on our property. It will take fill dirt to fix, but we don't know how a truck will get in here."

"Gotta carry it in bag by bag, most likely," intoned the mover. "Just like they built the pyramids, stone by stone."

Louise didn't hear. She stared out at the yard and the hovering forest so close to their house and was filled with momentary panic. She knew what it was: the moving blues, moving in. Out there was the strange new yard. Another yard. Gone for good their old one in New York, the yard of a rented house, but still *their yard,* its garden soaring with midsummer bloom. Tears formed in her eyes. All the new things to fix and contend with. New friends to make. What would happen here? How would just the fact that they moved here change their lives? She knew it would, just as in the Ray Bradbury story of the man who entered prehistoric time. By straying from the path and stepping on a butterfly, he altered evolutionary history. She shook her head. But surely not *that* significant a move. Roughly she brushed tears from her cheeks and turned back to the others.

Joe had remembered something. "You lads, didja set up that bed in the backmost bedroom? Nope? Earl, you do it while the other fellas load the pads onto the truck. Missus, go with him to tell him where you want it."

Louise was impatient now for them to leave. She unwillingly trailed the young man down the hall. He banged the frame together, then leaned over to set up the headboard. The bed was out of place by a foot. "Right about here is where we'll want it," she said, shoving the frame briskly. Then the skirt of her dress caught in the steel, forcing her to remain crouched over, close to Earl. "Oh," she cried.

Without saying a word he slid his hand around her right breast and pulled her toward him.

She lurched awkwardly backward as far as the dress would allow. The hand was reluctantly released. She hissed at him: "For heaven's sake, what do you think you are doing? My dress is *caught. Please get me out.*"

"Oh," he said, his face aflame. "I guess I thought . . ." His strong hands busily parted the two pieces of steel and gently removed the dress fabric. "There—there, you're free."

She straightened and looked at him, her eyes flashing.

He got to his feet slowly. She could smell his sweat, or maybe it was her own. In spite of herself she felt a little twinge in her groin and her body flush with heat.

He looked at her with frightened eyes and said, "I'm sorry. I'm sorry. I'm *truly* sorry. *Please* don't tell him."

She glared at him. "I won't tell him, because I suppose it would mean your job. But I'm really curious: what made you *possibly* think that I . . ."

"You were so nice to me. I thought you were comin' on to me." He raised his chin a little. "It wouldn't be the first time."

She sighed and shook her head. "You know, Earl, you really should try to go to college. I think you're probably a nice person. But . . . get out of moving."

"I'll talk to my mom. Maybe I should. You know, you're sort of like my mom—real nice." He smiled at her. "No hard feelings, okay?" He put out a timid hand for her to shake. She shook it. It was callused and rough and made her feel guilty. This person at eighteen was already a poor, working stiff with calluses a half inch thick. She retracted her own smooth, manicured hand.

"Okay, Earl," she said, all business now. "Let's get going."

"Louise," called Bill from down the hall. "Are you coming? We have to say good-bye to these folks."

She joined him at the front door and they drifted with Joe and the moving crew down the front walk to the large truck at the curb. Parked nearby were the scarred and dented cars driven by the mover's helpers. Bill shook Joe's hand, transferring several folded bills into his palm, then shook the hand of each of the others. "You did great for us."

"Good-bye, ma'am," they said to Louise. All except Earl cast a last appreciative glance at her legs.

As they walked back to the house, Louise and Bill slipped their arms around each other's waists. "I can't believe it," Louise said. "They acted just like Janie said they would—and we acted just like Janie said we would. We plied them with beer and bourbon, tipped them, and sent them off in their twenty-ton truck and dilapidated cars to drive drunkenly home."

"You've forgotten, Louise. That kid understands everything much better than we do."

"Scary," said Louise.

Bill looked at his watch. "It's five o'clock. Moving in took seven hours. That's not so bad; beats our last move-in by an hour or so. And you know what I'd like to do now?" He slid a hand down to her hip and gave it a jaunty pinch. "Test our bed. How about it?"

She looked up at him. "You must be kidding. Or as Joe would say, 'You gotta be kiddin'.' " She looked at him again. "You are kidding."

"You don't know," said Bill, propelling her gently into the house. "Maybe I have no other motive than that we just lie down for a minute and relax. I have to prove to you I'm as charming as that young guy Earl."

She looked at him. "You noticed. What a hunk, hey?"

"So did he put the moves on ya in the bedroom?"

"What if I said yes?"

"I'd say, I'd have beaten the guy up if I'd known it."

"It's okay, darling. I'm still all yours."

They went into their bedroom, dodged empty boxes, and plopped back on the bed together like two children. They rested, hand in hand.

Then Bill murmured, "This isn't going to work, you know."

"Why not?" asked Louise, already half asleep.

"Something . . . somebody will disturb us." Seconds later, he began snoring noisily.

The delicate net of near sleep was broken, and Louise's eyes popped open.

She lay very still and stared up at the skylight over their bed. Lying here reminded her of games she had played in her youth. At dusk in summer she and her brothers had lain in the empty lot by their house, hiding from their mother's call to come in for the night. She had lain on hillsides in summer with young men who wished to possess her but were lucky to get a kiss or two. She had always felt that, even if you were an attractive female, lying down and staring up was not a submissive position but rather, an inquiring mode in which to study sky, sun, moon, and stars, and possibly God. She had no idea when they bought the house how delightful it would be to lie here with their private view of the universe. On the left was the top of a tall forest tree, probably sweetgum. It swayed ever so gently in the August night. In the rest of the frame she could see pale stars emerging. Maybe later the August moon would climb into the picture.

Louise suddenly felt at home. It was as if a load had been lifted from her. They had moved everything they owned from one place to another place hundreds of miles away. And they had survived. And now this was home.

Like a cat she wiggled her neck and her back against the familiar mattress. Then, unbidden, she felt a rush of sexual desire. She hoped Earl had nothing to do with it.

She sighed. A lot of good it would do her. Bill had stopped snoring but was motionless beside her, his hand heavy in hers. For a moment she contented herself with staring at the hovering tree in the skylight. Then she impatiently moved a leg, preparing to get up.

"No, I'm not."

She turned her head and looked at him. "You're not what?"

He smiled, but his eyes were still shut. "I'm not asleep any more. You thought I was asleep."

His eyes opened then and he leaned over her and threw a hand over her belly. She could smell his familiar buttery smell. "It's been a long time, baby," he said. "Nine days, I think. It's always, 'Honey, I'm too tired—we're moving.' "

"I've been thinking the same thing. But do you think we're too sweaty?"

"Who cares?" He murmured into her neck. His hand sought out her breast.

"And Janie . . . Janie might come back."

"No worry there. I checked it out. Some dishy lady lives across the cul-de-sac. Her daughter's Janie's age." He moved his hand and began gently massaging the muscles down the length of her back. "And I've taken the liberty of locking you in here with me."

"You devil, you." She turned to face him.

Bill stopped his massage. He leaned his head on one elbow and gently tapped her on the breastbone with a forefinger. "But before we go any further, do you promise me you'll shed no more tears for the old friends we left behind?"

"Oh," she moaned. She sat up abruptly and put her hands on either side of her head. "Why did you remind me? In my mind I'd almost moved; I'd almost forgotten them. And the garden . . . I'd almost stopped thinking about the garden."

Bill gently pulled her down again beside him. "I'm sorry, honey. Please don't go away from me. I just want you to be all right." He grinned. "And yet I don't know why I worry about you. Today you're mourning lost friends and in about two months you'll be in the middle of something, people will be running in and out the front door again. . . ."

She began to snuggle in comfortably against him. "We already have our friends from the last time they made us move here. I'll just hop on the Beltway and in forty minutes I'll be out there." She stiffened a little. "But they won't be home. Beth teaches, and Ann has her business. . . . I've just got to decide what *I'm* going to do. Maybe freelance." She turned and gave him a searching look. "Don't you think it's time I grew up and got a real job? Don't you get tired of always being the one who brings home the bacon?"

He gently smoothed her dark hair and outlined her lips with gentle fingers. ''I like bringing home the bacon to you and the girls. You can do what you like. You won't have any problem: If you don't find excitement first, it'll reach right out and grab you.''

''Oh, you don't say,'' she said, slipping her arm around his stomach and pulling his shirt out. ''Well, I could use a little excitement right now. I've waited long enough.''

They kissed, then tumbled Bill's clothes free, but the buttons on Louise's dress impeded them. ''This dress . . . where did you get this infernal dress?'' muttered Bill. ''It doesn't want to cooperate.''

''It's been nothing but trouble today,'' murmured Louise. ''I bought it for Janie or Martha. They wouldn't wear it, so I decided to. . . .''

He mastered the last of the buttons and stripped off her garments. ''Give it back,'' he said. ''It's too old for you.''

She laughed and reached over to him.

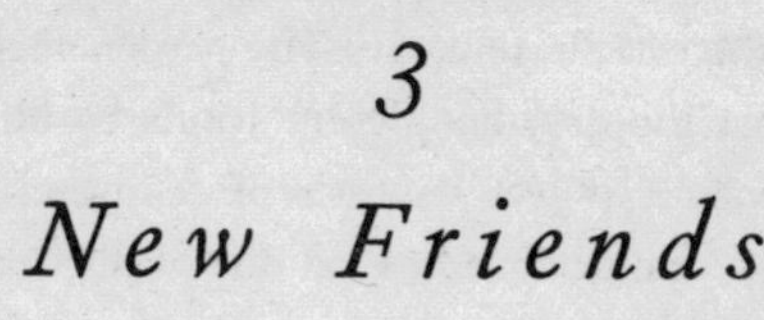

3
New Friends

THE VIRGINIA NIGHT TREMBLED WITH WET heat. Out-of-sync cicadas screeched in the woods so that the eleven people on the patio—the entire adult population of the cul-de-sac—had to raise their voices to be heard. Louise noted how wet they all looked, herself included, despite the powder she had dabbed on her face before she and Bill crossed the street to join the party. Sweat glazed faces, bare arms, and legs. She smiled in the light of the high torches, thinking of another patio, her favorite, the one in Tel Aviv. The garden there had been buffered against the dry, hot desert winds by filigreed brick walls. Once inside, it was an oasis of calm and color, with soaring palms, clamoring roses on the walls, and Turkscap lilies swaying in the breeze. Prize stands of tulips, an ancient heritage of the Middle East, bloomed in spring, so perfect the blossoms seemed to be carved of translucent soapstone. Amidst this beauty, she and Bill and friends sipped their gin and tonics and talked about the state of the world. That seemed so long ago.

Her eyes refocused on the present, and on the strangers-cum-friends in the lively circle around her. She knew Washington well, not only its unrelenting tropical summer heat, but the political heat present in almost every activity, and the competitive heat as people clamored for success and status.

This Washington fever was represented best in the question people asked soon after they met them for the first time. "And where did you get your degree?"

"Cook County Community College," Louise always felt like answering, but didn't, of course, being a well-trained foreign service wife. Bill's Harvard degrees conferred immediate approval. Her degree worked two ways: Northwestern was good; English, wimpy. She had gotten used to it years ago, but these days, tart retorts came to mind.

Now she studied her neighbors and wondered how much of this Washington pressure burbled within them. Some had paid welcome visits during the past few weeks; a few they were meeting for the first time. The sweat and vocal competition from the cicadas made everyone seem a little frantic. And the alcohol was obviously working faster in the heat, as if introduced intravenously. Suddenly she conjured up a mental picture of everyone in the Washington area sweating and straining and getting drunk together in this soupy summer night.

It was obvious these people were used to having fun together. Bantering, jousting, silly, a close-but-not-too-close-knit group of people who genuinely liked each other. With hosts Eric and Jan gracefully leading the way, they had gathered her and Bill in like old shoes.

Louise had learned a little about them all: Sam Rosen, a congressional aide, living next door to them. Roger Kendricks, on the international desk at *The Washington Post.* His wife, Laurie, owner of a thriving boutique in nearby Alexandria. Eric VandeVen, the host, Washington city planner. Hostess Jan, an elementary school teacher. Ron Radebaugh, consultant on businesses in the Pacific. His wife, Nora, a poet, of all things. Then Richard Mougey, a State Department employee like Bill, an expert on the Middle East. His wife, Mary Mougey, a fund-raiser for international causes. An interesting collection, thought Louise.

No sexual jealousies here that she could perceive, although Nora, who was leaning over talking to Bill, was a smoky woman with eyes luminous in the torchlight. She looked like the sort that all men fall in love with.

Richard slumped down beside Louise and turned his pale Modigliani face her way. "I can see you're suffering, my dear. You should be drinking gin like me instead of that 7-UP. Or maybe Eric and Jan should have entertained us all inside in the air-conditioning."

"Oh, no," she said, smoothing back her long, damp hair. "We might as well get used to it again. I didn't remember it being this sticky but tonight brings it all back to me: One is *insane* to stay in Washington in August. One should just go off to Maine, or Michigan.'' She didn't know why she had fallen into this pompous style of speech. She was downgrading Richard Mougey by assuming this drivel was what he wanted to hear. She sounded like the kind of person she hadn't liked in the foreign service crowd. The kind who talked in their own little code and sent each other little verbal signals like ''n.o.c.d.,'' standing for ''not our class, darling.'' And spouted worldly little aphorisms beginning with ''one should'' or ''one is.''

She tried to relax her hands against the metal arms of the deck chair.

What she thought was pompous was obviously everyday fare for Richard. He didn't blink an eye. ''You're so right, Louise. We shouldn't be here at all.'' He slid an arm around the back of her chair. ''Mary and I were planning to be in Austria, but we had to postpone it.''

As he talked, she noted that he slyly looked her over, from her breasts to her legs. She wondered if his slight drunkenness would go beyond the garrulous level; she guessed not. As he examined her, she did the same to him, noting that he was not a healthy-looking man. Maybe fifty. He probably had smoked and drunk much more than a person should all through what Bill told her had been a solid if not illustrious career in foreign service.

''In Foggy Bottom,'' Richard continued, waving his highball glass in a northerly direction, ''where your husband and I both work, we have always called Washington a hardship post—''

"Too bad we don't get hardship pay," finished Louise, smiling.

"Oh, come on, Richard," said Roger, a balding, professorial man with surprising red plastic frames on his glasses. "A little hardship is in order for you guys. It makes up for all those years you were posted to Paris and Bonn, drinking fine wines and taking in all the good rathskellers and restaurants."

"Yeah," agreed Eric, the host. Eric was big, blond, muscular. According to what Louise had heard, he drove his family into the hardest sports. "While Roger and I were back here solving the problems of the city and the country, respectively, you were across the pond collecting wines."

"And that brings us to the subject of wine tasting," said Laurie, Roger's handsome red-haired wife. Understandably, she advertised her boutique on her back. A layered look with checks, in an array of patterns—a little hot for tonight?—matching perfectly with her patterned shoes and patterned earrings. Louise noticed *she* wasn't sweating; what was her secret?

Laurie prodded Richard: "When are we going to have a wine tasting again?" She made a wide gesture. "Oh, why do I ask you when it's Mary who will plan it. Mary, we're overdue. Set a date, and we'll all bring something for dinner."

Mary was pale and quiet. Louise guessed her blond hair once was beautiful, but now, untouched by dyes, was faded comfortably to half white. This made Louise like her before she uttered a word.

Mary leaned forward and began. "I'm *afraid*—"

"She'll do it," interrupted Richard. "She'll do it in mid-September. Won't you, honey?"

"As I was saying—" She gazed amiably at her husband. "—I'm afraid we'll have to make it later, Richard. I think you're forgetting Austria." She looked at the others and gently shook her head in regret. "Our light bags are all packed for Austria. It's been an exhausting summer, with so much travel involving our latest fund drive." She looked straight at Louise. "I raise money for world hunger, I don't know if you knew that. It's extremely satisfying, if enervating, with all the travel and the speeches. So now, Richard and I are going to recuperate for a couple of weeks—hide in Vienna with old friends." Louise was entranced. The woman, so small in stature, had a deep, mellifluous voice. Then she remembered hearing that Mary was a singer when a young woman. "How about doing it in mid-October, instead?" She smiled over at Louise. "But I hope you and I have a chance to get together before then. Can I come over and spend a minute with you?"

"I'd love it," said Louise.

The bourbon-damaged Richard no sooner unwound himself from the chair than it was commandeered by Eric. He sat erect but slightly swaying, no more immune to the heat and alcohol than his guests. After Richard's low current, Louise found his athletic presence high-voltage, and he had a faint aura of a gutsy men's cologne clinging to him that she rather liked.

Eric opened up with a little host speech: "Louise and Bill, we are happy to welcome you here in Dogwood Court. It's obvious by Bill's long, compulsive working hours and Louise's energetic enhancement of the woods, you fit into this place like a couple of old shoes. Why, from the very moment you moved in, it was obvious nothing would remain the same over there. And it doesn't really intimidate us too much the way she reels off the Latin names for all those new trees and bushes: Why, we just run home and call up the library reference department and plead with them to tell us what a *Lobelia syphilis* is, and assure us it isn't contagious.'' This was followed with appreciative laughter. Louise remembered the day Eric had come over and hung around while she laboriously planted a half-dozen of the plants.

She responded before she could stop herself. ''It's *Lobelia siphilitica,* actually, a kind of wildflower category. Has unobtrusive blue flowers, spreads well, and is much more reliable than *Lobelia cardinalis.*''

Eric put his arm around her shoulders and everybody applauded. ''See, the woman cannot stop talking about plants even at a dinner party.'' Louise blushed and grinned, and he settled easily back into his welcoming speech. ''Well, we hope you have us all straight now. It's easy. Just think of all the men here as dreamers, working somehow for the perfection of man; metro Washington, the EEC, the State Department, the—whatever *The Washington Post* stands for, the Pacific Rim—that's Ron's specialty, and a very damned profitable one, too.'' More laughter.

''While the wives, now''—he saluted them—''and I salute you—do the important jobs. They're the realists. Teacher, merchant, fund-raiser—''

''Wait a minute,'' said Roger. ''Mary funds idealistic causes. That surely throws her into the column of those working for the perfection of man, doesn't it?''

''And how about Nora?'' asked Bill. Louise immediately tensed. ''What do we say about her?'' He looked at the woman sitting beside him in a way Louise hadn't seen before. It was the way she was used to him looking at *her*.

All eyes turned to the smoky woman. Even in her worn, sleeveless dress, gray denim, it appeared, plainer than all the other dresses, the woman was utterly striking. Louise felt embarrassed to look at her and yet did not know where to turn her eyes. She was not accustomed to this feeling, which she realized was jealousy.

As if reading this, Nora looked straight at Louise and locked in the connection. "I think the whiskey is talking in all of us. With that disclaimer, I can say this: As a poet, I hope I can communicate with both the realists and the dreamers."

"Hear, hear," said Sam, chortling. He was a slight but handsome man Louise and Bill had talked to several times in the yard. They had stood as if on either side of a nonexistent fence—fences were not fashionable in Sylvan Valley—while his friendly little dog did figure eights around their legs. "You've expressed a noble sentiment, Nora. It's dated nonsense to divide people into categories, especially us. Although of all of us, I'd identify Nora as one of the true dreamers of this world." He turned all his attention to her. "I can tell from your garden alone—all those lilies, and thistles, pretty little white things scrambling over the rocks . . ."

"She is a dreamer, indeed," said her husband, Ron, in a lazy baritone voice. Large, elegant, with white hair, he seemed much older than his wife, whom Louise had pegged to be about her own age. "Any person who can back our new car into a concrete wall at the rear of a parking lot because she was thinking so hard about a poem surely qualifies as a dreamer."

Everyone laughed. Nora smiled and put a garden-worn hand gracefully on her husband's knee. "Darling," she said in a soft, low voice that caused the others to lean closer to hear, "please don't give Louise and Bill a distorted picture of us." She looked first at Bill and then at Louise. "Despite his remarks, he is not a chauvinist, and I don't want you to think that he is. As for the women being the realists, I see more than just that: I see in Jan and Laurie and Mary people who help other people achieve their dreams, whether they're schoolchildren, or shoppers, or people in developing countries. As for myself, well . . ."

All ten of them waited, silent, while she paused. "I am not *just* a poet; I am a published poet with an agent who gets fifteen percent—which places me, just like all of us here, with one foot in the order of dreamers and the other foot in the order of realists."

Merry applause greeted her words. Nora smiled gently at them. Ron grinned and reached over and massaged his wife's supple arm. Eric took final drink orders.

This woman could make an interesting friend . . . or would it be enemy?

4

Lunch at Pomodoro

PETER SCOOPED IN THE LAST FORKFUL OF creamed herring, then carefully patted his mouth with the white linen napkin. His eye caught that of one of the other diners, and he realized this person and probably others in the restaurant were watching. It wasn't him; it was because the president's well-known chief of staff, Tom Paschen, sat opposite him. They occupied Paschen's favorite table at Pomodoro, apparently the man's favorite restaurant.

Peter knew most celebrities liked tables in corners. But this one was in a bay window overlooking the restaurant's on-the-street herb garden, where even now through Belgian lace curtains Peter could see a Mexican planted in midstoop, picking large basil leaves off thriving two-foot bushes. These were for use in their renowned hors d'oeuvre, toast with fresh tomato slice and fresh mozzarella, topped with basil leaves and drizzled with olive oil. Which Paschen was finishing right now. Peter wished he'd ordered it rather than the herring.

He leaned back and in the process dwarfed the captain's chair with his large frame. He peered down through thick-lensed aviator glasses to be sure no herring had landed on his tie. Satisfied that there was none, he looked over at his diminutive host. Time to open business.

''So, Tom. To what do I owe the honor?''

''Let's say it's that long line of people who have lusted after big government jobs—Supreme Court, Cabinet, federal judge—or even lower-level jobs, like deputy secretary of defense . . .'' Paschen's eyes glittered maliciously at Peter as he wiped traces of olive oil off his fingers. His British tailored suit could not conceal the taut energy in his body, a tiger's energy, caged in serge.

Peter waited.

''. . . and fell on their asses because they somehow screwed up.''

''Yeah?'' said Peter belligerently. ''You'll forgive me if I don't identify with that.''

Paschen smoothed his already smooth hair in a gesture familiar to watchers of Sunday morning TV news shows, where this guy was the president's Answer Man. He settled his forearms on the table and gazed straight at Peter. "Normally, Hoffman, as you and I both know—or maybe you don't—these approvals at deputy secretary level are pro forma, not to be compared with higher-level positions. You know the drill—or do you? One senator plus you and your sponsor in a Senate hearing room. A written statement, which you need to read with sincerity. A few good words from Senator So-and-so, and that's all there is to it."

"Unless, of course—"

"Unless the nominee tends to talk to the press, which is what you've done this week. Now, I have the utmost respect for you"—Paschen put up a hand as if to indicate his utmost respect—"and I know you did this in total innocence, without realizing the harm that could be done."

"Jesus Christ, Tom, I was just putting a little color into a story of how an honest arms dealer operates—"

Paschen threw both hands up wide. "See what I mean? What could arouse more interest in the press than that kind of story? A hotdogger: The press can smell one a mile away. And what happens to hotdoggers? They eventually take a real bad fall and break their goddamn necks." The chief of staff leaned over the table, pointing his finger in Peter's face. "You have to learn how to use the press and not let them use you." The eyes were shining with superior knowledge. "The press, Hoffman, is a monster, a big, unkempt monster. You've got to know how to keep it in check. You can use it like your pet, if you know how, like me. I jolly it, push it, con it, and use it to my purposes. I *don't* feed it too much red meat like you are doing right now. It goes crazy if you do, and latches on to *you* and''—Paschen sat back in his chair and snapped his fingers—''gobbles you right up.''

Peter was restraining a smile. The guy was living up to his reputation, every inch of the way.

He continued. ''Let's not further belabor the Middle East situation with stories like the one you gave the press. You are not privy to exactly where we stand these days on the area because you are not yet in the loop. Although we were tilting one way, this has changed somewhat over the past days, and we don't like indiscreet stories in the media—we want to do nothing to tip our hand.'' He folded his hands in front of him and leaned forward conspiratorially. ''And in any event, even if you have been a resourceful arms peddler, drop 'arms sales' from your vernacular. We phrase it differently; it's termed 'security-enhancement agreements.' Got that? 'Security-enhancement agreements.' You've got to get the phraseology down. Things are a little more complicated when you get to this level. I hope you realize that.''

Peter smiled and dislodged a piece of herring from his front tooth with his tongue.

The president's chief of staff gave him a sour look. ''And another small problem: You've got to keep your old war stories to yourself—including the intelligence stuff. Everybody knows what intelligence is. We'll tell you when, if ever, those war stories will be suitable for publishing, so to speak.''

''When? When the next little war starts? And what would that be called? Publicity-enhanced memoirs?'' He gulped down his sauvignon blanc just as the veal arrived and occupied them both. There was a quiet little clatter, as their knives effortlessly sliced through the flesh of the tender baby steer, and

Peter thought reflectively that the little fellow had never had a chance to get big, and even if he had he would never have had the chance to enjoy the fruits of manhood. Then the animal image receded, and there on his plate lay the puny slice of veal. Washington restaurants were notorious rip-offs: For the price he was paying, he should have had twice as much food.

Paschen pressed on. "Back to these individuals who make it hard for themselves to reach office. You don't know President Jack Fairchild that well: Underneath his straight exterior is a straight interior. Although his kids occasionally were caught with their pants down or some minor drug thing, this was not a pattern, and they all grew out of it. He doesn't like drugs and is suspicious of womanizers."

"Has to be, doesn't he, in today's climate? Funny how I remember him quite differently years ago. Always smart and glib, I'll give you that. A real stud, for another thing"—he slid a mischievous glance at Paschen—"and full of derring-do back then—huh, he's changed a bit on that score, hasn't he? Willing to do anything back then—almost *anything* for his country."

The chief of staff eyed Peter suspiciously but said nothing. Then he turned full attention back to his veal. Peter watched him pile the meat and vegetables meticulously on the back of his fork, continental style. Peter ate the same way, albeit more sloppily, from years of living in Europe. But for this guy it was just bullshit airs.

Peter drawled, "You sound like you're suspicious of me and my lifestyle. What do you suspect me of, snortin' coke or something? Who've you been talking to?"

"I've just heard a couple of things—nothing major, a little

about women, a little about coke use. What we need is a clean slate.'' Paschen grinned. ''You know damned well about the political climate these days. I'd like you to get busy and see that your slate is wiped clean or I'll just blow you out of the water next time I talk to the boss. So. To summarize: If you fail in this, the worst-case analysis is that you then won't get confirmed. The best-case analysis is that you *will* but you'll forever remain outside the envelope.'' He spread his hands open in an appealing gesture. ''And then what good would you be to us?''

Peter stared at Paschen with mouth slightly agape. ''I've heard about you,'' he said. ''I guess I didn't believe it until now. Sure, I can clean my slate—a little. But I am what I am. I have a past I'm mostly proud of, and a damned lot to offer as deputy secretary. Shit, where would you guys be without the weapons I invented?''

''No one's saying you're not talented,'' said Paschen coldly. He set his napkin carefully at plateside and beckoned the hovering waiter for a bill. Peter was disappointed, because the desserts in Pomodoro were some of the best in town. He could feel a distinct space in his stomach that needed filling.

Paschen scribbled his signature on the bill and said, ''Don't take offense, Peter. I'm only doing my job. Keeping pet whores in apartments is about as dated as romps in the Tidal Basin. Remember way back to Wilbur Mills? Free souls like yourself need to be aware of this.'' He pushed back his chair and got up.

Peter stood up, towering over Paschen. Taking a step closer to the other man, like a shark coming in for a kill, he grabbed his upper arm, pulled him close, bent his head to him, and said quietly in his ear, "Let me tell you something too, Tom baby. Just because I'm signing up again to work for the government doesn't mean I'm going to take chickenshit from you or anyone else in the White House."

Paschen flushed, trying to pull away. Peter held. He said, "Don't get upset now—everyone's watching us. Smile as if I were telling you a useful secret or something. One more thing: I know President Fairchild better than you think—from way back in the Diem days in 'Nam. Ask him. And then there's the money." He widened his eyes. "Aren't you aware I've become a big contributor? Check that out too. And I'll be seeing you, but not too soon, okay?" Then he released him and walked out of the restaurant. When he glanced back at the door, Paschen, his face a dull brick red, was still standing where he left him.

5
The Swim Club

LOUISE TRUDGED UP THE HANDSOME WINDING steps, admiring them as she went. Each step was outlined with weathered wood and filled in with small river stones set in concrete. This grand approach was in sharp contrast to some she had seen in Sylvan Valley that were no more than simple Indian-style footpaths.

The hill was carpeted with ivy. Out of this sturdy ground cover emerged graceful clumps that stubbornly represented the fading summer: pale rudbeckia and globe thistle, fall asters, lamb's ears, sedum Autumn Joy, and other perennials she couldn't recognize in the gloom. All planted, it seemed, by an artistic hand. Soaring up behind them were graceful masses of ornamental grasses, swaying in the faint evening breeze. These last remainders of the summer were like separate presences on the hill, many faded to neutral shades of rose, pale blue, tan, gray, and off-white, with an occasional accent of rust or deep ruby.

Off to the side, but still visible in the waning Virginia evening light, was a picture that in the dimness looked as if painted in watercolor by a Japanese artist: sharp-angled, bony-looking branches of a trio of oakleaf hydrangeas set in front of an evergreen backdrop. An irregular drift of spiky-leaved carex growing low in front added a grassy accent. She noted the large seedheads that festooned the hydrangea branches had changed from the white of summer through the pink of fall, and now were the palest peach-beige. They would hang in there, she knew, all through the worst kind of winter, a kind of assurance that this sturdy plant would do it again next year.

After climbing twenty-four steps, she reached the house, and realized coming in the front door of this house, though interesting, was really doing it the hard way. The place sat on the top of Sylvan Valley's highest hill and belonged to Mort and Sarah Swanson. He was a lawyer with Wilson and Sterritt, and she was one of the many neighborhood potters and said to have been a beauty in her heyday, whenever that was; Louise had not yet met the woman.

She had heard that when it was built, twenty-five or so years ago, the house was featured in *Architectural Digest*. Probably, she decided, because of indecent exposure. She could see its innards through two floors of floor-to-ceiling windows.

Sarah Swanson was chairman of Sylvan Valley's Swim and Tennis Club and was hosting the first meeting of the season. Louise's neighbor Jan had involved her in this—plump Jan with her pretty blond hair and earnest blue eyes, making her pitch with such disarming grace that Louise's intended "no" came out "yes." Not the least of it was Jan's mention of the location of the first meeting. Louise's curiosity had been aroused; she couldn't resist checking out *any* house in the neighborhood, much less a designer house. She wondered if they led different lives than people in more ordinary houses. As Bill put it, she was just plain nosy about things like that.

The door opened just as she raised her hand to ring the bell. "And you must be Louise Eldridge," said a large woman Louise knew was Sarah. She wore an apricot gauze caftan. Long, curly, graying blond hair was swept back at the nape with an apricot-colored bow, exposing a good cheek line and handsome, large gray eyes. Her feet were bare. She extended her hand gracefully, and Louise took it but would have shaken it loose again had she dared. It was like a horned beast's. "I . . . ah, I'm pleased to be here," stuttered Louise. "You're . . . Sarah." The woman released her hand and laughed. "You handled that terribly well, Louise. Potters, you know, don't have the skin you love to touch. I know I shouldn't shake hands with newcomers, but I do like to touch people. But come." Then she flowed in front of her up flagstone steps into the living room.

Louise saw now that the house was glass on not one but two sides. "It is simply beautiful," she said, staring. Just enough furniture here, all muted gray and white tones, tan wood floors, no interruptions to the eye, so that the forest and the last trails of colored light in the west became part of the room.

"I love it," she cried. "It's as if we're standing in the forest."

"Most people say that," said a thin balding man with horn-rimmed glasses. "I'm Mort Swanson. You must be the new kid on the court down the road." He grinned a lopsided grin. A $450-an-hour grin, Louise bet. She noted his very clean chinos and deck shoes, just right, she thought, for a swim club meeting. His hands looked soft, the nails manicured and shiny. "You have a nice house in the woods yourself," said Mort. "Yours is one of the houses that no one has deforested much, unlike some of the properties around here. I think yours has only lost two or three trees over the years. I think, if anything, that adds to its intrinsic value."

He beckoned Louise to a chair. She dutifully sank into its womblike design, then struggled to regain a more upright sitting position.

Mort waved his arm. "Sit back. Let the chair have you. Relax."

She leaned back slowly. "That impresses me," she said to Mort. "To think that you know that much detail about our house. Everyone around here knows everything about everybody else, or at least about their property. It's like a small town filled with real estate experts."

He laughed. "That's because they all started out like backwoodsmen here. Woodsmen know every tree in the forest. The water pipes and phone lines weren't even in when the first people moved in in 1958. This was open farm and forestland, of course. The very first settlers—Sarah and I were a bit later—fetched water from a well out near Ransom Road.'' He peered at her as if depending upon her for a proper reaction. ''That's damned hard, you know, carrying water in cans in the trunk of your car. So, with no running water and no phones, people were really dependent on one another for baby-sitting, running to the store for groceries, driving others to the emergency room, and just generally seeing that their neighbors were all right.''

''It must have led to some strong friendships.''

He gave her an approving grin. ''You hit the nail on the head. Need creates close bonds between people. Some of the friendships, in fact, got too close. We received some lousy publicity once in *The Washington Post,* in the sixties—''

''It was nineteen sixty-seven,'' said Sarah, who was floating through the room, a large, pastel presence, positioning small bowls of nuts on nearly invisible glass end tables. ''That was when they wrote that terrible exposé; of course, I must admit a lot of it was true.'' She laughed and disappeared in the direction of a delicious smell of strong coffee.

Mort leaned forward and rested his elbows on his knees. ''Yes, I guess it was nineteen sixty-seven. By that time, of course, we were all settling in. Sarah had set up her kiln and was beginning to sell her pots.'' He grinned another crooked grin. ''I must say I'm happy she has that—but some women, and some men, just as always, got bored, so a little wife-swapping developed.''

''Wife-swapping?'' asked Louise with a faint smile. ''Not husband-swapping?''

He looked at her levelly. ''You have to remember this was

before the woman's movement.'' He touched his breast with a hand. ''That's not what *I* called it. That's what the *Post* called it back then: wife-swapping. Here we were, a modern little subdivision, surrounded by acres of traditional colonial houses inhabited quite often by military . . .''

He was warming to the subject now, even as others drifted in for the meeting. They smiled at Louise understandingly. Mort continued. ''And who were we? Lawyers, doctors, lots of newspapermen, artists . . . a suspect lot here in conservative northern Virginia. An enterprising reporter decided to extend the metaphor. Modern houses, modern lives, modern morals. Actually, there was only one swap; that was the extent of it.''

''But it made a helluva story.''

Louise looked up and saw a tall, rather attractive blond man with aviator glasses staring inquisitively at her, then at her legs. She felt an immediate bond, because he was dressed as informally as she was, in a shaggy old sweater and tan pants, and worn sneakers.

''Peter,'' said Mort jovially, standing and extending a hand. Louise leaned forward, as gracefully as she could in the chair, for the introduction that was coming. ''Louise Eldridge, meet Peter Hoffman, neighbor, and slated to be the next deputy secretary of defense.''

''Hello,'' she said.

''Hello.'' He leaned down and took her hand gently in his large one and gave it an imperceptible squeeze. ''I see Mort didn't take long dealing you in on the dirt,'' he said, in a voice with a penetrating, rather nasal quality. ''I'm a relative newcomer, too, and the first thing I heard when I moved here was all those tall tales about Sylvan Valley."

Mort stepped forward and put his arm around Peter and guided him away. "Excuse us, Louise. Peter and I are not part of your committee. We have a little legal work to do tonight while you people talk about replacing the swimming pool. But so good to meet you. So good to talk with you."

Peter looked back at Louise a fraction longer than politeness required. "I'll see you again. The wife's on the board, too."

Ninety minutes later Louise folded up the little notebook in her lap and replaced it in her purse. In the space of that ninety minutes she had become acquainted with nine new people, some of whom she wasn't sure she liked.

She had heard in detail about the decayed condition of the Sylvan Valley pool, every last rusty pipe and cracked surface. No one was discouraged by this tale of entropy, however. The treasurer, a quiet man named Bob Wilson, had devised a plan to raise money to rebuild it, amortizing the cost over a span of years. Louise, to her dismay, had been persuaded to become grounds chairman of the club. Jan, again, telling people all about her. But grounds chairman? Is this what she wanted to do? And what would it entail? The club owned six prime acres right in the middle of Sylvan Valley, and like her yard when they'd first moved in, the six acres were rather unkempt. No expensive groundskeepers, they had told her, but just a high school boy hired to mow the grassy sections.

She brushed her long hair away from her face, and gave the matter some thought. She knew herself to be a fussy gardener. She wondered if they could afford her. If she took over the grounds chairman job, she'd want to improve the whole place:

nagging members to get out and help neaten it up, wanting to spend real money on new plants and trees.

On the other hand, did she have to give way to her gardening lust at every turn? The club did not have an enormous budget, it was quite obvious, and it was all going to be gobbled up in those hideously expensive swimming pool repairs. Maybe this would be a good experience for her—learning to manage a very big garden on a small budget: It might force her, for once in her life, to curb her garden excesses.

As she attempted to get up from the chair, Sarah grabbed her hand in her rough one and effortlessly hefted her up to her feet. "We should have a pulley to remove people from that one." She stood close to Louise and looked for all the world as if she would like to hug her. "Don't look so serious, my dear. People here—including my husband—are actually nicer than they sound; I think they were showing off a little for you because you're new and you seem especially interested in this place." She nodded her head as if Louise had agreed with her. "I have difficulty with this Washington preoccupation with houses and neighborhoods, and how much houses are worth. I agree with Yeats." She laid a hand on her ample bosom; her gaze moved somewhere beyond Louise while she recited, in a low, eloquent voice, " 'I will arise and go now, and go to Inisfree, And a small cabin build there, of clay and wattles made: Nine bean-rows will I have there, a hive for the honey-bee, And live alone in the bee-loud glade.' " She smiled with satisfaction. "I memorized that in ninth grade. But we both know life's not that simple, and, anyway, cabins of clay and wattles must be very drafty. Now, as for *grounds* chairman"—she made it sound as if Louise had won the lottery—"it's just great fun. It means no more than getting the troops out next spring to pull weeds and rake leaves. We have a wonderful time, we all catch poison ivy, and then we eat hot dogs, no matter how cold. Later, you pop in a few petunias near the clubhouse door and we'll all think you're *wonderful.*'' She squeezed Louise's arm companionably.

''Or you could do what some have done—fill large containers with flowers and place them near the pool.'' This drawling speech came from Phyllis, Peter's wife. She was very small and thin, with gold hair falling in a pageboy over green eyes. Dyed, thought Louise. She was wearing beige slacks and top with high, sporty heels and bulky gold jewelry. During the meeting she had said little but had paid close attention to what others said and scanned Louise from head to foot, from her casual jeans skirt to her L. L. Bean suedecloth shirt and worn tennis shoes.

''Containers of flowers sound beautiful,'' said Louise. ''Would you like to help me?''

Sarah laughed and put an arm around her. ''You're a natural. Spoken like a true recruiter.'' She turned to Phyllis. ''Well, Phyllis, how about it? Will you be part of Louise's committee?''

Phyllis had pulled out a brown cigarette and was about to light it. ''You don't mind, do you, Sarah? I have to smoke this before Peter comes back or he will go into a rage.'' She lit up, inhaled, and exhaled deeply. Then she looked levelly at Louise. ''I'm so undependable, Louise. I'm a decorator and I travel. I have a few special clients I work with and for whom I buy antiques and things. That means I'm running off to shows, or maybe just taking a break with friends. . . .''

Rich, thought Louise. Rich and restless. Then Phyllis's eyes grew wary and she quickly tamped out her cigarette in a nearby glass dish—an ambiguous dish, Louise noticed, not quite an ashtray, not quite an objet d'art.

Her husband, Peter, and Mort had returned. Peter sniffed the air like a German shorthair. "Ah, the smoker's here," he said. He walked over to his wife and looked down at her without smiling. "You realize, of course, your smoking is harmful to others, not only yourself. When are you going to put that patch on?"

"Please, Peter, not here," she said, and turned to Louise with a hastily mounted smile. "I told you he was a bear about smoking. Forgive him."

"Wrong one to forgive. Let's go home. Louise, do you need a ride?" He turned to her in surprise. "My, you're a tall woman."

"Just the right height, my husband Bill always says." She did not know why she felt she needed to call up the name of her husband. "I don't need a ride, thanks. I only live down the hill and over a few steps."

Peter looked down at her. "You're new here." His voice was concerned. "You can't be too careful, even in this neighborhood." He stood so close that she instinctively drew back a little. "There are crazies down there on Route One who could wander over here into our neighborhood—who's to stop them? I never let Phyllis walk around at this time of night alone. Come on. We'll drop you off." He slipped a large but gentle arm around her shoulders and guided both Louise and his wife out of the room.

At the car, which was silver and low-slung, Louise demurred again, this time more firmly. "I thank you for the offer. But I can't ride with you. It is just not necessary."

His wife said good-bye and slid gracefully into the car. Peter lingered for a moment, looking at Louise. "All right, Louise. But I'll see you again."

Strange man, she thought, as she sauntered home through the oak leaves. But interesting. She liked his directness. It was refreshing, and different from what she saw in a lot of people around Washington, who seemed to specialize in indirection, if not actual lies. She knew about lying: Her husband lived a lie, and she helped him live it. The difficult dance of deep cover. But she wondered if she weren't growing beyond that.

6
Little Things Mean a Lot

LOUISE STOOD IN THE LIVING ROOM, STARING out at the rainy woods, and experienced a moment of hysteria. She placed her forehead against the glass and closed her eyes for a moment. Would he never leave?

A few more ordered bangs from the bathroom told her she had not yet won a reprieve. She had been fulfilling a two-month-long sentence with this man. The carpenter. Al Woodruff. Highly recommended by a friend of a neighbor, who used him some years ago.

"Mrs. Eldridge!" he yelled in a raspy voice. "C'mere. I'll show you the finished product."

She straightened slowly and walked toward the bathroom. Just as she passed the kitchen, the phone rang. She could guess who it would be. "Hello?"

"Is my husband there, Mrs. Eldridge?" The voice was stretched thin with tension. The carpenter's wife. She was like a living radar, determined to keep her husband within telephone range. "*Please* don't tell me he's ducked out."

"No, Mrs. Woodruff, he hasn't ducked out. He's still here . . . but just finishing. I'll put him on the line." She went down the hall.

Woodruff, a large, balding man in plaid shirt and jeans, the ends of a dozen nails protruding from his mouth, looked at her. His bloodshot eyes asked the question.

"Yes, it's your wife."

"Christ," he muttered out of the side of his mouth. He continued removing the nails quickly one by one and pounding them into a prestained molding strip. "There!" he boomed. "I'm finished." He passed her, trailing alcoholic fumes. "Better take that call before she *really* gets pissed—uh, 'scuse me—upset." He lumbered into the kitchen, and Louise could hear low-pitched combat.

She wondered how long it had been going on. Al had to be in his midsixties. His wife sounded about the same age. Had he been a drunk for years? The wife obviously didn't trust him. But then, neither did Louise. He wanted her there when he worked, but he had stood her up at least ten times after he said he would come. This had stretched the job beyond two months. To reduce the aggravation, she continued to improve the yard. With no trouble at all, she found new places to plant things, beyond those that she and Bill had budgeted for when they first moved in.

A climbing hydrangea went alongside a tall pine at the edge of the patio; someday it would flower in a column of glorious, puffy white blossoms. She moved a stand of bamboo to a small hillock in the side yard; she also had a local quarry deliver enough rocks for Bill to construct a partial wall to buttress the little incline.

It wasn't the first time that patient Bill had been called upon to build a wall for her: He teased her about trying to replicate Roman ruins wherever they lived. On top of the wall she planted a couple of jasmine plants, their arching branches cascading gracefully down over the rocks, looking as if they had been there for years. In spring, it would be a shower of tiny yellow blossoms.

Bill hadn't minded building the wall, but he had disapproved of moving the bamboo nearer to the house. In fact, she had tussled with the big, awkward, soggy clumps all by herself, for fear he would talk her out of the project. This left her muddy, and with a sore back from digging, but with an unbounded sense of accomplishment. She had lassoed the bamboo like dogies with a hunk of sturdy rope, and dragged them from the back corner swamp, one by one. Bill warned her she was creating a future southeast Asian jungle, skeptical that the twelve-inch black plastic edging she imbedded around them would keep them in check. He had looked at her darkly: "Do you realize bamboo has been known to uproot *whole houses*?" She promised him to keep a constant eye out to be sure it didn't grow beyond her plastic boundaries.

The Leyland cypresses were the last straw. When she brought the three of them home a few days ago—and, granted, they were big, so they were pricey—Bill had asked her to sit down to talk. It didn't matter to *him* that the cypresses were needed in the near distance to give real depth to the yard.

With extra politeness, he brought out the family accounts and went over them with her. He didn't even have to say it: It was obvious that she had become a horticultural spendthrift again. And right when they had taken on the biggest debt load of their lives. When he had gone on to suggest that she was overdoing the gardening because there was something missing in her life, Louise could hardly keep back her tears. She listened in this taut state, as he talked about the gardening "situation"—she would have laughed merrily at this euphemism had she had any sense of humor left—and, chastened, told him she would do the bills with him in the future, to get a better handle on their finances.

Louise knew she had a problem. She was a binge gardener, not much better than the binge drinker, Mr. Woodruff, now busy fighting with his nervous wife by phone in the kitchen.

She slumped against the handsome new bathroom sink and tried to dredge up one happy feeling about life.

Woodruff slammed down the receiver and rejoined her in the bathroom, his head down, muttering under his breath. But his spirits seemed to lift as soon as he looked at his completed work—new skylight overhead, Mexican tile on the walls, touches of wallpaper, and custom cabinets.

"It is lovely, Mr. Woodruff," said Louise, meaning it. Fortunately, his skills had been ingrained so deeply that they overrode the effects of alcohol. All those bad days when he had stumbled in half drunk would soon be forgotten. She would pay him and he would be gone, and she could get on with her life.

But no. No, he said, she needn't pay him today; he would send her a bill.

"And can I ask you one more little favor?" he asked. In his red and scarred face with its fattened jowls and knobbed nose she could see dimly the handsomeness that must have been in the young, strong, talented Carpenter Woodruff.

"What's that?" she asked, raising her chin to take any last blow.

She realized he was cajoling her the way he must have cajoled his wife in better days. "I sure would love one last cup of your nice, strong coffee." He smiled. With the exception of a couple of gleaming gold fillings in back, his teeth had grown old gracefully.

She smiled back. "Come on, let's sit in the kitchen. I have a couple of sweet rolls, too. I'll pop them in the microwave." She led the way down the hallway. She could see light at the end of this tunnel. But right now she had to make one more conversation with the man. Her mind sought vainly for a topic, and then one came. "By the way, Mr. Woodruff, do you know there is a valuable ground cover with your name?"

"Is *that* so?" he asked, his voice rising with desperate interest. "Tell me about it."

After she closed the door on Woodruff, she felt strange. On a sugar high from the sweet bun, but no place to go. She wandered slowly through her house, trying to look at it objectively. Time to take stock of things.

She had done well up to now, hadn't she? After all, weren't the pictures all hung now, and with only a few polite arguments with Bill? She wondered why he liked them hung higher than she did; it was one of their small incompatibilities. She straightened a small print that had moved from its assigned place.

And Janie was doing well. Apparently she liked tenth grade at her new school. She was filling out, not quite as thin as she used to be. She had a few friends, the best one the boy across the street. True, when she got in a glum mood she disappeared for long, solitary walks. But since Louise used to do that herself, she was sure it was normal.

Their highly social Martha, who didn't know how to be glum, liked Northwestern University and loved being away from home. She and Bill were comforted by the fact that Louise's parents lived three miles away in Wilmette, so that their daughter had a place to go if she needed family. When Louise went to Northwestern, she found, as she joked to friends, that her folks were about 497 miles too close. Now, it was perfect for Martha to have a grandmother and grandfather near at hand.

Except Martha was spending little time with her grandparents. And her phone calls home were becoming less frequent. Louise felt she had lost a daughter and Chicago had gained a social butterfly. ("The quarter system is hell, Ma. It gives us *no* time to have fun.") "My, my, Martha," Louise had said, "your profanity sounds so natural." A snapshot of one-year-old curly-headed Martha flicked through her mind. "I'm not that profane, Ma. Just when I think of everything I'm supposed to jam in my mind in ten weeks! It sucks!" Louise would try to talk about language when she came home for Thanksgiving. "The hardest class is the English seminar on feminism and Marxism. Now, don't worry about my becoming too rad— I'm more of a middle-of-the-roader." Louise had smiled at this moderate position from her opinionated offspring. "But it's this phallocentric stuff. It *pervades* our culture, Ma. I'm really going to have to bring you up to speed when I come home at Thanksgiving . . . *if* I come home.")

Phallocentric? Maybe she had better check some feminist writings out of the library before Martha arrived.

As for making friends near home, she and Bill liked the neighbors, but nobody was a real friend yet. They preferred to travel back to Bethesda to see their old-time friends. Because Louise had been persuaded to take the job of grounds chairman of the swim club by Sarah, the potter, she had felt obliged to study up on landscape effects at the library. Another woman in the neighborhood, Sandy Stern, played tennis with her every week, enabling Louise to keep up with her game. But now it was too cold. She, Sandy, and the elusive Nora from across the street seemed to be the only women at home during the day, although there probably were young mothers ensconced in other houses. The interesting Mary Mougey came over one afternoon, and they had tea. Mary's life seemed full of travel, to all parts of the United States and many countries of the world. As she told of the cruel plight of the millions of refugees in the world, Janie joined the two women, and sat on the floor at Mary's feet near the white couch. Her stories of distressed children brought tears to the girl's eyes, and Mary stretched out a hand to show she understood. As Louise saw the instant bond between the woman and the girl, she recognized Mary's enormous talent at reaching out to people. The only trouble with Mary was that she was seldom home.

Bill's experience was different. As soon as they moved in, he had started playing poker with the neighborhood men; he was developing bosom buddies faster than she was. As usual, her husband was right at home in a new place. Maybe that was because his family had moved many times when he was a child, while she spent her entire early life in the same house, with the same friends and neighbors.

As for the job search, she'd made some progress, hadn't she? She had borrowed an updated version of *What Color Is My Parachute?* from the library and answered a half dozen or more leads from friends and from the paper for writers and editors. So far she had had two interviews. Each time the job sounded so dull that she could hardly wait to get away. In both cases the offices had been modern, gray, electronically overburdened, and just not her kind of office at all. She would have to work on that.

Summing it up, Louise could say everything had been going along fairly smoothly. There were little things not quite set to rights: the smell and the swamp in the yard. The smell was in a closet within a closet. Mr. Woodruff, on seeing it, dismissed it. "Y'c'n fix it yourself," he assured her. "All these slab houses, from California on out east, have no basements so they have dead air beneath them. Usually smells like a rat died."

It was a small linen closet with a long, thin door in its side wall. This allowed access to some pipes for the adjacent bathroom that ran from underneath the concrete slab the twelve feet up to the flat roof. When she had first opened this access door she recoiled backward, holding her nose against the strong, moldy odor, and noted fleetingly before she closed the door that it would have made a good hiding place for her precious jewels, had she owned any.

Bill thought the odor inconsequential and had it low on his list of household tasks. She, on the other hand, put it first.

This smell was her enemy. It was the distillation of all the strangeness and the adjusting she had had to do in the past two months.

"It sucks!" she muttered. "It's got to go." Noting only fleetingly that she had absorbed daughter Martha's raw language, she went to the kitchen cabinet where Bill kept assorted tools and found a big roll of silver duct tape. According to him it was capable of holding the whole world together. Now she'd find out if he was right or not.

She ripped off stubborn hunks of the stuff and sealed the little door on all sides. Then she crouched down and sniffed from bottom to top. She smiled: only a trace of odor left.

One more small battle won. She got into her Wellingtons and rain jacket and went to the kitchen and fetched the colander filled with daily food scraps—vegetable peelings, coffee grounds, and eggshells—and went to the living room and slid the tall glass doors open. As she stood on the semicircular patio, raindrops pelted her face. She took deep breaths of cold air that hinted at the coming of winter.

She took a spade from the toolshed and dug a careful, deep hole in the garden alongside the patio, avoiding the little patch of pale lavender autumn crocus, *Colchicum speciosum,* which she had tucked amidst the *Geranium sanguineum* *"Album."* She found a spot and dug energetically, dumped in the contents of the colander, then carefully replaced the earth. It made her feel good that every useful scrap and ort of food was going back to recirculate in the earth. Each time she buried garbage, she thought of her grandmother, who had buried her scraps in her sunny, old-fashioned garden, winter and summer. She mused sadly on the fate of that old lady, who after having lived, loved, and gardened for eighty-two years, was now confined to a wheelchair in a retirement home. Only her bones, and not her mind, had deteriorated.

Thoughtfully, Louise returned her spade to its place in the toolshed, trying not to dwell on the realization that her grandmother was nearing her last days. Then she came back into the yard and turned her eyes toward the final garden problem: the swampy corner.

The trees were so numerous on the property there was no way a truck of fill dirt could be driven into the area. Even if it could, she reflected guiltily that she had spent her last dollar on garden materials—at least for this season.

She frowned and stared at the spot, then went down the steps and across the forested yard to look at it more closely. This tiny corner was a bog in dry weather and a pond in wet. On this dank, rainy day, the water poured evilly into it, imparting an ominous feeling that reminded her of a dark poem by Robert Frost about a forest pool.

Yet she had to admit that there was an awkward charm to the corner. It was due to the flagrant, big-leafed plants sprouting from the edge of the wetness. Skunk cabbage, with their mysterious, mottled purple and green spathes emerging in early spring, and turning showy yellow as spring grew older. In England, she had seen magnificent varieties growing near pools. The British used them in abundance, not being as skittish as Americans about the bad odor that was emitted when the leaves were crushed.

She was beginning to see possibilities out in this dank corner, and for a moment considered giving the swamp a reprieve. Her mind conjured up a picture of a lush bog garden, with plants that liked their feet wet. Japanese iris, Cyperus, Lysimachia, Japanese sweet flag, and horsetail would be perfect here.

Then, like a sign, a new burst of rain came splattering down on her face. Her heart hardened: She *wasn't* going to maintain a swamp in her new backyard. But how to get rid of it?

In an instant, a solution came to her that would spare her the expense and labor of buying and hauling bags of fill. She would just gather the fall leaves that her neighbors were putting out for the trash men, dump them out here, and bring up the level of the land. She heaved a sigh of satisfaction and headed for the house for a hot cup of coffee.

Scuffing leaves as she went, she walked quickly with head down around the corner of the house, nearly running into the figure wearing a hooded loden cape.

"Oh, hi," she said, recognizing the calm face beneath the hood. It was Nora, mysterious Nora, with whom she had not spoken since the cocktail party at Eric and Jan's when they first moved in. Louise felt unaccountably nervous. The smoky woman. The woman that men liked so well.

"Louise." Voice warm and lilting. Gray eyes irritatingly beautiful and unlined, although she appeared to be in her early forties like Louise. "I'm so glad I found you. When I rang your bell no one answered." She tilted her head back and looked at the sky. Her hood fell off her dark, straight hair.

Then she moved close to Louise. "Rain's stopped. D'you want to try sitting on a log out in your backyard?" She pointed to Louise's supersaturated woods.

"Wouldn't you rather go inside?" asked Louise. "It's so . . . chilly out here."

The big eyes studied Louise seriously. "Not really. I would always rather be outside, with the squirrels and birds."

"I'm dressed for it, I guess," conceded Louise, leading the way, clumping down the slight decline to a large log. The termites that had once feasted on it had contributed to making it a good seat. Nora would have a good view of squirrels here: They were working furiously, cleaning and burying oak nuts for winter.

"How about this?" asked Louise, and plopped down.

"Perfect," said Nora, smiling. "We're right in the spirit of Robert Frost." She settled her body down gracefully, then drew cigarettes and matches from a pocket and languidly lit up. Louise noticed she didn't inhale much; could she be smoking just for the effect? And how could she smoke if she were such a nature lover?

For a moment Nora said nothing. Then she turned her gray eyes on Louise and said, "I see you've had a contractor doing things to the house."

"Yes, a very *slow* contractor. He finally finished renovating the guest bathroom before Bill and I died of old age."

Nora chuckled. "We could tell from the things you put out to the curb."

"I'll show it to you if you like." Her voice was not enthusiastic. At the moment, nothing interested Louise less than her hard-won remodeling job.

"And you've populated your woods with the most wonderful-looking plants."

Louise took a sidewise glance at Nora's serene countenance. How unruffled the woman appeared, in contrast to Louise's churning inner discontent. "I didn't know if you'd noticed all the activity. I've just been trying to achieve—oh, that Japanese thing with near distance." She opened her hands on her lap. "I think, however, I've done enough this fall." That was surely an understatement.

Nora's cigarette was now at rest in her graceful hand, like a small, magic wand. Her bearing, as she sat on the termite-ravaged log, was as royal as a queen's. She turned her serene gaze again toward Louise. "I know you've been terribly busy, Louise, and done wonderful things. But are you happy here?"

Louise, who thought she had composed herself against domestic disorder, erratic contractors, closet putrefaction, the onset of empty-nest syndrome, and the psychic anguish of moving, looked for a moment at the poet sitting beside her on the log.

Then she burst into tears.

7

Invisible Janie

JANIE SNEAKED QUIETLY OUT THE REC ROOM door, closing it soundlessly behind her. Leaning against the house near the door was her bamboo walking stick, one her father had found for her and neatened up by cutting off its small branches with pruning scissors. She grasped it firmly and took off, loping through the woods that were her yard and down the street toward the nearest park. She left behind parents talking money. Specifically, Martha's college costs. By the time Janie went to school, think how much time they'd have to spend "talking finances," as they called it. By then, Martha would be a senior and the family probably would be penniless. They wouldn't sit there and tell comfortable little jokes to each other while they did their figuring. They would probably look grim and resentful, the way poor people always looked when they discussed their problems on TV shows. Janie was afraid of being poor. Maybe she had better get an after-school job; her mom didn't seem in a hurry to go to work. Having peeked at Martha's quarterly tuition bill, Janie didn't want to be the one to bring the family down.

She entered the park, walking quickly, enjoying the smell of rotting leaves and the gathering damp of night. She kept her stick at the ready. Then a tree root tripped her and she had to grasp a nearby scrub tree to keep from falling. "Clumsy," she condemned herself, and slowed down. She was walking in what she liked to call her "canyon." It was a narrow valley with a little creek running through. Next to the stream was a well-worn trail that had felt the tread of the feet of schoolchildren bound for Sylvan Valley Elementary. On either side of the park were lines of houses built on top of ridges.

Janie loved to walk here. She couldn't believe people lived in glass houses and didn't even pull the curtains at night. Well, some people did, but a lot didn't. She didn't know everyone yet; sometimes she and Melanie walked around on weekends or after school, and Melanie of course knew everything about everyone. But when Janie walked at night like this by herself, she often crept up through backyards and peeked in windows. Once when she did this, she met a chained dog in the backyard, a big dog who magically remained silent. A large, silent, golden dog. Rebuking her with its silence. Saying (silently), "Don't you know Sylvan Valley people do not reveal their normal curiosity about their neighbors? So what are *you* doing here, you misfit?"

She must not appear to be a threat to anyone, not even a dog. At this thought, she brandished her stick like a sword and leaped forward at an invisible foe and warned: "En garde!" Then, dropping her pose, she sauntered on. Maybe she would fill out like her sister, Martha, and then people would notice her more. Dogs might even bark at her.

Janie noticed that some houses had little additions, some had great big additions, while others had separate buildings similar to the one at her house. Her mother was now using this addition as her writing studio, which meant Janie rarely could entertain friends there any more. Instead she had to bring them into her bedroom, which wasn't nearly as cool. This had all happened after her mom talked with Nora, Melanie's mother. Although Janie liked Nora ("Call me Nora, Jane, and I'll call you Jane," she had said in that low voice of hers) she noticed that Nora was another housewife who didn't go to work. She wrote poetry, and Melanie said her mother got paid for it, too, but not even minimum wage if one counted up all the time it took. And now Nora had influenced her mother not to work but write instead, which was a little embarrassing, because Janie worried that her mother would never get published. So that left two of the women in the cul-de-sac as housewives who wrote, which was kind of funky. Secretly, it's what Janie could see herself doing when she was married. Secretly, she would like to be a Shakespeare or at least an Elizabeth Barrett Browning.

But the rest of the mothers had jobs with real salaries, like Mrs. Mougey, who was becoming a kind of friend of Janie's. She raised money to help needy children in the world, and probably earned lots of money, which always meant the family could more easily pay for things like college. She thought that type of job would make you feel good about yourself, although it was giving *Mrs. Mougey* more gray hair. She worked so hard, coming home late almost every night, leaving her husband alone all the time in the evening. Janie had a perfect view of their house out of her bedroom window.

She was torn. If only she didn't have to worry about money. Then she felt guilty: She was well aware of the homeless when the family drove through Washington. They made her ashamed to drive by, a passenger in a big, new car, wearing clean, new clothes. She knew her family would never suffer like that, and wondered how God figured out what was fair for people.

She saw the outlines of a big tree ahead. This was where the trail curved sharply up. Here she had a good view of one of those outbuildings, with a man working inside. A saw whined faintly. Janie scrambled up the small incline for a closer look, the leaves crunching like cornflakes. She crossed the yard. The man, who seemed very large, slowly moved his body with the saw, with an occasional forward thrust as if he had hit an easier spot in the wood. The saw's whine rose to a higher pitch when he hit those easier spots. Her father always talked longingly of having a saw so he could make his own furniture, but she knew somehow that this was just talk. Her dad was more of a reader than a carpenter. She came a few steps closer, then realized the saw had been turned off. Had he heard her? She froze. He was right there on the other side of the glass, blond, with thick glasses, wearing jeans and a big plaid lumberjack shirt like one her dad wore. In his hand was some kind of a planing tool, which he grasped like a weapon. He slowly turned around and stared at her, his eyes blue and dangerous.

She was visible! He could see her blond hair, her blue eyes, her skinniness, her jeans jacket, her tan Levi's, her dirty tennis shoes . . . he could see it all, she was sure. If only she had been a brunette, he wouldn't have been able to see her! Dropping her stick in terror, she turned and stumbled out of the yard, tripped and sprawled down the shallow incline, and landed in the path.

She pulled herself up to a sitting position. "Oooh," she groaned, and gently touched her face. Then a light shone on her. She looked up and there he was, standing motionless on the edge of the yard. She put a hand up to shield her eyes from the glare.

His voice was low and threatening. "My, what a pretty girl you are. But this is the last time I want to see you hanging around my house. You understand?"

Janie mumbled, "I . . . I understand. I'm really sorry. I won't ever do it again."

"And take your stick with you. Here it comes. Heads up." He threw it down at her and she brought a hand up to catch it but missed, and it caromed against her body, then flipped out into the darkness.

The man and the light had disappeared. Limbs trembling, she heaved herself up and ran back on the trail the way she had come, out of the park and down the street to home, leaving her stick behind.

She stood in her own backyard, panting for breath, her mouth and throat dry, her body cold but wet with perspiration. She slipped up the timbered steps leading to the patio and watched through the expanse of glass windows her parents sitting at the dining room table. Her father's arm was around her mother, and she knew this meant that later they would probably make love. If he had been sitting without touching, it would have meant one or the other had given some signal that they weren't going to make love that night. She had figured this out recently. And the rest of the world could figure it out too, because it was all right there for them to see. Her family was just like the others—no curtains drawn—families all over this neighborhood were living in fishbowls! No wonder kids were window peepers.

She retreated to the other side of the house, coming in through the rec room door, then quickly retired to the bathroom and locked the door. She looked at her face. The scratches were on one side only; she pulled her long, curly blond hair over the area. She was pleased to see that not only did it hide the scratches but it made her look very pretty, actually very grown-up, like that blonde in an ancient movie with hair over one eye and a lisp. Her eyes, for another thing, were still wild with excitement. The eyelashes were like little curtains sweeping the edges of her cheeks. Very becoming, she decided. Then she shuddered, remembering the man. Hoping she would never meet him again.

"Darling, are you taking a bath?" Her mother was at the door of the bathroom. "I thought you were still doing your homework."

"All finished, Ma," Janie said in a breezy voice. She

thought guiltily of the array of open books in her room. Yet any proper investigating mother would know that a person as neat as Janie would never leave them like that if she truly had finished her homework.

She turned on the water to almost the hottest range. She took off her torn and dirty clothes and sneakers and carefully bundled them to wash later. Her mother would ask too many questions if she found them, so they would go temporarily into Janie's superhiding place.

The bath was now quite full of steaming water. Into it went Janie's thin body. She lay back and put her blond head on the back of the tub.

"Gosh, this is living," she said to herself, and closed her eyes.

8
Kristina

PETER REMEMBERED WHEN HE'D FIRST MET HIS current mistress. One night, because his wife hadn't done it earlier, he was stuck with taking the dog for a late walk. It was spring, and the air smelled of spring's earliest flowering blossoms. It must have been near midnight. He walked down the path in the woods and then for some reason up to Martha's Lane. She had been standing among the trees in her front yard. Wearing white, looking up. Looking like a nymph conferring with the moon.

He had called to her. "Are you all right?"

"Oh, yes, I am all right," she had called back softly, a lilt raising the "yes" to something special. "I am only out here at this hour to enjoy the beautiful smells."

It turned out she was Austrian. He had gravitated toward her as if she had been a magnet, and had been held ever since. Translucent sort of beauty. That charm that only European women possess. Small, lithe, very sexual. And with the ability to love him like his current wife or his ex-wives had never done.

Her name was Kristina.

They met next for lunch at Le Steak in Georgetown. Then he had taken her to his place on Q Street. They had tea in the tiny garden. The acrid smell of the boxwoods hung in the damp air and somehow turned them on. They did their mating dance while sitting on French wire garden chairs. She was witty without once talking about Washington politics. They had a proper conversation but smiled conspiratorial smiles, knowing what they would do next and relishing it. Finally they looked at each other and decided the preliminaries were over. They took the tea tray into the kitchen—she carried it, and he put his hand on her silk ass—then rushed to the bedroom and fell at each other.

Two hours later the sheets were sweaty with their lovemaking, and they were fully acquainted. Comfortable with each other. After that, they met weekly and spent long hours in that bedroom, sometimes going out later to eat, sometimes just eating in.

That had been spring. Now it was fall. A seven-month affair: a little shorter than his average. The bitter, unexpected cold of early November had hardened the ground just as fast as it had hardened his heart.

Kristina had cried too much when he told her they had to break it up. He could tell there would be trouble. At first he had been moved. Did this one really love him? For a fleeting second he considered another divorce, then a marriage to this continental, warmhearted woman. But a second terrible picture flashed across his mind: another bitter, rejected wife to get rid of. An open scandal the press would devour. His nomination down the tubes. No thanks. No woman was worth that.

It was then he realized how unhandy it was to have acquired a lover who lived in the same neighborhood. What if, in one of her hysterical moods, Kristina let something slip? She had seemed like the perfect woman. But even she must have woman's mischief in her; what if she decided to squeal to his wife?

He knew that Paschen, an arrogant, hypocritical bastard who probably ran around on his own wife, would leave Peter no room for error.

Now he stood in Kristina's living room. He had been here only once before, on that first night they met. Dangerous to be here but necessary. Just two blocks from his own house—perilously close. But it couldn't be done at his place in Georgetown; the noise of a saw would carry through the walls of the row house.

He had it all planned. He had even practiced in his workshop. He had to do it right.

She was to leave tomorrow for one of her foreign buying trips. Gone for two months. Once he had resolved to do this, he had acquired a detailed knowledge of both her business and her personal habits. It had been pathetically easy; Kristina construed it only as an intensification of his love for her. It had been just as easy to acquire samples of her handwriting. He'd write to the few people in the States who would miss her, regarding her plan to live abroad. At the proper time, his Hong Kong connection would send the letters.

A more sophisticated letter would go to her company, severing her relationship with them—a move that she had been contemplating anyway, and that the company knew about. Mail would be forwarded to his Hong Kong source, and then back to him in the States.

No one would miss her for quite a while.

And then the messy part. He thought nostalgically of the ease with which he had disposed of bodies in the jungles of Vietnam. A quick shot or knife thrust, and kick the body into the underbrush, where the animals and insects would take care of it within hours.

Here, he would have to use her laundry room. A bloody mess but no way around it. Store—in her freezer—the parts that could be identified. Deep-six them later in the Potomac. Dispose quickly of the rest. A perfect crime. As chance would have it, she had provided him with just the right type of innocent containers sitting out in front of her house. Otherwise, there would have been a storage problem bigger than the one he already had, in stowing somewhere the readily identified parts—or elements. Elements. That was the euphemism that readily came to mind; he grasped it gratefully.

With a start, he broke from his reverie. He looked over at her, sitting on the rose couch. Thinner than usual. Her hair looked like hell. He loved her hair. It was light brown with a rosy tone. So he'd teased her a lot about her pink hair. And her eyes; he loved her eyes, with their slight slant. Some Mongol barbarian blood in there.

But now she looked like hell. Yes, and nervous. Could she read his mind? His gorge rose in his throat. He fought to keep his face smooth, noncommittal. He took a deep breath and strolled across the room. In his pocket he fingered a coil of strong, thin wire, fashioned with a padded loop on either end.

Her brown eyes followed him as he approached. He sat down beside her and draped a hand gently around her.

"You're tense, my dear. Turn a little and I'll massage your shoulders, like old times."

She exhaled and took a deep, relaxed breath. "Oh, I'd love that so." As he started kneading her shoulder muscles, she turned her face and quickly kissed one of his hands. A current ran through him of remembered sexual pleasure. She said, "We're having our troubles now, Peter, but we can find some solution. Just don't forget how much I love you."

The words, the touching, sent a message right through him down to the groin, hardening his penis and softening his resolve. Then he pulled in his breath, bared his teeth in a grimace, and pulled the garrote out of his pocket. At that instant she turned and saw his changed face.

"Peter!" She howled it like an animal. Her eyes near his were more terrifying than any Vietcong's had ever been. Then she attacked him.

Blown it! This 110-pound woman was fighting him! Shoving him in the face, scratching him, twisting away . . . how dare she!

"Bitch! Die!" He roughly grabbed her arms and wrenched

them back as if breaking wings off a chicken. She screamed. Then quickly he slipped the wire around the small neck, avoiding those large, angry brown eyes. Now it was easy—just a matter of keeping a tight hold. The screams turned to gurgles. Her objecting body arched up in a parody of lovemaking. The fingers—God, he thought he'd neutralized those arms and fingers—clawed at her neck where the wire was now buried deep.

Finally, she drooped like a dead flower.

And he, he who was twice her size, was left gasping for breath. It had always amazed him what superhuman strength invaded humans when they were being killed.

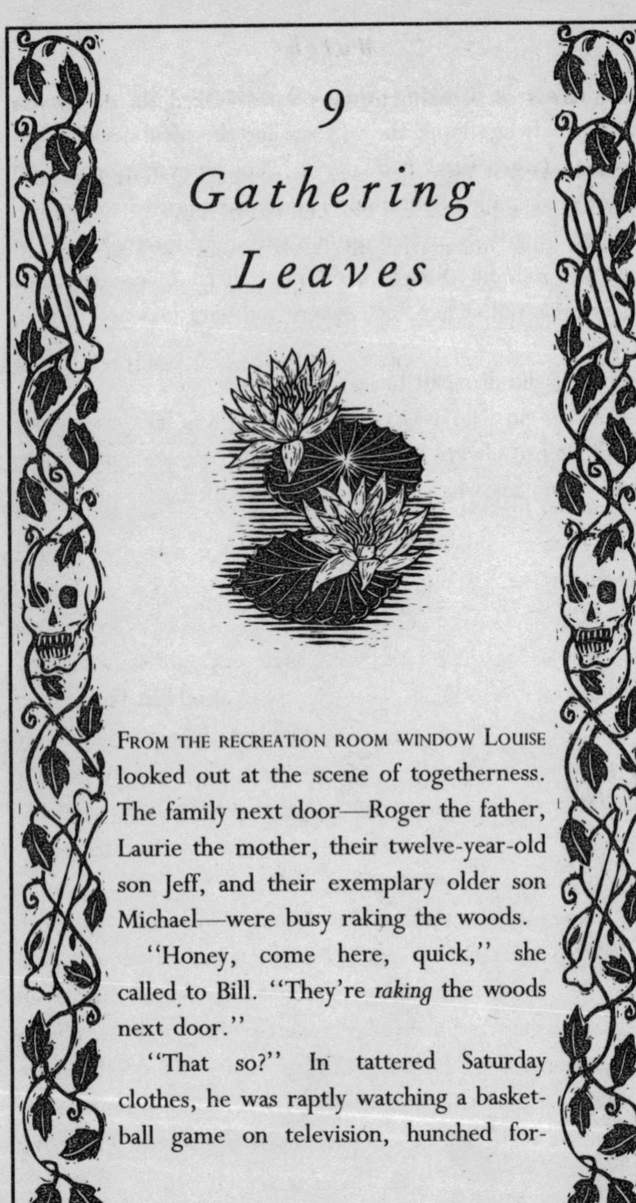

9
Gathering Leaves

FROM THE RECREATION ROOM WINDOW LOUISE looked out at the scene of togetherness. The family next door—Roger the father, Laurie the mother, their twelve-year-old son Jeff, and their exemplary older son Michael—were busy raking the woods.

"Honey, come here, quick," she called to Bill. "They're *raking* the woods next door."

"That so?" In tattered Saturday clothes, he was raptly watching a basketball game on television, hunched forward, hands on knees. His eyes were locked on the sports action.

She looked at him, her eyes narrowing. Quietly she said, "The house is on fire and our child is burning."

"That so?" murmured Bill, then sat forward and yelled, "Shoot, baby, shoot!" She looked at him in disgust and went to get her jacket out of the front hall closet.

"Ma," summoned Janie as Louise passed her room. "You leaving?"

"No, I'm going outside to play," she said, smiling. She came in and sat on the end of the bed where Janie sat propped up with her French II workbook. A neat pile of notebooks was stationed next to the bed. "Actually," said Louise, "I'm going outside to beg the neighbors for their leaves."

Janie hid her blond head in her hands. "Oh no, Ma, tell me no," she said in a pleading voice. She opened her hands and peered at her mother in disbelief. "Is Michael out there? And you're going to humiliate me by asking for their *leaves?* Can't we get some more on our way to Bethesda?" She swung her feet down and sat on the edge of the bed next to her mother. "Tonight. Tonight I'll even help you swipe them in the neighborhood if you'll just—"

"Janie, just cut it out," said Louise. She stood up. "You are being so sensitive I can hardly believe it. I thought you were the environmentalist. I thought you would have read about mulching and using the resources that we have. Leaves are just something else that needs recycling. There's no sense in sending them to the recycling fields of Fairfax County when we can use them in our own backyard. All I'm doing is asking neighbors who are nutty enough to rake their woods to save them for me."

Janie, more composed now, got up, stood very tall, looked her mother almost eye to eye, and said, "Okay, Ma. I get you. But you may be ruining a future romance before it even starts." Then she laughed, and Louise gave her daughter a little hug. Michael, the boy next door, was the same age as Janie but totally engrossed in, as Janie said, "being as perfect as his parents have always planned."

Louise put on her work jacket, gloves, and gardening boots. She went outside and strolled casually over to where Roger was raking. "Beautiful day," said Louise, and then felt foolish. It was one of those overcast, chilly Saturdays when many people simply threw up their hands and hit the local movie house. "On second thought, it's kind of gray . . . kind of like the world is." Roger's favorite subject was international affairs. He was considered an expert.

"Hi, Louise," he said, smiling at her. "Not so bad out here after you work up a little sweat. As for the world situation, that's also causing me a lot of grief. I should be at work right now; probably have to go in for a while tomorrow."

"Hello, Louise," called Laurie, walking over, her red hair attractively windblown. Jeff and Michael came over, too, and Louise realized raking wasn't their favorite occupation.

"Do you always rake your woods?" inquired Louise politely.

"Well, it *is* a yard," said Roger, adjusting his glasses and studying her more closely. "Even though there's no grass. But Laurie's going to plant some ferns around in here." He pointed to the now bare ground.

''I'm pretty excited about it,'' said Laurie. ''I've talked to a landscaper, and he's recommended that I order six dozen ferns to be put in in the spring. They're supposed to spread. Then he also suggested a grouping over here—'' she pointed to a spot where nature had already planted a gracious clump of small trees—''a few azaleas and a few variegated cotoneaster.''

''That will be great,'' said Louise. She turned to the children. ''And how are you, Jeff . . . and Michael?''

''Part of the slave labor around here,'' said Michael, batting his rake like a tennis racquet. ''I'd rather be doing my physics than this.'' He was slim, with dark red hair like his mother, and vivid brown eyes. Jeff, several years younger, seemed drab in comparison. He watched his brother and smiled faintly.

''Physics. I didn't know students took up physics in tenth grade.''

''A special program they used to have at Sylvan Valley but don't have any more,'' Laurie explained. ''Kids who tested at one-fifty IQ level or above''—her eyes skidded toward her son, who continued to pat the air with his rake as he stared into the distance—''were admitted in sixth grade, so by ninth grade they're at least a year ahead in science. Michael is one of the twenty or so who went through this program.''

''Well,'' said Louise. The look on Jeff's face made Louise want to change the subject. ''Maybe I can save you a little work out here. Rather than have you bag your leaves, can I please have them? We have a low spot on the edge of the property near the stand of bamboo, and as you might have seen, I've been gathering bags of leaves to put in there and raise the level a bit.'' She looked at the large piles of leaves the

Kendrickses had labored to achieve. ''Bill and I have a large drop cloth. We can just come over and gather them up with that.''

''Oh, no, Louise,'' said Roger. ''We have lots of recycling stuff. We'll just bag them up and leave them on the edge of your property.'' He looked at Michael, a strange look from a parent to a child, thought Louise. As if Roger were in awe of this handsome boy at his side, in awe perhaps of the fact that he, the father, was still in charge. ''No. What we'll do,'' said Roger with finality, ''is have Michael carry the bags to your backyard and put them with those others you've collected.''

''Oh, my goodness,'' said Louise, ''you'll be doing all the work.''

Roger waved imperially. ''It's done. No trouble.''

Louise looked closely at Michael. ''You don't mind?'' she said, smiling.

''I'm not permitted to mind,'' he said, with a flourish of his rake and a winner's smile.

Louise went inside the house. Janie stood in the living room, well away from the windows so as not to be seen from the outside. ''What's Michael doing?'' she asked shrilly. ''He's carrying those leaves for you. What did you say to him?''

Louise went into the kitchen, pulling from the refrigerator the makings of pepper steak. ''His family has commanded it, and it is being done.'' Then, under her breath, ''Would that this family helped me without squawking.''

With dinner finished, the leftovers were put away and the dishes nearly done. Janie was helping dry the pans. ''Okay, Ma, any time now I'm ready.''

Louise was feeling that special satisfaction that comes when dishes again are done. She added a final victorious wipe to the stainless steel sink. "You're ready. Now let me see. What are you ready for?"

Not to be outdone by her mother, Janie took the last of the pans, the deep skillet in which Louise had cooked the pepper steak, and with a flourish she dried it and slipped it into its appointed place in the cupboard. "I am ready to willingly . . . under the cover of darkness . . . help you go get some more leaves." She looked at Louise hopefully. "Unless maybe with the Kendrickses' you don't need any more?"

Louise grabbed Janie's arm. "What a good sport you're getting to be! Let's go. I could use some more. Oak leaves are mainly what's left, and they're acidic, you know—really good as mulch under the rhododendrons and the azaleas."

Janie said, "Ma, why are you giving me another gardening lecture? Let's just go. Take the wagon, it holds more. Besides, it's already dirty."

Mother and daughter drove around the neighborhood in the dark. Louise was disappointed to see no bags of leaves. Maybe they were waiting until closer to trash day. They drove past houses with people partying or watching TV and other houses that were totally dark. In front of such a house, in the cul-de-sac on Martha's Lane, they found the bonanza Louise was seeking: a dozen well-stuffed bags of leaves. She stopped and Janie helped her crowd six of them into the rear of their elderly station wagon.

"Is that enough?" said Janie.

"It will have to be. This is the end of the leaf season." She looked over at her daughter. "It was pretty nice of you to offer to do this tonight."

''That's okay, Ma. I'm just like Michael—nothing better to do. Might as well help the family.''

Louise looked in the rearview mirror. A car facing the same way as theirs had turned on its parking lights and was slowly keeping pace with them. She had not noticed it in the cul-de-sac on Martha's Lane, where all of the houses had been dark. She slowed down for the turn onto Ransom Road. The car behind her slowed down, too. ''Hmmm,'' mumbled Louise.

''What?'' asked Janie.

''Oh, nothing,'' said Louise, her mind already on how tomorrow she would get the family to help her spread the leaves she had collected and close up gardening for the season. She needed to get back to work on her writing.

❧

It must have been 12:30 Sunday morning when the phone rang.

''Bill, sorry to wake you—you were asleep, weren't you?'' It was Sam Rosen, their neighbor. ''I wanted you to know I heard someone in the yard a few minutes ago. Your yard or my yard, I couldn't tell, but I'm pretty sure yours.''

''Should we call the police?'' Bill asked sleepily.

''If you want to, but I'd say, let's don't do it. This is Sylvan Valley. It's probably kids returning from a party, just cutting through. I know they didn't hang around long. I just wanted to tell you to lock the doors in case you hadn't.'' Sam chuckled, and Bill could tell that, unlike him, his neighbor was wide awake and full of chat. ''Lots of people around here have never locked their doors, since the day they moved in—can you believe that? I'm a little more paranoid, maybe, mostly to discourage kids from being tempted to do something they shouldn't. That's why I put in those floodlights. I've turned them on now and you and Louise ought to be able to sleep peacefully. Better still, I put Missy out on her line. She'll yap her head off if any strangers approach."

Bill thought of Missy, a black and white mongrel, maybe eighteen inches long, maybe fourteen inches high, tops. "Thanks, Sam. Sounds like you've taken care of it. G'night."

"G'night."

10
Distributing Leaves

LOUISE CLOSED THE BOOK REVIEW SECTION AND looked above her half-glasses at her husband. He was a pleasant sight, thin face and lined brow relaxed, handsome in his white dress shirt and Sunday dress sweater. The family had been to church, had breakfast, and since then had burrowed into the Sunday papers with a delicious disregard for time. He looked up from the sports section as if she had sent him a telepathic signal. He grinned and looked at his watch. "I can always tell when my time is up. You want us to help now in the yard, don't you?''

Still in her blue church-going dress, she gave her husband a conciliatory smile. Despite his protestation, he liked yard work. She said, ''You're right. But it won't take us long, dear. And then, if Janie has her homework under control, we can go to the movies.''

Janie, sprawled on the floor, reading the funnies, said morosely, ''I wonder what other kids are doing this afternoon. Going to the Smithsonian maybe, or a concert, or just being left alone to do their homework in peace. . . .''

Bill got up and, passing Janie, reached down and unceremoniously tousled her blond hair. ''Grumble, grumble. Other kids are probably just like you: at home and buggin' their parents. C'mon, Janie, time to suit up for our big leaf-spreading project. Get on your most disreputable clothes.''

Janie changed to her new jeans jacket and tan pants, Bill to his tattered chinos and lumberjack shirt, and Louise to her usual yard uniform, Japanese garden pants, boots, and heavy wool sweater. They went out into the crisp, sunny November day and surveyed the backyard.

''Oh boy,'' said Janie, ''this place has turned into a graveyard for old leaves. I'm glad we're getting rid of them. The neighbors will begin to talk. What other mother on earth would swipe other people's leaves?'' The big tan bags stood against each other at angles, like a platoon of slightly drunken soldiers.

Louise was all business now. ''Here's what we need to do: There are about twenty-six bags here. Bill, can you take six bags—be sure they're oak leaves—to the front yard? They'll be just enough to mulch the rhododendrons and azaleas. Do that first, will you, darling?''

''Yes, ma'am,'' said Bill, bowing a little. ''Whatever you say.''

''Good. Then Janie and I will start dragging the rest to the back corner, where we will dump them. Except, Bill, will you also take two bags with oak leaves and put them near the addition, because we need to mulch the little hollies I planted along the west edge.''

''Your wish is my command, ma'am,'' he said. He walked off, dragging a bag of leaves in either hand as if he had the Katzenjammer Kids by the scruffs of their necks.

Janie put her hands on her hips and looked at her retreating father. ''Ma, why does he always tease you about gardening? What is it, anyway? Why doesn't he just do it? *He's* the father.''

Louise gripped a bag firmly and said, ''Don't worry about it. Men tease when they can't think of what else to say. He really loves working in the yard, but I can't see him standing here like Wordsworth or Shelley or somebody, going on about it.'' She looked at her frowning daughter. ''After all, darling, your father is a political scientist, not a poet.'' She began dragging the bag of leaves. ''Come on, let's get on with it.''

Janie followed her like an unhappy puppy, her mouth turned down, her brow furrowed with the same kind of wrinkles her father had in his forehead. ''That's another thing,'' she said, trailing behind her mother. ''I think he's more than just a State Department foreign service officer. I think he's doing something secret. Don't you ever think that?'' She looked at her mother with her chin held defiantly high.

Louise stopped and looked at Janie. "Let's you and Dad and I talk that over carefully one of these days"—she grimaced—"but not today. I'd like to get this job finished first."

Janie dropped into a thoughtful silence as one by one they took the bags to the rear corner of the yard.

Louise herself was panting with the effort. "Gosh," she said, "I think these are heavier . . . although I don't know why. It hasn't rained or snowed since we brought them here."

Bill, carrying a rake, joined them, and they quickly moved the rest of the bags.

"Now comes the fun part," said Bill. "Come on, Janie, let's empty the bags. Louise, you do the raking. Try to keep the leaves in a neat, high pile." He looked at his wife through the corner of his eye and said, "I'd estimate a five-foot-high pile, which we will undoubtedly achieve in this little corner of the world, will—given the proper incantations and phases of the moon—disintegrate into about four inches of mulch."

"Exactly. You're such a good helper you can kid me all you want. But this probably will solve our water problem. We'll never have another puddle out here. And try to avoid stepping on that dessicated plant out there—I want to save it."

Bill and Janie started upending the bags, Bill working quickly, lifting them effortlessly and throwing the contents in Louise's direction.

Then they all saw it and heard it at once. Two thuds, as two plastic-wrapped objects flipped through the air to the ground near their feet.

"My God, what's this?" said Bill.

"No wonder these bags are heavy," complained Janie. "They've mixed trash in here . . . what . . . what *are* these things?'' She reached down quickly and picked up one of the packages, holding it like an unwelcome present. ''Gol, this looks like an arm!'' she cried. ''But it can't be an arm—but *heavy.* And this one . . .'' She picked up the second package.

''Janie.'' Bill barked it. ''Drop it!''

She stopped and stared at her father. ''Gee, Dad, just because someone puts some old meat or something in with their leaves . . .'' She glared at her father.

Louise ran over to Janie and took the package from her. She dropped it on the ground and turned her daughter's shoulders toward the house. ''Janie, please go in the house. Just go. Dad and I will take care of this.''

Janie's eyes had grown round and terrified. She jerked out of her mother's grasp. ''No, Ma. Don't do that to me. Don't act as if I'm a baby. I've already seen something; I've got to see the rest.'' She looked at her father. ''After all, Dad,'' she added, ''it's my yard, too.''

''All right,'' said Bill, ''but stand well back.'' Janie and Louise backed up a few feet through the rustling leaves, as cautious as if he were investigating a bomb. ''Now let's all try to keep calm while we figure this out.'' He knelt down and picked up the longer package with his gloved hands and gently felt it. ''Let's be sure what we're looking at first. It's probably just . . . a ham bone, maybe.'' He made a face. ''Lots of plastic wrap . . . you can see that.'' He carefully unpeeled the outer layers of plastic until they could all see through the remaining layers a flesh-colored object with large, dark smears on it. Bill sniffed, then pulled back in revulsion.

He put the object down quickly and looked up at Louise. His voice was very low. ''Louise, let's go in and call the police. And Janie, whether you want to or not, I want you to go with your mother into the house.''

''What is it?'' cried Janie. He stood up quickly and swayed a little, his mouth contorted as if he were going to spit. ''Let's go,'' he muttered. ''We've all seen enough.'' He hustled Louise and Janie through the leafy woods and back into the house, the warm, friendly house with its strewn newspapers and empty coffee cups.

Within what seemed only a minute of Bill's phone call, they could hear the sirens crying, louder and louder. Police cars with blue flashing lights wheeled around in the cul-de-sac, like a covey of grounded UFOs, and stopped in front of their house.

Four dark-clad policemen hurried down the woodland path to the front door. Bill opened it, looking much older and thinner than a few minutes before. The officers talked to him in low tones, as if not wanting Louise and Jane to hear. Bill accompanied them to the backyard while Louise and Janie watched out the back windows, prisoners in a glass house.

The police went to the leaf pile, crouched down, and examined the packages without moving them from where they lay.

''I think they're unwrapping one,'' said Janie, pulling her breath in sharply. Suddenly, in unison the men moved back, recoiling from the opened package. All stood up except the policeman handling the package. Bill bowed his head solemnly.

''Oh, God,'' whispered Louise. Janie was silent.

They watched the officers walk around and carefully upend

each of the remaining bags of leaves, as if performing a solemn ceremony. In each case they placed the bag alongside its contents.

Janie turned to her mother and smiled lamely. "They're not getting those leaves in the corner where you want them, Ma."

"I noticed. Not a lot we can do about it, is there?" She squeezed her daughter around the waist, noticing how large her eyes were. The child would never sleep tonight, but then, would she or Bill?

Suddenly all the policemen gathered together around the leafy contents of other emptied bags.

"Oh, no, they've found something else!" cried Janie. She opened the patio door and they stood there, waiting as the men crouched down, first at one pile, then at the next.

After a minute Louise said, "That's it; I'm going out." She shoved the patio door completely open, strode down the timber steps, and quickly crossed the sixty feet to where the men were.

"Bill—what is it now?" she demanded.

He turned to her, startled. The officers broke their huddle and looked at her distractedly. Now she could see the packages on the ground. Her eyes fixed on their rough, angular lines. The unmistakable shapes. The dried blood. She dropped her jaw in horror. "Oh, no!" she wailed. "It is. They're body parts!"

Bill came toward her and put his arms around her. "Louise," he said quietly, "maybe you don't want to be here. I don't want to be here either, and I'll be in quickly. There are four more packages. They say they're part of a woman's torso, and leg, and another piece of . . . her arm.''

She swallowed and looked at Bill. ''I'm going to be sick.'' She broke away from him and ran back through the leaves up the steps onto the patio. She vomited near a large *Pieris japonica* bush, then lost her balance and nearly fell into its thorny arms.

Her daughter came out and guided her into the house. ''Ma, come on with me. It's going to be all right.'' Louise stumbled in and slumped onto the couch. Janie got her some tissues to wipe her mouth.

Louise leapt up again. ''Coffee,'' she muttered, as if this were the solution to all problems. She hurried to the kitchen. ''I have to put on a pot of coffee,'' she called back to Janie. ''Your father will need coffee. It's getting cold out there.'' She filled the kettle and put it on.

''Uh-oh,'' reported Janie from the door. ''More men are coming now, Ma, a big fat man in a brown suit . . . no overcoat. I wonder if he's a detective. And another man in an overcoat; maybe he's the boss . . . but cute . . . maybe too young to be the boss. Maybe the guy in brown is the boss.''

Louise got the coffee beans from the freezer and poured them with trembling hand into the coffee grinder, then pressed the start button and held it so long that they were pulverized to powder.

''Now they're putting tags on the bags of leaves,'' reported Janie, ''and they're taking them away. And those packages . . . they're putting them in black bags of some kind. I guess they're taking them away. The cute guy and the big man in the brown suit are coming this way with Dad. I think they're going to come in. And one of the cops is walking all around the edge of the yard rolling out some yellow tape.'' She gasped and caught her breath and looked over at her mother in the adjoining room. ''That's to mark off the scene of a crime! Criminy! Our backyard is the scene of a *crime*?'' Louise leaned against the kitchen cupboard and stared into space.

Janie returned to her surveillance. ''I can see Sam next door; he's coming to see what's going on. And here come the VandeVens too—boy, they're here in a hurry.''

Louise sighed and opened the refrigerator. ''The whole neighborhood's probably dying to know what's happened.'' She poked around the refrigerator shelves aimlessly, as if looking for something lost.

Bill opened the patio door. ''Louise, Janie,'' he called in a tight voice. Louise turned around and walked slowly into the living room to meet them.

''These are Detectives Morton and, uh''—Bill turned to the heavier man in the brown suit—''Geraghty, right?''

''Mike Geraghty, that's right,'' said the man. He went right up to Janie and put out his large ham hand and enveloped Janie's thin one in it. Then he shook hands with Louise. ''We know you've had a shock,'' he said to Louise. He had large, blue, staring eyes that she somehow found reassuring and a thatch of white hair. ''But still we need to ask you some questions. I understand Jane knows something about all this, too.''

''What *is* it all about, Detective Geraghty?'' asked Louise. ''We don't know either.''

"Well, first let's sit down," ordered Geraghty in his easy way.

They sat around the dining room table, with Geraghty taking the seat at the head of the table, which Bill usually occupied, and Morton at the other end of the table. Morton was handsome, Louise noted, but with a face like a mask. Wordlessly he took off his overcoat and put it on an empty chair. Then he sat down, put his notebook and pen to his left on the table, and folded his hands. Bill and Louise, on opposite sides of the table, looked at each other forlornly. Then Bill's face broke into his beautiful grin and he reached both hands across the table and briefly squeezed Louise's hands in his.

Geraghty looked at them with unabashed curiosity. He leaned back, relaxing, and his suit coat fell aside, revealing a rotund belly. Louise had read that as people aged, women, being hippier, tended to become pear-shaped, while men, with their slimmer hips and bigger stomachs, ended up shaped like apples. She could see that this man had achieved his goal early.

He waggled a finger first at one and then at the other. "So you two get along pretty well, hey?"

"We get along very well," said Bill, without smiling. "Now, Detective Geraghty, let's get down to it. Tell us what you need to know—beyond what I've already told you."

The voice that interrupted was low and harsh. Morton. He was looking squarely at Louise. "We want to know how you come to have those packages in your bags of leaves."

"Well . . . they aren't, ah . . . our leaves," she stuttered. She looked closely at the young man for the first time. Morton's upper body was the better part of him, so his head was well above the rest of theirs, giving him a giant quality that Louise found unsettling. Were these men playing good cop–bad cop with them? If so, what on earth for?

His dark eyes bored into her face. ''Well, the leaves are in your yard. What do you mean they aren't your leaves? Where'dja come by 'em if they aren't yours?''

''I, we picked them up here and there.''

''In the woods, right?'' the detective persisted. ''Getting 'em ready to set out for the trash men, right?''

Faintness enclosed her like a light blanket, and her heart thumped hard for a moment. Then it stopped thumping, leaving a little curlicue of pain in the middle of her chest. She was glad it had stopped, as if she had a new chance. ''Let me explain, Officer Morton.'' Her voice was dangerously sweet. ''We are organic gardeners, Bill and I. We collected these leaves from other people. We were using them to mulch our plants and to enrich the forest floor.'' She looked steadily at Morton as if daring him to quibble with their organic gardening techniques.

''You needed thirty bags—*that* many bags, to enrich the forest floor?''

''Twenty-six. There were only twenty-six.''

''Thirty, ma'am, I counted. And by the way, why don't you just call it the ground, Mrs. Eldridge, instead of a floor?'' He looked at her as one might look at a sassy child.

Louise slumped back in her chair. ''You're right, Mr. Morton. Why did we get all those leaves? It was so much work, and look what we got for it.''

''You must have had some reason.''

She looked at the unpleasant man. "You just take whatever you get when you pick up other people's throwaways."

Morton and the others looked at her, alarmed.

Bill said, "Louise, are you all right?" Then he turned to Morton and said, "We collected them mostly to fill in a low spot in the corner of the property. Right where you found . . . the packages. That's where we were emptying them. It was really a good idea on Louise's part; it saved buying a bunch of fill dirt."

Morton looked at Bill and then at Louise without expression. Then he said to Geraghty, "I guess I've heard everything now." He dove into his notebook and busily wrote.

Geraghty heaved a big sigh. Louise looked at him and knew what he was about to do. Smooth the rough waters or, as Bill would put it when feeling crude, follow the circus horse to pick up his mess.

"Mrs. Eldridge," said Geraghty in a friendly voice, "your husband says you picked up these leaves all over the place. Can you please try to remember just where those places were?"

She turned to Geraghty. "Oh, let's see . . . Foxhall Road, in Washington, just beyond Canal Street, by those big embassy houses . . ."

Morton's head jerked up and he and Geraghty exchanged weary glances. Louise could read the situation: It was bad enough being pulled out on Sunday evening to investigate some stray body parts found in leaf bags, without dragging in another jurisdiction as well.

"Bethesda," she continued, "where we have friends, though not from the friends' houses, but along the route." This time the detectives masked their dismay: three jurisdictions! She continued: "And of course, here in the neighborhood, including quite a few from the next-door neighbors."

"Next-door neighbors?" echoed Morton ominously, and Louise suddenly visualized relations with her new neighbors deteriorating under the strain of a criminal investigation.

She said dryly, "I'm sure that a *Washington Post* reporter who's a specialist on international affairs has just the mind-set to murder someone, chop them up, and then toss the parts in bags he thereupon gives to me for mulch. Or his wife, Laurie—very suspicious there in her Belleview Boutique. Why, she could be plotting murders while rearranging the earring display."

"Now, now, Louise," said Bill smoothly, patting her hand, "we mustn't get sarcastic. But, I'm sorry to say, guys, I just remembered another collection spot—the Westmoreland subdivision." He looked blandly at Morton, while addressing his wife. "Don't you remember, Louise, we picked up that batch after church last Sunday?"

Morton put his pen down. "Well, it's a good cover, I'll say that."

"Good cover," said Louise dully. "What do you mean by that?"

"It's a good way to get rid of a body; just chop it up and tuck a couple parts in one bag, a couple of parts in another bag. . . ."

Janie, sitting beside Louise, was listening intently to every word. Suddenly she turned to her mother. "I . . . I don't think I feel very well." Her voice was hollow.

The girl lurched up from the table, tipping her chair over, and ran from the room. Bill went after her. Louise got up from the table and turned angrily to Morton and Geraghty. "Can't you people get finished and get out of here? The whole family is sickened. Haven't we told enough? *We* didn't commit the crime. We . . . we just happen to live here." She started crying, her whole body shuddering as if from intense cold. Flanked by detectives and nowhere to turn her face, she covered it with her hands.

Geraghty stood up and came over to her. "I'm sorry, Mrs. Eldridge. You're right. We've done enough for today. This has been a long afternoon for you. We'll push on and come back tomorrow—how about ten o'clock?" He leaned over her and put a gentle hand on her shoulder. With an effort, she stifled her sobs.

"Mrs. Eldridge, you okay now?"

Louise nodded and wiped her nose with a tissue. Geraghty continued. "Your husband can go to work if he likes, since you seem to remember everywhere that you picked up the bags of leaves. We can talk to him later at his convenience." He looked down at her reassuringly and patted her on the shoulder. "Now, don't you cry any more. And I hope your daughter feels better."

She went with them to the door. Morton turned to her and said, "You have to realize, ma'am, even if you are upset, that this kind of discovery raises a lot of questions. The whole thing revolves around *your* property, *your* family. We don't want anything disturbed in the backyard. Stay out of it. We have someone posted back there just to keep people out who might want to nose around. We'll be back tomorrow when it's light to cover the whole area with a fine-tooth comb. And we'd just as soon have your daughter stay home from school so we can get a complete statement from her, too. Right, Mike?'' Morton looked at Geraghty.

Louise's mouth was agape. ''Are you telling me *we're* under suspicion . . . even *Janie*?'' She laughed, then pulled in her breath in a little gasp and shook her head. ''What is the matter with you people? How could you possibly think—''

Geraghty quietly interrupted. ''Mrs. Eldridge, let me explain. It isn't that we think that you're directly involved. It's just that so far everything is centered here. But I'm sure we'll find out more tomorrow and then our investigation will branch out. Meanwhile, you try to get a good night's rest.''

Down the hall Louise could hear Janie's crying and Bill's soothing voice. She had leftover sobs in her own breast. ''Yes,'' she said quietly, ''we'll try to have a good night's rest.'' She let the policemen out and closed the door.

''But if we do,'' she yelled at the closed door, ''it will be no thanks to you!''

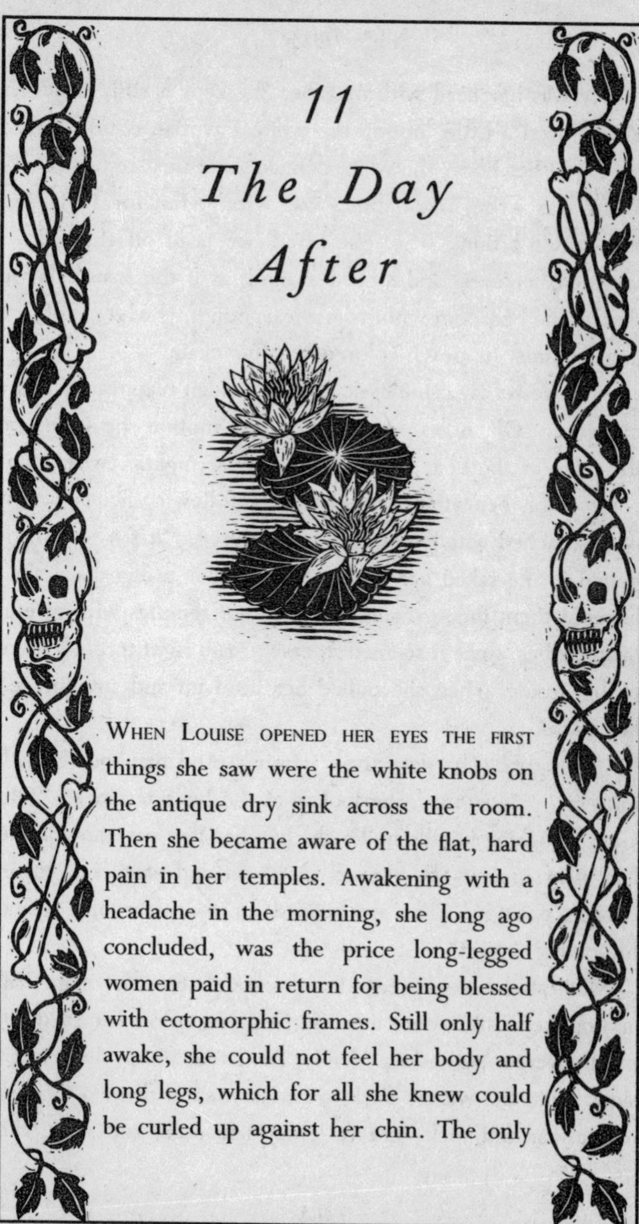

11
The Day After

WHEN LOUISE OPENED HER EYES THE FIRST things she saw were the white knobs on the antique dry sink across the room. Then she became aware of the flat, hard pain in her temples. Awakening with a headache in the morning, she long ago concluded, was the price long-legged women paid in return for being blessed with ectomorphic frames. Still only half awake, she could not feel her body and long legs, which for all she knew could be curled up against her chin. The only reality was her head with its ache. She kept it still. Only her eyes moved a little, noting the white Egyptian cotton spread on top of her body, the white percale sheet next to her cheek. What was wrong? Something was wrong, but for an instant she couldn't think why. She lifted her head off the pillow, squinted her eyes, and looked around, as if the answer lay in this serene bedroom with its gray carpeting, its white walls, its taupe blinds, its peach-colored boudoir chair.

Then yesterday came back like the sudden reappearance of a monster. "Oh, nooo . . ." With one motion she sat up on the edge of the bed, her pink charmeuse nightie twisted uncomfortably beneath her, the headache following her up as if it were attached with springs. She murmured, "It's true, it happened." She raked her fingers through her brown hair, then brought them forward and massaged her temples with careful little pushes, since it seemed so easy to rub right through there to the inside. Then she pulled her head up and straightened her back.

"Geraghty. The detective's coming. And that moron with him . . . Morton." She looked at the bedside clock. "Oh, God." Kicking blindly under the bed her feet somehow found her satin mules. She slipped them on and staggered to an upright position. Then she headed for the bathroom to find life-giving aspirin.

Medicated, she proceeded with careful steps down the hall and opened Janie's door a crack. Her daughter was curled up, head covered, still asleep. Louise hesitated, incapable of decision. Then she walked back to her room and dressed in fresh underwear and socks and yesterday's trousers and shirt, and went to the kitchen to find that Bill had made a large pot of coffee. "Bless you, Bill," she muttered.

A movement in the backyard caught her eye, but she did not look out. She had accepted the fact that the world was no longer normal, and there probably was a whole beehive of police activity out there. If she didn't move her head too quickly or nose into it too much, it might all go away.

She focused instead on a microworld: Bill's comforting beaker-shaped glass coffeemaker filled with aromatic mahogany-colored liquid. And her coffee mug reading "She Who Must Be Obeyed" that he had set out nearby for her use. She concentrated hard on pouring out a small third of a cup as a starter, then struggled to the refrigerator to add a dollop of cream. Then she leaned her elbows on the counter and cradled the cup in her hands like a small, precious prize and drank.

Two more cups and she might live.

The doorbell rang.

Detective Geraghty was alone. His large body filled the doorway. Louise looked at him and had to blink. He was dazzling. Rosy cheeks, roundish nose, bright white hair, bright blue eyes. Except for fifty extra pounds, the picture of health. "G'morning, Mrs. Eldridge. Sorry Detective Morton couldn't come."

"Well, I'm not." Her eyes flashed. "Come in. Would you like coffee? I'm just starting mine."

Geraghty settled down at the dining room table again. After laborious efforts that seemed to take forever, she brought a tray that included buttered toast. "I'm sorry . . . I just got out of bed a few minutes ago. I—I'm not in very good shape. And I have to tell you, Janie isn't awake yet. I don't feel like waking her for you.'' She looked at Geraghty to see how this struck him.

He nodded his head to show that he had heard but didn't necessarily agree. Louise went on, encouraged. ''Everything was just too much for us. None of us could get to sleep until very late. And the TV trucks! Their lights all over the place. The street full of reporters.'' Again her eye caught a movement in the yard and she turned and stared out at her little piece of woods, all outlined with garish yellow police tape. Two policemen were slowly walking in a line, their eyes poring over the ground, in their hands rakes with which they gently moved leaves around. An ancient picture of reapers came to her mind.

She looked at Geraghty and he nodded. ''Our men have been out there for some time, examining the yard for further evidence.'' He leaned forward and put his boxing-glove-sized hands on the table in front of him. ''Mrs. Eldridge, I'm not surprised you didn't sleep last night. Let me give you some advice. The reporters may or may not ease off after a few days. Just remember: You have no obligation to say anything to them at all. I advise you to listen to the answering machine before you pick up on phone calls . . . at least for a few weeks. But the press—especially Channel Nine—they're going to hang around like ghouls until we solve this crime.'' He patted her shoulder. ''So just acquire a thick skin for a while. Your family has been thrown into the world of crime . . . no fault of your own, most likely.''

He patted her hand for emphasis. ''We aren't trying to persecute you and your family. But we do have to get all the answers to the questions we have.'' He carefully withdrew his hand and proceeded to drink his coffee, all the time looking at her with his blue marblelike eyes.

Louise sighed. "Thanks. That makes me feel better, Detective Geraghty, that you don't suspect us. It seems so ridiculous. It's bad enough what happened." She touched her stomach. She felt primitive: hungry, headachy, unbathed, wearing yesterday's clothes. Then she took a piece of toast and spread it with a little homemade jam. "Now you go ahead. Ask your questions." She gave him a fleeting smile and took a big bite of toast.

Geraghty looked more sober now. His smile was gone. "Well, ma'am, I told you I thought this situation was no fault of your own. That doesn't mean there won't be some suspicion attached to someone in this house. . . ."

Louise gulped the toast down her unwilling esophagus.

The lawman leaned forward as much as his stomach would allow. "The reason being that in the majority of crimes, the perpetrator is someone nearby—in the same family, in the same house, maybe in the same neighborhood in this case."

He extended both large hands outward in a gesture of helplessness. "That means we have to do a thorough check of this family, this yard, all your movements . . . and all your past associations."

In a low voice, Louise said, "Incredible."

Geraghty readjusted himself in the chair and looked down at the table. "I am afraid that although this check will include you and even your daughter, it will focus heavily on your husband." He looked up at her, his face redder than usual.

She felt queasy again. "Tell me just why that is."

"Well, the body is a woman's, relatively young. Young

woman killed; points to a man usually. Only rarely another woman. Dismemberment points to a man, except . . . for some historic exceptions.''

Louise's voice was dull. ''This was a young woman. Who was she?''

Geraghty hesitated, then said, ''We don't know that yet. You know we found only about half of her body: two freckled forearms, two upper arms, part of a leg, and part of a torso. No head. No feet. No hands . . . hands are gone.''

Louise began breathing deeply through her mouth. ''Oh, God,'' she said, rested an elbow on the table, and put a hand over her mouth.

''Mrs. Eldridge, you're not feeling well.'' The detective leaned forward solicitously.

She took her hand away from her face. ''I don't. But it's all right, Detective Geraghty. I want to get on with this and get it over. Exactly what do you want to know about us?''

''Not us, Mrs. Eldridge. I want to know about you. So why don't you just finish your breakfast there, and then we'll take a little ride around the route where you picked up leaf bags. That way we can kill two birds with one stone.''

Louise winced at his use of ''kill,'' but then returned to her toast and coffee and finished it with gusto.

When they walked out the front door, Louise put her nose up and breathed in the cold, fresh air. ''Aah, air. Life-giving air.'' She felt like a new woman. Geraghty glanced at her and said nothing. When they climbed into the unmarked black car, Louise was assaulted with the rank odor left behind by countless cigarettes. She struggled into her seat, fastened the seat belt, and clawed at the crank with both hands to open the window. It wouldn't move.

"Don't smoke, huh?" said Geraghty. "I don't either, but a lot of the other boys do. That window doesn't open, by the way. But I'll open mine." With one hand he rolled the window down; with the other he turned up the collar on his worn, brown wool coat. "Now," he said matter-of-factly, "you're the navigator. Let's retrace all your travels. Do we start by going into Washington and Bethesda?" He handed over to her a pen and a small pad of paper. "This might help."

As they traveled she jotted a list. She concluded that she and her family had stopped to get leaves at seven different locations, the first in Washington.

As Geraghty drove into Washington on the George Washington Parkway he asked Louise about her work experiences.

She chose her words carefully as she listed their tours of duty with the State Department: Turkey, Israel, Washington, London, Paris, New York, then Washington again. "We'll probably finish this tour about the time Janie starts college and then be assigned overseas again."

"So he's been around. What's his title, exactly?"

"Political officer. These days, on the European desk at State."

"Now, that still leaves unanswered my question about your work experience and how you met your husband."

"I graduated from Northwestern, and then took some graduate summer classes at Georgetown. That's when I met Bill—he was a Kennedy School of Government student at Harvard, visiting Georgetown's International Institute. He kind of swept me off my feet, and we were married August twenty-third, right after he completed his course work.''

She fell silent. Funny how she could remember times and places, whereas Bill often forgot their August anniversary, making amends with a lavish late present when he did remember. What was it about men, and remembering family events? Sometimes she felt a keen dividing line between them: He was CEO and controller, and she was secretary in charge of keeping everything else straight.

''And then?'' Geraghty prodded.

Louise's mind returned to her chronology. ''Martha was born in Washington a year later, and by that time Bill was with . . . the Foreign Service.'' It was easy for her to slide over Bill's secret spy role with the CIA, since she had twenty years of practice dissembling. ''We immediately picked up and moved overseas. Then Janie was born three years later, when we were posted again in Washington. We went back to the Middle East for a couple of years. Back and forth, back and forth—that's about it.''

''You haven't mentioned a career for yourself.'' The detective's florid face was in silhouette; it seemed as if he were avoiding eye contact. He rolled his window back up, as if to give himself something further to distract him.

''I haven't worked outside the home,'' she said, looking at him in case he looked at her. She did not want to appear to be apologizing.

How could she have worked, seesawing back and forth on the oceans with two small children? She added hastily, ''But I've done a little freelance writing. I'm trying to get some writing assignments around here.''

"Oh," said Geraghty, with a condescending tone, the kind that nonwriters give to writers to convey interest in something that actually bores them silly.

Geraghty. There he sat, bright, shining, healthy-looking, and, above all, law-abiding. Looking over at her, unwashed, hair unkempt, jacket worn, sneakers dirty, and somehow guilty until proven innocent.

"So. Where do you do your writing?"

Between his "oh" and "so" was a world of time. Louise felt her face flush.

"In the hut," she said in a curt voice.

"The hut being that extension of your house across from your front door? It looks like part of the house, until you get close. By the way, why don't you attach it to the house? Would it be that hard?"

She gazed over at him, wondering if she could ever like such a simpleminded man. "We like it separate." She bit out the words. "Anyway, it's connected with a big pergola. Did you notice the pergola?" How could you *miss* it, she thought snappishly. It was huge, and the architectural focal point of the entire house.

"Pergola, that's what you call that archway? I thought it was just a grape arbor without grapes. Okay, okay." He moved uncomfortably in his seat and the car swerved a little, a first time for the detective; he was a skillful driver. "Mrs. Eldridge, don't get too annoyed with me." He shot a boyish glance at her; she saw that his good nature was not in the least disturbed. "I'm just asking questions. You can tell me if you object to something I say."

"I don't mean to be difficult. It's just this headache, but it's going away. Ask me anything."

After a little pause, Geraghty said, "Then let's talk about your gardening a little more."

"What about it?"

He cleared his throat. "You have a nice, interesting-looking yard, that's for sure, and you obviously are, uh, caught up in gardening. Since I don't do that stuff myself, can you make one thing clear?"

"I'll try."

"Do all gardeners, um, go around collecting other people's leaves—or is that just you?"

She slumped a little in the seat. She would never lose the tag "gardening nut" with these detectives. "I suppose that not a lot of people do that. It was just expediency, Detective Geraghty. It's very simple: Leaves are mulch. I needed mulch. And free mulch can't be sneezed at." Instantly, the power of suggestion took over and she gave out a huge sneeze, her olfactory system barraged again with the car's used air and evil fumes. She smiled. "But this police car can be sneezed at. Do you mind opening the window again?" She rubbed the dirty glass with her fingertips. "And better slow down: We're coming to the first place we picked up bags . . . beyond this long hill."

They were on Foxhall Road, passing estates set back behind iron fences and coming to smaller houses standing closer to the road. "Just a few more houses . . . this brown one. I think we must have picked up four bags here. That's what Janie and Bill and I all remember."

Then they traced their way through the crowded streets to

Bradley Boulevard in Bethesda, where Louise remembered another pickup. Wistfully, she thought of her friends living here, and wished she could visit them and tell them what had happened. They would take her in their arms and comfort her. But Geraghty wouldn't stop: He was like a bird dog searching out quail. Their friends would know soon enough, anyway. The story probably was already on TV.

After Bethesda they turned south again, snaking through the middle of the diamond that represented the District of Columbia, on Rock Creek Parkway; they emerged near the high-flying Watergate and the Kennedy Center, sped past an indifferent Lincoln and Jefferson in their respective memorials, then south on Route 1 through Alexandria and to Geraghty's headquarters, the Fairfax County police substation.

He parked in front of the building, which featured abbreviated large white columns of the sort found in public buildings throughout Virginia. Louise had been inside to obtain car stickers and had been amused to see that the faux colonial style stopped at the door. Inside was an array of grimy ivory walls and Formica counters. "Have to dash in here a minute, Mrs. Eldridge. Want to come, or will you wait in the car?"

"I'll wait here." She snuggled into her coat and closed her eyes, then opened them almost immediately, sensing people near. They were walking by to enter the police station. They stared at her, trying to figure out why she was in an unmarked police car. Louise felt like putting her wrists on the dashboard as if to illustrate, "Look, no handcuffs! I've merely been detained for questioning." Instead she put one hand up and casually rubbed her face, as if she were totally used to hanging around police stations.

Geraghty lumbered out and down the stairs; like a large bear on the move. "I wasn't too long, was I?" he said with a big grin. Louise bet he said things like that to his wife: a man who wanted the favor of women.

"No. Not too long. Now, the next place is east of here, near the parkway." They drove there, Geraghty again noting the address of the house, a large colonial.

"Now we come to Sylvan Valley," said Louise. She directed him to two homes on Ransom Road where she and Janie had picked up as many as twelve bags of leaves.

"And then the last bunch: They came from Martha's Lane." They drove up there, to the highest point in the neighborhood, where the houses had a wide view of the valley to the west.

"It's the house on the bend . . . right here," said Louise. It was one-story, at least in front, and shrouded with bushes and low trees. "We took six bags from here; they were the only ones that were out so early before trash day on this particular street."

"Oh? How so?" said Geraghty.

"I don't know why. Some people here are very, well, fastidious. They only put their trash out at the last minute, so as not to make the neighborhood unsightly." She smiled and looked at him. "Sylvan Valley is full of liberals, but they're fussy about appearances."

Geraghty left the car running and went up to the house to find out the address. He came back carrying a couple of advertising flyers he apparently had found near the front door.

They slowly made their way back down the lane.

"There's something else. . . ."

Geraghty turned toward her, blue eyes alert. ''Ah. What is it?''

The memory slipped away as quickly as it came, like a wisp of smoke.

''I . . . I just can't remember. Maybe nothing.''

''Maybe not,'' said Geraghty slowly. ''Can you do something for me?'' He stopped the car and turned full toward her. ''I want you to sit down with your family tonight and talk about all these places you've been''—he nodded at the list she had in her hand—''and get Janie and Mr. Eldridge to think of anything at all that happened when you were out at these places.''

Then he drove on Route 1 toward Louise's house. ''I think we've done it for today,'' said Geraghty. ''We'll do a thorough check on these addresses, for one thing. Although anybody could have done just the opposite of what you did.''

She looked at him. ''What do you mean?'' She put her hand to her head. ''Oh, of course.''

''Yeh. Anybody could have brought their bags of leaves and put them in front of someone else's house.''

Louise smiled wanly. ''That would leave you nowhere, right?''

''Right. That's why the forensics report will be important . . . and another report, too.''

''What's that?''

''Missing persons, Mrs. Eldridge. You see, this woman had a life. What kind of a life we don't know. But someone's bound to miss her.''

''Oh,'' sighed Louise. ''I don't envy you your job at all.''

''It's not so bad,'' said Geraghty. ''I meet lots of nice

people. Like you, for instance. So, Mrs. Eldridge, I'm hungry. Can I by any chance interest you in a burger? We're not far away. . . ."

"A burger." Her stomach flinched. She had recently read that most burgers contained about fifteen teaspoons of fat. On the other hand, the release of the iron grip of headache had left her with mushy feelings of gratitude toward the whole world. So she said, "A burger sounds very nice."

Geraghty turned into the fast-food place and parked expertly in a crowded lot. As they entered, Louise realized this was truly another world. Red and tan Formica everywhere, repeated in the uniforms of the youngsters behind the counter. The colors assaulted her eye, waking her up for good on this slow-to-get-started morning. The number of people surprised her. She and the detective stood at the end of a long line.

Then she became conscious of the smell, the smell of grease. Little globules of grease perfumed the air and must be entering all her apertures and fastening themselves onto her clothes and her exposed hair. She tried to restrain a shudder. Then, determined to be a good sport—after all, she had come here of her own free will—she shook the picture from her mind and concentrated on the customers, who almost filled the place up.

She looked at her watch; it was noon. The noon crowd, she noted, included students from the nearby high school and nondescript older couples, the women without makeup or pretence, the men equally plain, hunkering down with rounded shoulders to gobble their meals. There were a couple groups of young business people, perky, sitting tall, dressed and groomed for success in whatever the game was around here—

maybe the big insurance firm located nearby on Route 1. They acted no different than if they were lunching in Georgetown.

Sprinkled in were the young mothers. They were not the slimmest mothers she had ever seen, but they had pretty, plump faces and bright winter outfits that probably disguised figures heading for trouble. Their children seemed to hang on them and clamor for specialties. "Mom, I want the fresh apple pie!" yelled one little boy, then hustled over to the condiments counter to gather up expertly the ketchup, napkins, cream, and straws that the family needed. For these children, this place was like a second home.

She and Geraghty had worked their way to the front of the line. He grinned down at her, as if reading her mind over the past minute or two. "What'll you have . . . the treat's on me."

"Oh, I hadn't thought . . ." said Louise, straining to read the offerings on the wall menu. She had left her reading glasses somewhere. "Maybe a plain hamburger."

"You're willing to wait, then."

"Wait?"

Geraghty gave her a strange look. "You don't eat fast food at all, do you? Plain hamburgers are like a special order. They take, maybe, five minutes."

"Oh, gourmet stuff, huh? Okay." She squinted her eyes at the menu again and then looked straight at the smiling young black man waiting for their order. He seemed to have a twinkle in his eye. "I'll have your Super Burger," she said, pulling herself straighter and maintaining eye contact. "I'm sure it's very good, and a glass of milk." The youngster turned to

Geraghty, but Louise interrupted with an afterthought. ''Uh, what does it have on it?'' She shook her head. ''Not ketchup.''

''Yes, ma'am. Ketchup.''

She put up a restraining hand. ''No. I don't want—''

The young man hadn't stopped smiling since she began to speak. ''Hold the ketchup: no problema. How about our Russian dressing instead?''

''Russian?'' asked Louise suspiciously.

''Pink. Very tasty.''

''Okay, if you say so. And a big cup of coffee please.'' That would banish the very last strings of headache left in her brow.

''Super Burger,'' said Geraghty. ''Good choice. I'll have one too, with fries, slaw, and coffee, and a piece of apple pie.''

Louise asked the young man, ''You wouldn't have a few pickles, would you? Pickles to put alongside, not inside, the hamburger?''

He smiled again. ''Ma'am, pickles are our middle name.'' He rang up the total and Geraghty paid. Then, before their eyes, in less than ten seconds, the young man gathered their orders, set out their cups, and prepared and delivered a small cup of pickle slices for Louise.

''Enjoy,'' he said.

As they walked to an empty table, Louise said, ''I know why people like these places.''

''Why?'' asked Geraghty, placing the tray on the table and settling himself down.

She took off her old jacket and hung it on the hook, then slid in opposite him. ''Because it's instant gratification, as opposed to postponed pleasure.''

"Never thought of it quite that way before."

It was a very large burger, whose insides she did not want to investigate but whose sides were leaking pink sauce. Louise took her first bite and realized it had things in it that she would never have combined in her craziest recipe. Then she gave in. She chewed slowly, savoring the sharp tang of a pickle that—contrary to her likes—was embedded somewhere within; the sauce, also tasty; the enticing taste of beef; and then the crunchy aftertaste of tomato and lettuce. She took a sip of milk to wash it down.

"How d'ya like it?" asked Geraghty, his mouth half full. He looked as concerned as someone introducing a gastronomical treat.

"Not bad," said Louise, hunkering down and going for another bite.

Geraghty reamed through his lunch, wiped his mouth, and settled back with the big coffee.

Louise wondered how his stomach stood such abuse.

Geraghty said, "There's something we didn't go into yet, Mrs. Eldridge. It might be called 'what you know but don't know you know.' "

"You mean that memory of something happening on Martha's Lane?"

"The memory that won't shake loose. And there might be others, too. You and Mr. Eldridge, being highly educated, know the mind is like a computer and it has a lot of files. A lot of these memory files won't come open unless we have the password to open them. You need to spend some time concentrating on anything that might have happened to your family over the past month or two, but particularly the past few weeks. And then, there's another way to help you remember things."

"What, torture?" She grinned and carefully wiped pink sauce from her mouth. These burgers were messy but good. Not anything like the rather austere, lean ones Bill occasionally grilled in the summer.

"No. Hypnotism." He leaned forward. "Hypnotism has been used very successfully on occasion. And you, Mrs. Eldridge"—he sat back and waved a hand at her as if he had invented her—"I believe you know something you've forgotten."

She downed the last of her milk. "Hypnotism. Does the Fairfax Police Department have a resident hypnotist?" She couldn't restrain a smile.

He scowled back at her. "No. But we know where there is one—not here in Fairfax County, but in Washington. You might not take this seriously, Mrs. Eldridge, but it may be at your own peril. I think you know something that could help us."

Louise was sitting back, feeling comfortably fed, sipping coffee. And then his words sank in, and her brain communicated to her stomach a sharp unease.

She stated it flatly: "Then the opposite of that is that the something I know could hurt the murderer."

"Exactly. That's why the possible peril." Geraghty looked at her, his blue eyes wider than usual. Concern for her? "That is why we have to get going. We have to find out what you know. There's an outside chance you could be in danger."

She looked around at the crowd of students and oldsters and professionals and mothers innocently eating their rations.

None of them had overheard; she and Geraghty looked like part of the crowd; middle-aged couple, the man overweight, the woman with unkempt hair. And yet here they were talking about murder and danger. She stared down for an instant at her thin hands cupping the plastic coffee cup, then looked up at the big detective. "I can think of one good thing out of this, Detective Geraghty. You must not any longer think of our family as suspects."

"Not you, anyway, Mrs. Eldridge. And within a few days I believe we can safely eliminate any suspicion regarding your husband. What we want to do is to solve this terrible crime, and without hurting you or your family."

Her eyes teared up and she smiled at him. "You're a nice man." She got out her bandanna handkerchief and blew her nose and wiped her eyes. "And I didn't mean to make fun of the police and hypnotism."

"I know that, Mrs. Eldridge," said Geraghty.

She leaned forward. "I'll be hypnotized. I'll do anything you want. Tomorrow; I'll do it tomorrow if you want." She flailed her hands helplessly in the air. "I just want to be rid of this, get it away from my family."

Geraghty scratched his fingernail thoughtfully on the tabletop. He did not look at Louise. "I wish it was that simple. These cases don't solve themselves that quickly, unless the police have a stroke of good luck." He looked at her solemnly. "You've gotta be strong. And you can't have too high expectations. Six months from now we still might not have the murderer. Right now, we don't even know who the victim was. The fact is"—he looked down again at the table—"sometimes torso murders never get solved."

"Torso murders," muttered Louise, pulling in her breath. "So that's what you call this?" Suddenly the heavy dose of protein, fat, and carbohydrate overlaid with a dose of caffeine changed from a friend to an enemy in her beleaguered stomach.

12
The Investigators

JANIE'S SHOULDERS SAGGED AS SHE AND MELanie approached the corner of their street. She dreaded the sight of their yard as she had left it late this morning, all marked with the policemen's garish yellow tape. But with relief she could see through the trees that the tape was gone. She brushed her blond hair away from her eyes and said, "Oh boy, am I glad they took that down. It was . . . just so *embarrassing*."

"You wouldn't even know anything

had happened at your place any more,'' said Melanie comfortingly. She knew Janie was tired of talking about finding body parts in her backyard. The word had gotten out at school and Janie had had to answer questions all day from people she barely knew, including teachers, who seemed just as nosy as the kids.

''Want to play a little b-ball later?'' asked Melanie. ''It's really nice out. Like the weather guy says, it's Indian summer in November.''

''Sure, if my mom will let me,'' said Janie. ''It'll take me about ten minutes.'' Actually, she was tired and her stomach growled with hunger. It was an outside chance, but maybe her mom had something good baked. After all it had been through, the family could use some putting back together.

First Janie tried the door to the addition and knocked. Her mother wasn't in there busily writing as she usually was. She unlocked the front door and went in. ''Mother,'' she called in a tentative voice.

The house was empty. Through the tall windows she looked out at the backyard, her eyes searching out the spot where they had found the body parts.

''Oh, no,'' she said, taking a deep breath. ''I guess I'm alone here.''

She put her books carefully in her room and took off her good pink cardigan and replaced it with an old sweatshirt from elementary school that she had not quite outgrown. The only problem was the sleeves, which grew a little shorter every year. Comfortable now, she headed for the kitchen.

She found a note from her mother on the counter. It said she was out with Detective Geraghty, returning to all the places where they had picked up leaves. She wasn't sure when she would be home.

"Oh, Ma," muttered Janie as she tidily disposed of the note in the wastebasket. "If you weren't such a gardening nut this would never have happened." Then she turned her attention to the refrigerator.

Good. There were the makings of a real sandwich. French bread, two big slices. Gruyère cheese, three even-sized chunks. Baked ham slices, two. Tomato slices, two and a half, just enough to cover the surface of the bread. A dab of Dijon. Four hot peppers arranged in a square. Lettuce. A large glass of milk in a nonbreakable old plastic glass they had had ever since Janie remembered. And a pickle, her father's favorite kind: a half-sour dill.

She took these prizes and went to the family room, grabbed the TV remote control, flipped on "Jeopardy," and curled up in her favorite chair, the one that used to be Great Gram's. Between bites, she called out the answers she knew. During commercials her mind free-floated, often a prelude to giving up and taking a nap. But Melanie expected her. Better still, Melanie's brother, Chris, might be there. As much as she liked the thoughtful Melanie, she had come to like her brother even more. She hopped out of the chair, put her dishes in the sink, and ran out to the cul-de-sac.

Melanie was sitting in their spot. It was a slight depression almost in the middle of the asphalt circle forming the cul-de-sac. Water puddled here when it rained. When weather was fair, this spot caught the last rays of sun through the high walls of trees. Melanie and Janie had started meeting and talking here when they met in late summer. They would sit around the small depression as if in an Indian kiva and trade pieces of teenage wisdom.

Now Melanie sat cross-legged, scratching the asphalt aimlessly with a piece of stick while waiting for her friend. She looked up at Janie with thoughtful gray eyes just like her brother's.

"Hi. You forgot your ball."

"I thought you were bringing yours."

They heard a door slam and a figure dash out of Melanie's house. "Here comes Chris. He has one."

The tall seventeen-year-old sprinted across his yard and onto the street and immediately began bouncing his ball with practiced beat. The sitting spot was on the perimeter of the shooting area for basketball, with the free-standing basketball hoop and backboard in the parkway in front of Michael's house.

Chris sank a few shots, then came to join them.

"Want to play two on two? Michael's coming."

"Oh goody, Michael," said Melanie, her lip curled. Janie knew she liked him a lot.

Chris squatted down beside Janie, who was trying not to look at him. He lifted her hair away from her eyes as if he were lifting a tent flap. "Janie, hey, are you in there? Are you all right?"

Janie looked at him in all his blond and gray-eyed beauty and blushed to her toes. "Wha—what do you mean?"

"Well, if that had happened in my yard, I'd feel bad. I'd do something."

Janie pulled at a thread in the sleeve of her sweatshirt. "I don't know what I can do." She looked up at him, crouching there, as if ready to spring. She shook her head as if helpless. "What do you want me to do, go look for the criminal or what?"

Chris smiled his wonderful smile. "That's what I'd do. What're the police doing?"

"My mom right now is out with the detectives tracing where she went, where we both went."

Chris tugged at her worn sleeve. "That's just it! You know something. You could go out investigating."

"Chri-is," admonished Melanie. "Why would she do that? That's what police are supposed to do."

"Janie could help," said Chris, turning to his sister and then back to Janie. "You were right there when she went leaf picking, right?"

"Right," said Janie, "most of the time."

"Well, I'll go with you if you're scared, but you ought to go back to those places . . . find out who lives in the different houses . . . you know, stuff like that."

The sun was gone now and Janie was beginning to get cold. But she didn't want to move away from Chris. "I told you, my mother and the police are out doing that already."

"Yah, but who knows the neighborhood better than we do?" said Chris. Janie had never seen him so animated; as a rule he barely talked to her.

"Think of it this way, Janie. The more detectives you have investigating a crime the better, right?"

She smiled up at him. "I guess. Well, if you want to, we could do that, go around, retrace our steps and everything."

Melanie leaned over and grabbed Janie's arm in hers and

glared at her brother in mock anger. "What about me?" she said. "After all, I'm the one who's Janie's friend."

Chris stood up, towering above them. "Sure, Melanie. You can come if you want. When'll we do this, Janie? Tomorrow?"

Janie sighed and dropped her head for an instant. "Tomorrow. That will give me time to catch up on my sleep." When she looked up again, Chris was gone to the opposite perimeter, trying for a three-pointer.

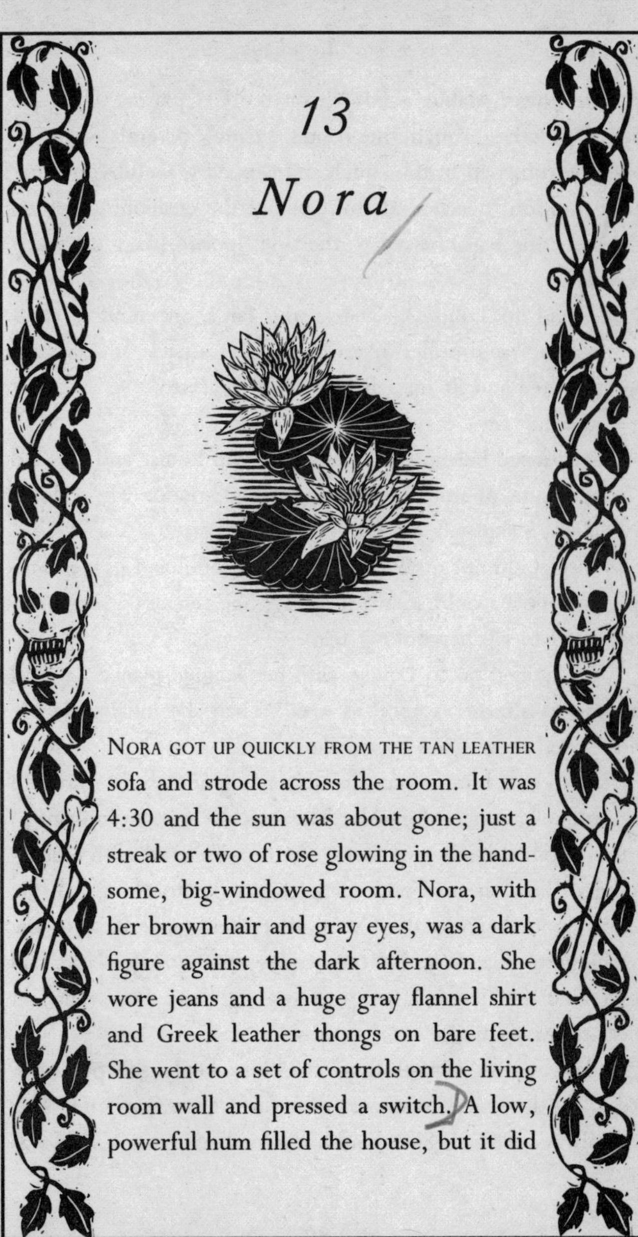

13

Nora

NORA GOT UP QUICKLY FROM THE TAN LEATHER sofa and strode across the room. It was 4:30 and the sun was about gone; just a streak or two of rose glowing in the handsome, big-windowed room. Nora, with her brown hair and gray eyes, was a dark figure against the dark afternoon. She wore jeans and a huge gray flannel shirt and Greek leather thongs on bare feet. She went to a set of controls on the living room wall and pressed a switch. A low, powerful hum filled the house, but it did not overpower Mahler's Fourth on the CD player. Then she moved quietly through the room, turning several lamps on low. She returned to the couch and slipped gracefully into her usual position, perched at the front of the cushion and, even with her long legs crossed to the side, looked like a cat ready to pounce.

She said to Louise, "There, the fan's on; now it can't bother you," and pulled from her pocket a pack of cigarettes and a lighter and lit up a long brown cigarette.

"Smoking isn't easy, is it?"

Nora turned her head a little away from Louise and exhaled a long stream of smoke. "You probably wonder why I don't give it up," she said, in her low, silky voice.

Louise could not think of what to say. "Bill and I gave them up years ago" would sound so smug. She remained silent and continued to sip her oolong tea.

Nora latched on to Louise with her languid glance. "I find smoking is almost as good as sex." Then she inhaled deeply and turned away again to exhale.

That did it. Louise was already feeling acutely overdressed and somewhat uncomfortable. This was the woman in front of whom she had burst into tears. She remembered with embarrassment how she had poured her heart out to Nora—all the details about her unsettled state after their move back to the Washington area. Was that only two weeks ago? But Nora had been kind and steered her into writing. And Louise had at least *started* writing.

Today was an invitation to tea. Mistakenly she put on a dress, the knee-jerk response of a foreign service wife. Tea? One always dressed. She should have realized Nora's style was totally casual, which on Nora came out looking like *Vogue.* And was this woman putting her on now with that remark about smoking? Louise decided that if they were to be friends at all, she would have to stop analyzing.

So she said slyly, ''Well, anything that's almost as good as sex has to be encouraged.''

Nora looked at Louise and then threw back her head and laughed. ''I don't think you mean that.'' Then she sobered. ''There is a physical thing with smoking.'' She made a lilting upward movement with one hand. ''A lift. With me it's a big lift.'' She looked more closely at Louise. ''And there's another reason. I tried to give it up before. I don't want to prove again to myself how little self-control I have. But enough of that. I'm not worried about me; I've been worried about you, Louise . . . even though I haven't come over like the others.''

Most of the neighbors had, commiserating with her and Bill about finding the body parts, realizing they had been plunged innocently into a terrible crime.

''The important thing, Louise, is, are you still writing?'' Nora looked as if her happiness hinged on the answer.

Louise looked down at her hands, empty in her lap. ''I've fallen off, that's for sure. It's just been so . . . distracting.'' She opened her hands in a little helpless motion. ''The media. You must see them hanging around sometimes, even going into the backyard. Calling, day and night. I never answer the phone until I hear it's someone I want to speak with. And I've tried to help the police. I'm even going to be *hypnotized.*''

Nora looked at her curiously. ''Hypnotized. Intriguing. What do you think your subconscious has to say?''

Louise blushed. ''Oh, nothing that important. Maybe something I might have seen when I went around collecting the leaf bags.''

''I hope it works,'' said Nora warily. ''It would be nice to clear the air. After all, someone did kill her. Which leaves a murderer out there somewhere.''

''Yes, there *is*. But it isn't my Bill, although they acted as if it might be for a few days there. They've kept questioning him, as if this woman were someone *he* might have been involved with. And of course Bill has his own priorities . . . he's very busy at work . . . and Janie, but you probably see Janie just as much as I do.''

Why was she running on like this? What was there about this woman, whose presence was uncomfortable one moment, and then so comfortable the next that she began to tell her everything? To defend herself against more words, she picked up the teapot on the table in front of her and asked Nora, ''May I pour you another cup?''

Nora merely nodded and continued to smoke and look at Louise. She stretched forward. ''You've got to be fierce, you know. They'll drive you away from what you want to do.''

''Who?'' asked Louise, pausing with the teapot in midair.

''Your family, my dear.'' The gray eyes were persistent. ''Your loved ones. You are so good, so giving. They will use you all up, and ten years from now, when the children are gone and Bill is thinking about the next phase of his career, you will be looking at that career you thought about and never developed—that book you started and never finished.'' She stared at a point beyond Louise and inhaled again, then slowly exhaled, while Louise remained silent. ''Janie is fine. I see her every day, at least out the window. My Chris loves her, you know. So does Melanie. A wonderful person. Don't worry about her. Now, let's talk about your husband. Bill is very attractive." She glanced over at Louise. "What do you think your husband wants of you, really?"

Louise's heart increased its tempo. Who did this woman think she was, always asking her the cosmic question? She shook her head a little as if to shake Nora's words away. "But I can't just ignore what's going on. A *woman* has been *murdered* and somehow I've dragged her remains into our life. I mean, I can't just go into a cocoon; I have to keep the family on an even keel; I have to be sure Janie hasn't been affected. . . ." Her voice was plaintive; to herself she sounded whiny.

Nora just looked at her and sipped her tea.

"I sound so whiny."

"Women are liable to sound whiny when they're looking for excuses not to do things for themselves."

"Oh, God," said Louise, capitulating. "I've done that my entire married life."

"I can imagine you have. You're in good company. There are hundreds of women who live for their families. I used to until a few years ago, but I don't any more—I leave plenty of time for myself. I've worked at my career very hard, and now I have part of what I want. I'm published, I do quite a few readings on the East Coast, and I'm well connected with the writing community."

Did she detect a little self-satisfaction in the woman's cool voice?

"And, of course, I teach, and surely, teaching is the best part of it—I *love* the young people. So no one except my Ron would call me a raging success, but at least I've developed a fulfilling life. I've given myself a voice. I think you would be happier if you did that, too.''

Louise searched her mind for a way to tell her neighbor how bad things really were with her. Finally she decided to tell her something that she had not even told her husband, for fear he would worry. ''Nora, it's not only the police and the press that are distracting. It's that woman herself, the woman in the leaf bags. She appears to me in my *dreams*.''

Louise was unprepared for the effect of these words. Nora swayed forward and with a trembling hand tamped out her cigarette in the ashtray. Then she moved warily back into the sofa pillows, as if trying to evade a ghostly presence hovering about the room. Louise realized that the calm-appearing Nora was just as much on edge as she was herself. But now all the pretenses were gone.

''I *sensed* it,'' said Nora, her pained eyes on Louise's. ''I sensed that the woman haunts you, too. I was trying desperately not to talk about it, to talk about anything *but* it. But now that I hear that you're having nightmares like me . . .''

''Almost every night.''

''Oh, Louise, the plight of that woman *horrifies* me. I feel as if I have entered her consciousness—her, and all the women victims that I read about in the news each day. Beaten. Sometimes slaughtered. Left like dross.''

Her voice dropped even lower, so that Louise had to lean toward her to hear her. ''This woman's murder has invaded my psyche, to the point that I sit in this house day after day, writing about it. Can you imagine what happened to her that night, or *was* it night? What kind of betrayal took place? How did he trap her to kill her? Was there a chase, and then he caught her? Or did he even have to pursue her: perhaps she simply tumbled willingly into his arms. And the saw: did he use a saw?''

The eyes pleaded with Louise for understanding. ''You see, don't you, that I am obsessed?''

Then abruptly she released Louise's arm and shrank back into the cushions.

Louise's mouth was agape, her breathing unsteady. Nora was a tormented woman. And she had just opened a Pandora's box of appalling images that Louise herself had kept carefully locked away.

Yes, she fretted almost daily about the unsolved murder and dreamed about it at night. But with great effort, she had forbidden herself to humanize the murdered woman; being newly-moved to a new place, and unsettled in every other aspect of her life, it would have been the last straw. It would have reduced her to the state of the distraught woman sitting beside her on the couch. She looked over at Nora. Had she invited her here simply to spill out her own agony?

Nora sat forward again, recovering a little, as if remembering she was the hostess for tea. ''Forgive me, Louise. I see you don't want to talk about it, and I can fully understand that. But you should be terribly cautious.''

''And I am. . . .''

The poet shook her head slowly. ''Oh no. I'm sure you think you are taking care, but there is something different about this murder. I feel it, rather than know it. . . .'' For a long moment, she stared out the big front windows. Louise, following her gaze, saw her own yard across the cul-de-sac, the house and studio obscured by the leafless trees, but still faintly visible. "It's not *all* in my head: There are strange things going on about your house, didn't you know? I am up late often and I've seen a figure about your place." The slim hand came out again and clutched Louise's hand, and the gray eyes locked on hers. "Oh, my dear, please tell Bill to take good care of you."

"But it could have just been a reporter hanging around—they are pests. When did you see this person?"

"That's it. I think it was even before the—the leaf bags were even opened. I would have called you, but it was so furtive—so fleeting. . . . Once, Sam Rosen even turned the lights on when I thought I saw him." Nora rose restlessly from the couch and lit up another cigarette.

Louise sat there, trying to remember that time period. She was fairly certain Sam, too, had seen or heard something. She shivered, though the room was warm.

Nora suddenly looked tired and drawn, standing there like a figure out of a Greek tragedy. "I'm so, so sorry, Louise. I didn't mean to frighten you. I shouldn't have shared my private nightmares with you." Her gaze dropped modestly, as if she were ashamed to reveal what she next was going to say. "I . . . have always had this terrible talent, or curse—some kind of ESP—that gives me forebodings of danger. . . ." She stared at Louise.

"Danger for whom?"

Nora continued to look at her without answering, and Louise felt almost suffocated in the atmosphere of near-terror that filled the room. She felt her temperature suddenly rise, and a desperate need to flee. She put a hand on either side of her body, ready to heave herself out of the couch. Then she changed her mind, sat back, and smoothed her hands against the plush cushions. She forced her body to stay very still, waiting for this moment to end.

She and Nora exchanged a long look. Then she took a deep, measured breath.

Nora had terrified her, but only for a few moments. She had called on her strengths—her sanguine nature and her Midwestern common sense—to override what she now decided were Nora's honest but neurotic fears about the strange death.

A death that probably would have no further impact on any of their lives except for the residual nightmares.

Nora watched Louise's face closely. Then she lifted her chin a little. "I see you have no fear. You are probably right: You mustn't pay attention to my wanderings. As Ron tells me, they're the product of a fevered poetic imagination. Everything I've said mustn't stop you. That poor woman is dead and gone, and you are alive. In the end, the very worst thing that can happen to you is centering your energies on all this, and not centering them on your work. You have something to say, and you must get back to work."

Louise left soon after, embracing Nora before she went. Worrying a little about this sensitive new friend, who spent each day across the street from her, brooding and writing on the subject of victimized women. With brow furrowed, she walked through the front yard, trying to leave the memory of the conversation behind her.

Almost immediately, she was distracted by the fall outfits of Nora's plants—the silken seed pods of the anemone, the spiky pods of the *eryngium,* and, since there had been no hard freeze yet, the still-blooming masses of some marigold species, with their spidery foliage, and inch-wide, single white blossoms with black button eyes, straying gracefully down a hilly garden that faced south. Nora's psyche may have been haunted by dark fears, but she had a garden of pure delight.

Once at the street, Louise started to hurry. She was practically running by the time she reached her own yard. She paused uncertainly at the front door. Yes, dinner could wait! She turned into the hut instead, where she flicked on the electric heat unit. Why bother with a wood fire?

Nora was right about one thing: Time was precious. She sat, turned on the computer, and went to work.

But her neighbor's nightmares had made their imprint. She went back to the door and carefully shot the bolt before returning to her keyboard.

14

Getting Warmer

A SOFT, DAMP NOVEMBER BREEZE BLEW through the woods as Chris and Janie made their way by the light of an almost full moon. It was a freakish fall night, as warm as if Indian summer had never departed. A good night for investigating.

Janie was carrying her favorite stick, and Chris had acquired one by snapping a dead branch off a tree. "This way, we're both armed," he said with a smile. She smiled back, trying to shake an agonizing self-consciousness.

Because of a break in the tall trees, a patch of moonlight lay on the path ahead of them. Chris grabbed Janie's arm and stopped her. "Look, Janie, a little pool of moonlight. Let's stand in it." They moved into the magic spot. Then he pointed up to the nearly perfect circle of light above them. "And look up there. Isn't that a neat moon? They say people are driven mad by a full moon." He looked at her, his eyes shining, his blond hair unkempt. "Do you believe that could be true?"

She threw back her long blond hair, cricked her neck, and squinted up at the moon. "Of course it's true. Haven't you ever seen *The Wolfman*?" Then she stepped out of the light and ran down the dark path. Chris ran until he caught up with her and then they both slowed down.

"You're not very scientific, are you?" he prodded. Janie felt very small; she knew he was a science whiz.

He prattled on: "You don't think that could be true, I bet. But cosmic things affect you. The moon affects the tides. You know that, don't you? Why shouldn't it have some effect on the mind? By the way, are you taking any science this year?"

"Of course I am—biology. But I don't know yet if I'm scientific. I think the right side of my brain is the dominant side."

"Hmm, right-hand side, huh? Didja ever read the book *Drawing on the Right Side of the Brain*? It shows you how you can use the right side of your brain and become artistic, even draw stuff."

"I'm trying to tell you that's the kind of book I *don't* have to read. The kind I have to read is about Einstein's theory of relativity, or something."

Chris shrugged and beat his stick against the small shrub trees on the side of the path. "I can see we'll never be in a science class together. I'm way ahead of you. But anyway we can get scientific about this investigation. Where're we going, for instance?"

"I wanted to come this way, because this is where the man scared me."

"What man scared you?"

"We're coming to it; that big place up there."

"Oh. That's the Hoffmans'. He's some big shot. No kids."

"He has a workshop in the backyard."

"Good for cutting up bodies!"

"Oh yeah, I bet. It's a really fancy house; he must have lots of money."

"Who says he killed for money?"

"Who says he killed? I'm just telling you, I went up in his yard and peeked in his workshop and he didn't like it. Then I dropped my stick and he threw it at me, only it missed and landed in the creek there." She pointed to the small stream to the left of the path.

"So what does he have to do with anything?"

"Only that when I went back to get my stick the next day, he had pulled the shades down on the windows in that workshop—see it right there? The shades are still pulled down; they're always pulled down now when I walk through here. I guess he didn't like me messing around his yard."

"Well, put him on our list of suspicious persons. But we're headed somewhere else, right? Where did you and your mother go to get those bags of leaves? And by the way"—

Chris paused and looked carefully at Janie—"isn't your mother a little odd, I mean, to go around and—"

"No," said Janie firmly. "I don't want to hear that any more. She's just an organic gardener. She can't help it; she's no worse than my great-grandmother, who had a farm in Illinois. She used to bury garbage in the garden and mulch like mad. You know about mulching, I suppose? But I swear: Otherwise, she's pretty normal. Now she might get some little job writing gardening articles, but like your mom, that wouldn't get her out of the house."

"Yeah. I know what you mean." Chris threw back his head to get his long hair out of his face. "I think it's very good for mothers to get out of the house."

"And as for my great-grandmother, know what happened to her? She's old and in a wheelchair, but she still gives other people advice on gardening. They take her around from the Home to different places so she can give lectures."

"Your mom's just like your great-grandmother."

" 'Cept when Great Gram could still walk, she and my mom looked really funny together—like Mutt and Jeff. Great Gram is tiny, and Ma's pretty tall."

He looked down at her. "So? You and I are a lot alike, and look how different we look."

She smiled. "Yeah—you're ugly, and I'm beautiful." Suddenly self-conscious, she added brusquely, "Let's get going—it's not far."

They walked to the end of the park in the woods and turned right onto Martha's Lane. "It's down at the end. Race you!" And she sprinted down the asphalt street. Chris followed and they were neck and neck. Then Chris surged ahead and out of sight.

Janie slowed to a walk, and Chris trotted around in a circle and came back to walk in tandem again. "Which house?" he asked quietly.

She pointed. "The one with all the bushes and trees in front." They walked across the parkway in front of the house, the leaves crunching underfoot.

"You picked up leaf bags right here?"

"Right here," said Janie, and pointed out the spot.

"But the yard is still all filled with leaves. It's a woodsy yard, just like ours. You don't even rake them."

"They must have a lawn in the backyard that they raked," said Janie.

Chris looked at her, as if to gauge her mettle. "Want to go look?"

"Okay." Janie's heart was thumping again.

With care they walked up toward the house, past the shield of evergreens that hid the front door from the street.

"Look at all those ads thrown on the front porch," whispered Chris. "There's nobody home here. Let's go out back." He led the way into the backyard. There was a large lawn strewn with leaves and beyond it a thick woods.

They stood for an instant, taking it all in. Then Chris looked at Janie, another challenge in his gray eyes. "Nobody's around. Let's go peek in the house."

They made their way quietly across the yard and looked through a crack in the drawn curtains. Two table lamps threw dim light on the room. "It's pretty," whispered Janie, "all rose and white. It looks like nobody lives here."

"Maybe used to, but doesn't any more," whispered Chris. "This place is creepy."

Janie looked at him in alarm. "I think I'm getting scared."

"It's okay. I didn't mean to scare you. C'mon." He took her hand and they made their way back to the front yard and the street. "All I can say is, it doesn't look like anyone raked leaves around here."

"It's probably a new leaf fall."

"Leaf fall," said Chris sarcastically, dropping her hand. "Where'd you get that expression?"

"Trees have a succession of leaf falls. Oak leaves hold on later than other leaves. Look up there." She stopped and pointed to a tree outlined in the moonlight. Colonies of silvery leaves still clung to the black branches. "See, they still have, oh, I'd say about ten percent of their leaves. They stay there all winter, through all the wind and snow and rain. Then they let go in spring."

"Huh, 'let go in spring,' " said Chris, scuffing his tennis shoes against the asphalt. " 'Successive leaf falls.' Who talks like that?"

Janie gave him a smug smile. "My mother." Then she took off with her long, thin legs and ran toward home.

15
Going Under

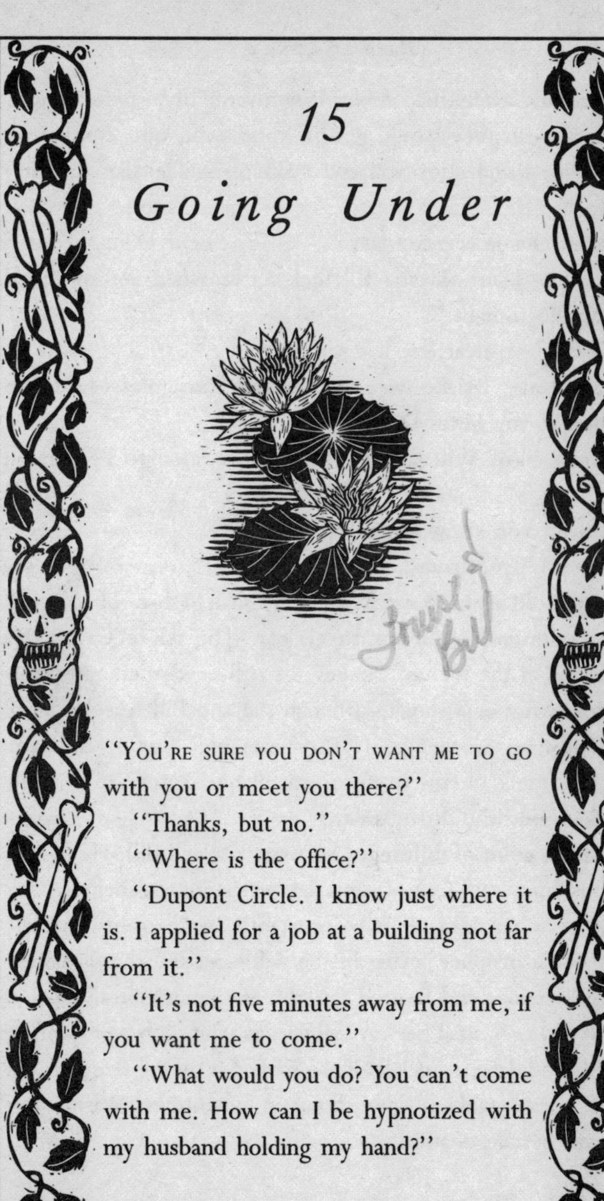

"You're sure you don't want me to go with you or meet you there?"

"Thanks, but no."

"Where is the office?"

"Dupont Circle. I know just where it is. I applied for a job at a building not far from it."

"It's not five minutes away from me, if you want me to come."

"What would you do? You can't come with me. How can I be hypnotized with my husband holding my hand?"

"It would really help things if you remember something."

"You mean they would get off your back, quit coming to your office to question you and making you feel like a criminal?"

"Well. *You're* crusty today."

"I guess I am. Maybe I'll feel better when we see each other again tonight."

"Good-bye, dear."

"Good-bye. By the way, can we trade cars, please? I'd like to listen to my Miles Davis tape."

"Good idea. Will jazz get you in the mood to be hypnotized?"

"I'll let you know later."

"Okay. 'Bye, Louise."

It was cold again so she put on her full-length wool coat and dress boots and went out to his car. The white Camry. It started up at the turn of the key. Its still-new smell and plush interior gave her a shock, although she and Bill traveled in it frequently on weekends. Her six-year-old wagon, redolent with the smells of cow manure, was like a creature apart from this sleek one she drove today.

It was a point of difference between her and Bill. He had to have his fancy car. Out of some leftover student rebellion—or was it from her minister, who constantly spoke against materialism like a prophet crying in the wilderness?—she disdained new possessions and favored the old. She knew one thing: No one would ever steal her car, while this white job would make a good candidate, especially if she parked it on the street in the rather questionable neighborhood in downtown Washington that was her destination.

She turned on Miles Davis and let her mind ride free. Just as she feared, this was becoming another winter of her discontent.

Bill was all settled in his job. Janie and faraway Martha were both snuggled in again with their schools and friends. She had tried, and tried again, and still no job. Her closest companion had been a sodden contractor who had occupied her life when they moved in. Now even he was gone. She refused to wimp out and become a volunteer again. Both in foreign service posts abroad and in their homes here in the States she had been the consummate volunteer—the one who set up children's library reading programs, fund-raisers, whatever was needed most and was up her alley. No more; her next job was going to yield a paycheck. And she *might* have a job, if that garden book editor would only call her.

In the meantime people thought of her as an unemployed housewife. Not only that—the unemployed housewife who had found the body parts in the mulch!

Tears came down her cheeks. Miles Davis's oblique, wailing trumpet was a perfect accompaniment. The minute she got up this morning she knew she would feel like crying.

She realized expectations were high. Her husband and the police glibly anticipated that she would lie on a couch, get hypnotized, and throw up to them out of her dutiful subconscious a handy clue to solve the crime of the body in the bags.

She parked on the street, looking around suspiciously at passersby and hoping no one would steal the dratted car; that would surely be the final indignity in her troubled life.

The offices of the hypnotist were fancier than the street—

modern, with decor in the pleasantest hues of pale apricot and beige. Hypnotism must pay well, she decided.

''Mrs. Eldridge? Dr. Gordon.'' His handshake was vigorous. He had white hair, slicked back to cover a widening baldness. He looked to her as if he used a sun lamp. His suit was dark blue with a stripe that to her tastes was slightly too wide. He was just a little taller than she, but then she had high-heeled boots on today with a deep red woolen dress. The somber dress she thought appropriate for such a serious business as being hypnotized and having one's mind, soul, and body put in the hands of another.

He invited her to use the women's lavatory. She demurred. ''I'm fine as is, thanks.''

Briefly, they sat and he told her what they hoped to accomplish.

''Have you helped solve crimes before, then?''

''On occasion, yes,'' he answered, in his mellifluous voice. He offered no further details.

He invited her to sit in a reclining chair near his. She did so, pulling her dress well down and crossing her legs at the ankle, as if following the dictums of a prim mother.

Then he began talking, in a sonorous tone that seemed to echo in the room. ''I want you to relax . . . to feel yourself letting go . . . going into a deep sleep.''

She noticed he repeated ''deep,'' ''relaxing,'' and ''letting go'' many times, and it rather annoyed her. He needed editing. He asked her to close her eyes and she did.

It was relaxing, and she felt herself slipping off a shelf into another level of consciousness. He was counting now. ''You are going deeper, deeper, deeper. . . . You're doing excellent."

Doing excellent! The improper usage clanged in her brain. Although wide awake, she kept her eyes closed.

"You're doing well."

She relaxed a little.

"Take these moments to enjoy and feel the wonderful relaxation of your body and your mind. . . . There now, you're doing just excellent."

She opened her eyes and looked at the man. "I'm sorry."

He looked startled. "You're not asleep." He looked at his watch. "Ten minutes, and you're not asleep at all." He looked puzzled. "Mrs. Eldridge, are you troubled by something?"

"Mmmm. Not exactly. I just don't think I'm going to be hypnotized."

"Can I ask why not? Something about me—does it make you uncomfortable?"

"Well . . ." Briefly she considered telling the truth, then thought better of it. How can you tell a man he sounds like a charlatan? "You have a very nice voice. But I know I am not going to be hypnotized. I just can't be."

"Ah." He sat back and nodded as if at last understanding. "I think you are a woman who is afraid, or shall I say does not want to give up control."

"Not any more I don't." Her voice sounded very cool. She liked the way it sounded. She flipped the wooden handle that allowed the recliner chair to right itself and stood up. The doctor stood up, too.

"This is a little disappointing, Mrs. Eldridge. The police

suspect you know something that you haven't remembered yet.''

She looked at him with widened eyes. ''Are you trying to make me feel guilty, Dr. Gordon? I don't believe that's called for. I'm not the criminal. As for the police, well, I guess the police will just have to solve the crime the old-fashioned way.''

She left the office. The receptionist, who apparently sensed something was awry, had Louise's coat ready for her to slip on.

As she strode out of the building onto the deserted street, she realized her challenge to Dr. Gordon was so much hot air. Actually, she felt guilty as sin, and that made her angry. ''Guilt sucks,'' she muttered fiercely, as she strode down the sidewalk, grateful again to her college daughter for widening her vocabulary.

Two preteenage boys approached, appearing to come out of nowhere. Both casually brandished sticks, acting exactly like Janie with her stick, bopping them on the ground, waving them in the air, hitting out at trees. But this was not Sylvan Valley—it was an empty street in downtown Washington. And here she was, looking like Mrs. Big Bucks in her fancy clothes and inviting purse, ready to climb into her $30,000 car. She clutched her purse strap with tight fingers and gave them a Clint Eastwood glare that said, ''Don't even think about it.''

They looked back at her with innocent faces, two young black kids going home for lunch. Feeling foolish, she opened the car door, got in, and drove away.

She maneuvered through the heavy late-morning Washington traffic, yielding not an inch to pushy drivers in sports cars who went ballistic if another driver got in front of them. But she did not mind driving these studs wild this morning: Today, no one would get the best of her!

But Geraghty had gotten the best of her. He didn't bother to keep her informed about the murder investigation. All he had done was interview Janie once, and Bill about three times, and shoo her off to the police psychologist. The crime had to be top priority since it was the grisliest murder Fairfax County had seen since the slashing death of a young couple last year in their Alexandria condo. No, the police were still hot on the case, but certainly not bothering to share any of the details with her or Bill.

The guilt produced by her failure to be hypnotized—and at being mean to two little schoolboys—lingered like a bad taste. The very least she could do was to retrace her steps again, from her leaf-collecting days. She plotted her route home so it would take her by every house where she had stopped, starting with the one in south Bethesda, and ending at the place on Martha's Lane in Sylvan Valley.

Finally, she returned home and pulled into the driveway, exhausted and starved. "I am a lousy sleuth," she muttered to herself as she stomped out of the Camry. Not only had nothing clicked in her mind. No lightbulb had gone off that suddenly and brilliantly illuminated a lost fact. And near the houses in question, she had seen a set of human beings straight out of Norman Rockwell. Charming old lady and man. Ebullient young mother with preschoolers. Grade-school kids romping home to be greeted by a flustered suburban mom. Clean-cut father working on his garage. It was hard to visualize any one of them killing, sawing, and packaging a human being.

And yet, who could tell from outward appearances? Maybe that suburban mom had reason to become jealous. . . .

Louise shook her head in disgust, went in the house, and kicked off her boots. That was it: This was the beginning and the end of her investigation of the mulch murder. It was just as she had told that strange Dr. Gordon: The police were going to have to solve it. She had no business poking around in murder.

16
Inside State

BILL RIFFLED THROUGH THE PINK MESSAGE SLIPS on his desk, then placed them neatly in a pile, selecting one out and putting it on top. Then he slowly pivoted his chair around, as if the movement would force to the top of his consciousness the thought that was troubling him. Instead of seeing the lights of the capital from his vantage point in Foggy Bottom, he saw only himself: a tired-looking blond man, blue shirt with shirtsleeves rolled up, hands knitted and resting on top of his head. A man who looked fretful, guilty. What was he forgetting to do that disturbed him so?

"Why aren't you on your way home to your wife?"

Startled, Bill swirled his chair around and sat up straight. Ed worked in the office next door. He stood in the doorway in coat and hat, a fat briefcase in one hand. Bill's mouth dropped imperceptibly as the man sauntered in and slumped down in a leather armchair.

He eyed the briefcase thrown carelessly across Ed's lap. "I was trying to clean up a few things so I wouldn't have to do what you're doing."

Ed smiled and took off his hat, revealing a balding head with only a rim of dark hair left. He wrinkled his nose—Bill thought he resembled a rabbit when he did this—to persuade his glasses back in position. "I have something for you before I go, Bill. Try this on for size: The president's theme in future is going to be SMO: supporting military operations."

Bill said: "Funny, I thought it was going to be SPW, supporting public works."

Ed shook his head. "Nope. That's what we thought it was going to be, but it's not. Anyway, not since the economy appears to be coming out of its slide again. Of course we know our economy is in for a long, slow downhill ride—no matter if the Dow reached a new high this week and my biotechs went up eight points. But the president's theme is not going to be economics; unfortunately, we're as bad off as when we were fighting the Cold War, he thinks. His mission is to lead the world out of trouble again." He laughed. "Isn't that the mission of all presidents? But the country cries out for more military budget cuts. So the key to it all"—he threw his hand back in a godfather gesture—"is supporting military operations."

Bill's patience was wearing thin, yet he showed no sign of it to the garrulous man sitting opposite him. "How to get the best intelligence and the best military backup for the least amount of bucks, so we can continue to facilitate the UN policy of assertive multilateralism."

"That's it!" Ed looked pleased, as if in the presence of a brilliant subaltern, although Bill outranked him on the European desk where they both worked. "And right here at home, the challenge of how to get that result out of Congress. Ergo the emphasis on strategic arms—small, smart arms"—Ed rolled his lips around the *s*'s—"with the ability to stop the bastards without sending in fifty thousand men every time." His eyes twinkled behind his thick glasses. "And you know what else?"

Bill looked at him soberly. "I don't know, but I think you're going to say it."

"Truth is, this is a very scary time for the country. Economy very rough, even if improving. Trouble everywhere you look abroad. Hell, the chief has his hands full. You *know* he'd love to get rid of the secretary of defense. That's why he's signing Hoffman on board. Small-weapons expert. Wants him to drive the secretary out. Hoffman's kind of a wild man, I hear. But maybe just what we need. He was in on the very beginning in Vietnam." Ed was a rambling conversationalist, but he tried to reward his listeners with a little pithy gossip, like the dollop of whipped cream on a stale piece of cake.

Bill suddenly sat forward and picked up the pile of phone

messages. "Ed. I'd love to talk more but I have to make a phone call. Catch you later, okay?"

"Right," said Ed cheerfully, put on his hat, and left. Bill waited until he would have time to clear the hall, then got up and closed and locked the door to his office.

He fingered the top phone message. Tom Paschen, the president's chief of staff, had called him. Not good. The whole burden of Bill's hidden life weighed on his shoulders. He and Paschen had worked together years ago in the old Executive Office building, when both were assigned to the National Security Council. Paschen must know that he still worked for the company, under State Department cover. Then what did he want?

He got him on his first try. "Hi, Tom, how's it going? What's up?" Bill and Tom had no need for extra words.

"It's Peter Hoffman—you know, the president's candidate for deputy secretary of defense. Christ only knows why he wants him."

"Yeah. Peter Hoffman. People here have been talking about him. And he talks to the press. So tell me about him."

"East Coast money, nouveau money . . ." said Paschen. Bill remembered Tom Paschen's family was Boston old money.

"MIT. Veered into Army intelligence as a very young man, in the early sixties. Bloody time then—remember? You and I were kids. A president was assassinated over there. Priests died. Monks conflagrated themselves. Christ, Bill, who knows what the *president* did back then. He and Hoffman met over there, served together; you've probably read Hoffman's self-serving account in the papers. Hoffman developed as a soldier of fortune type. Jack Fairchild went into politics. Then Hoffman grew up a little, began inventing weapons. He's a genius at it, I'll admit that."

Bill could hear the dislike in Paschen's voice; he knew the praise of Hoffman's work was grudging.

"So that's what the chief's after—the weapons know-how. He invented that A-Fifty-five hand-held gun. A revolution in automatic weaponry. And his hawkish persona—shit, the president *loves* his hawkish persona. He even thinks that stuff's going to carry him up in the polls."

"Any details about his service in 'Nam?"

"None that you can put your hands on. Records are wiped clean. It's the recent years that are potential trouble. He manufactures small arms. Acts as a broker. Makes a killing. Has connections all over the world. But he's kept his nose clean."

"That doesn't sound like trouble."

"I haven't got to the sleaze part. There are stories out there we don't like. Stories about women, always women . . . out of Europe, so they're hard to check. He's married again now, although I hear he always has a piece on the side—actually, a series of women, from what FBI surveillance has picked up."

"You're having him tailed by the FBI." Bill's heart thudded. "What would you want to know from me, then?" As a CIA agent, Bill would be flouting the National Security Act if he spied on an American citizen like Hoffman. Paschen must know what a bind he was putting him in. Didn't he care?

Fatigue rolled over him. He wondered if he'd even have enough strength to get up and go home to Louise and Janie.

Paschen continued: "I want to know if you think the president needs to pull back on this nomination—have the guy withdraw.''

Bill said: ''I suppose he ran with Secord and Hakim and all that crowd.'' Asking for more history. Buying time to think.

''Yeah,'' said Paschen. ''But not involved in Iran-Contra. And if he had been, well, nobody cares any more anyway. And then he only blew the way the country blew with Saddam. As I said, he's kept his nose clean, for an arms dealer.''

Bill sat back in his swivel chair and gently rocked. The niggling worry in his head had still not stepped forward and declared itself, and now he had this Paschen thing on top of it. ''What do you want from me, Tom?''

Tom's voice was cold. ''I don't like this guy. We've met a couple times and all my instincts tell me, 'Don't do it.' He's smart. He's cunning. But you can't just put some idiot savant in a deputy secretary job. I warned the guy about flagrant womanizing, and from what the FBI says, he's quit operating dames out of his Georgetown place. But there's something there I can't put my finger on. Hey, you know me, Bill. I'm no pussycat. . . .''

Bill smiled. Paschen was smart, tough, and ruthless. He never could figure out how they became friends. He guessed because despite the means Paschen occasionally used, Bill usually agreed with the end he was trying to reach; because the man, like him, did things for love of country. Mostly, the damage Paschen did was to the egos of those not quite as cunning as himself.

''Yeah. You're no pussycat.''

''But this guy . . . he's like a savage underneath a thin veneer of respectability.''

Bill turned one side of his mouth up in a cynical smile. "And my role in this? Do you want me to scrape him and see how deep the veneer is? After all, mankind in general has only a thin layer of respectability."

"He lives in your neighborhood, you know."

"He does? Not in our immediate neighborhood—maybe in one of those homes on the parkway."

"Nope. He's just inside your Sylvan Valley paradise there, close enough to the colonial houses to make him feel better, maybe." Bill was not used to the conversational tone coming from Paschen, but he knew it must presage the asking of a favor. "All I want you to do is ask him over," proposed the chief of staff. "I know you like your privacy now, after all those years of batting around the world. And then, of course, I heard about that body they found in the bags in your yard—that's damned unpleasant. But that's all resolved now, isn't it?"

"Not exactly resolved." Bill laughed ruefully. "We don't answer the phone until we're sure it isn't 'Hard Copy.' "

"No kiddin'. I guess that's right; a crime brings the media. It must have been a zoo."

"It isn't quite past tense yet, Tom. Someone from the press tries to get through almost daily. And the police . . ." Bill's face flushed red, and he was glad Paschen couldn't see his anger. "This caricature of an Irish cop—I should say *prototype,* named Geraghty. Three times he's been here at my office." He laughed briefly. "It's almost funny." He wasn't going to tell Paschen any more—about Louise's failed session with the hypnotist, about his nagging worries. . . .

"Sorry, old chap," said Paschen. From one of the country's busiest civil servants this was a lot of sympathizing. "You should have sent him to me. I could have told him right off the bat *you* didn't do it. But seriously, maybe I shouldn't be asking so much of you."

"No," protested Bill. "Go ahead."

"I was hoping your wife—Louise, isn't it?—could have a dinner party. I remember being at one of them; she's great at it. I bet she's already met this guy, knowing how friendly she is."

"Well, she hasn't been able to move that fast." Bill knew how tough it had been on Louise, job-hunting, trying to get acquainted, dealing for months with difficult contractors, then the murder. Paschen wouldn't understand. And it hadn't helped matters that she failed to go under when the police psychologist tried to hypnotize her. Now she would barely tell him anything about it.

Thankfully, yesterday, the garden editor she had been talking to for months finally threw her a crumb by offering to buy an article on ferns and pay her $300 for it. Bill hadn't been able to tear her away from the computer since. She was slipping fern plants furtively into the house—strange varieties he had never seen before. By the time the article was completed, he would know more about ferns than he ever cared to, and possess an inordinate amount of them, probably about $300 worth. Both of them knew it was a small first step toward the career she wanted.

Staring out the window, he said, "I suppose I could ask Hoffman to my neighborhood poker group; I'm the host in a couple of weeks."

"You lucky sonofabitch: I haven't played poker since I was in high school."

Bill grinned. "I believe that. We met once already at our house. Had a lotta laughs. From then on, Louise has called it the Giggling Men's Club."

Paschen chortled. "You're kidding. I love it. I bet you play rock crusher and shit like that."

"You got it," said Bill.

"I'm jealous."

"Come out and play sometime. Nice bunch of guys. It'd do you good."

"You know I'll never take the time. But how about inviting Hoffman?"

Bill shifted the phone to his other ear and put his feet up on the edge of the desk. "Actually, they're too nice for this Hoffman guy. On second thought, I'd rather ask him out to a dinner party. We can invite a combination of people, including some neighbors. I know what you want."

"What do I want?" said Paschen.

"A nice, loose party for this guy to operate in. You want me to decide how big a bastard he is, what's his capacity for embarrassing, what's his capacity for becoming part of a first-class scandal, what's his capacity for ruining the chief's chances for a second term."

"That's it in a nutshell," said Paschen, sounding pleased.

17
Bill

Once Bill remembered what was bothering him, he closed up shop at work and retrieved his Camry in the almost deserted underground State Department parking lot. Distracted with his own thoughts, he barely noted that he was passing most of the other cars on the crowded George Washington Parkway. Then a dark car loomed on his left, and with a start he realized it might be a policeman arresting him for speeding. But it was not. It was a proud-chinned young man in a Porsche, who paused a minisecond alongside Bill, gave his sedan a sidelong glance, and then spurted ahead. Bill smiled and relaxed his foot on the gas pedal.

He pulled into the carport and hurried up the front walk, a tumble of oak leaves crunching underfoot as he went. He frowned. Although he and Louise loved their wooded lot, he would have preferred something a little neater. Tonight he would get out with a broom and sweep the leaves from the walkway.

As he approached the front door, he heard a faint "yoo hoo" from the studio. He opened the door and entered the studio. There sat Louise, looking a lot friendlier than she had for the past couple of days. Her long chestnut hair was tousled, and she wore her winter season outfit: gray turtleneck, and garden pants tucked into her boots. She was sitting at her computer, books and papers spread out on the table. On the wall in back of her was a daybed with Navajo throw, and within reach was a small black woodstove, with embers glowing. On it sat her favorite beat-up aluminum coffeepot that she swore made better coffee than his Chemex. Her coffee mug stood near her left hand. On the other side of the room were two easy chairs, looking out the wide-windowed door at the end of the studio.

Without getting up, she reached her arms out to him. "Hello, darling. Give a little kiss to your working wife." He went over and kissed her lightly on the lips, then pulled away from her embrace.

"It's getting wild around here," he grumbled. "The sidewalk is going to disappear completely with all the leaves you've thrown around this yard.'' He saw her expression change to dismay and felt a pang of regret for his gruffness.

''What's wrong, Bill?'' Her eyes were round with concern. ''Is everything all right at work?''

Bill sat on the nearby daybed. Louise swiveled around in her chair to see him. He sighed a heavy sigh but didn't look at his wife. He was hunched forward, elbows on knees, holding his hat in his hands. Hat in hand. How many times does a man plead, hat in hand, for one thing or another? ''Louise,'' he said, ''I am getting concerned, and I didn't even realize I was.''

She looked alarmed. ''About what?''

At last he raised his eyes to meet hers. ''I'm worried about you.'' She looked as if she were going to object, and he put up a warning hand. ''No, don't say anything yet. Just let me get my thoughts together.'' He looked at the stove. ''That stove sure gives off a lot of heat; I'm roasting.'' He shrugged out of his coat and folded it beside him, putting his hat on top of the pile.

''You know what's happened before with you; you've got yourself involved in things. . . .'' He spread his hands, as if she would immediately know what he meant.

''Involuntarily,'' said Louise, her mouth set firm. ''I have never meant to get involved. I've been in a lot more danger those times I was helping *you.*''

She was right. It was the agency's belief that with a married undercover agent, it got two for the price of one. Louise had helped him on occasion, once with surveillance, a couple times as a courier, continually as a deft hostess who brought the right people to their dinner table where he could learn things. And once, in Turkey, he had put her in real danger, not realizing how her curiosity would overwhelm her caution.

He decided he had better change course. "Now look, honey, I don't mean it's been your fault, your doing, that got you into situations, but sometimes they were dangerous. It's when you get too involved—well, take the Turk, that time . . . or even that young moving man, for instance."

"You take him," she snapped. "I don't want him."

"Now, Louise, I didn't mean any harm."

"So, what is your point?" Louise sat very straight in her chair, her eyes an angry barrier. "That I'd better stay out of trouble, right? Never inquire about how someone else lives—what harm can that do?"

"Louise, you're *already* involved in something. *That's* what I'm worried about: Those body parts you dragged into our yard—you're involved whether you know you are or not."

Louise sat back in her chair. "Have you been talking to Nora? You sound just like her. She's really spooked about that woman who was murdered. Has some kind of premonition of evil, and she even writes *poems* about it."

Then, with no bidding, the hollow terror she'd experienced in Nora's living room that day came back to her in a rush. She sat unsteadily on her chair, giddy as a spinning top. Again, she could feel that heated, buried-alive feeling that nearly made her run from that room, Nora's ominous gray figure, standing there like a blind soothsayer, warning of approaching evil.

She reached back and put a steadying hand on the table, hoping Bill wouldn't notice, and tried to shut down those terrifying memories.

She had handled it then, hadn't she, and she didn't need to

dredge it up again. Nora's poetic predictions were just that. Practical people like her didn't rule their lives with the hunches of poets with extrasensory perception.

To her relief, her voice, when she spoke, sounded normal. "And then," she told Bill, "there's those shadowy figures that she sees around our house—"

Bill jolted forward. "Around *our* house?"

"Bill, wait: I'm not sure if that's real, or just her imagination—she has an imagination that won't quit. In fact, I'm a little worried about Nora. She's so otherworldly that—"

"Shadowy figures around our house, come on! When? Where around our house? Why in hell didn't she tell us? I thought that woman was smart."

Louise put a hand on his knee. "She did—she told me just the other day. But don't worry: It happened way back, around the time Sam Rosen thought there were kids in the yard. Well, Sam's lights are on every night now, so I'm sure we're much safer. I'm feeling better every day they don't find the killer, because that means the crime is more and more distanced from us. You know what Mike Geraghty thinks—it's an unsolvable kind of murder. It's probably somebody we picked up in Washington." Her eyes widened and she put a hand over her mouth and then burst out laughing. She laughed hysterically, rocking up and down in her chair.

Bill had to chuckle in spite of himself. He reached over and took her nearest hand while she recovered. "I'm glad you can make a joke out of it. I just wish you had more of a sense of danger." He squeezed her hand and looked at her with pleading eyes. He made his voice very smooth and calm. "Louise, this is not really funny, although what you just said is funny. I love you and I don't want you to be in danger."

"Then what do you want me to do?"

"Well, first of all, just consider yourself out of this thing." He put a warning hand up. "Don't try to think it out. Let's not have you investigating. Let Geraghty—Mike Geraghty as you now call him—run with the ball. I'm also worried that Janie may be snooping around with that boy, but that's probably all right, because I sense it's more the boy-girl thing than a real investigation. And that boy looks fairly sensible."

In a quiet voice Louise said, "That 'boy' is almost voting age, and his name is Chris."

"Chris. Whatever. But let's get back to you. I want you to do some simple precautionary things: Stay in phone contact with me. Don't take chances. Don't even talk about this to the neighbors any more—"

"Bill." He could tell she was getting angry again.

"Don't get mad at me, sweetie." He reached over and grabbed both hands this time. "I love you. I don't know what I'd do without you. I want you to close your eyes—go ahead, close them. Now, think back on that woman's body. It was hacked up with a power saw. Did Geraghty bother to tell you that? Blood went all over the place, somewhere. So what kind of a person do you think did that? It's a crazy person who obviously doesn't have any respect for life. If by some quirk he happens to come from around here, I don't want him zeroing in on my wife just because she happened by accident to discover the body." He raised her hands to his lips and kissed each one.

The expression in Louise's eyes had changed from anger to

tenderness. She leaned toward him. ''Oh, Bill. I do love you. I'm really not doing any of those things. I'm not even very social. And from now on, I'll just be sitting here writing about ferns. Trying to meet my deadline with the publisher.'' She shook her head. ''I am not a nosy housewife. I don't intend to let my life be that limited again. I'm *working.* Not only that, I'm getting *paid.*''

''Sweetie,'' said Bill, and pulled her over to him and sat her on his lap. He gave her a tender kiss. She returned it with interest, and they fell over onto the narrow bed and grappled, laughing.

Louise said, ''I don't think there's enough room, and your coat's in the way, but I certainly enjoy making up after a fight with you.'' And she pulled him closer.

Bill nuzzled against that special place in her neck below the jawline, and was just going lower when he thought of something. ''I suppose Janie's coming home.''

They pulled apart a little. ''Yes, but maybe we could hear her coming when she steps on those crunchy leaves.''

He groaned and sat up. ''Knowing Janie, she won't make *any* noise.''

She sat beside him. ''And there is the reality of starvation,'' she said, rubbing her stomach. ''I don't know about you, but I haven't eaten anything but a Granny Smith all day. I need to start dinner.''

He held on to her arm, preventing her from getting up. ''Before you go, tell me now what happened when they tried to hypnotize you.''

Louise slumped back comfortably against him. ''Oh, I don't know,'' she said, in a dismissing tone. ''Dr. Gordon essentially told me I was a failure as a subject. I politely told him to shove it.''

''Louise, *you* don't talk that way.''

''I didn't *say* it, I just intimated it.'' She looked up at him. ''Are you disappointed in me?''

''Disappointed? For not going under? Maybe a little. But I don't blame you for it.'' He smiled. ''After all, it's *your* subconscious.''

She smiled and poked him gently in the ribs.

He was serious when he continued: ''But that's the nub of it: The killer, if he's around here anywhere, might believe, just like the police, that you know something you're not remembering. So promise me: Don't tell anyone they tried to hypnotize you.''

''Too late, I'm afraid.''

''Oh,'' he groaned. ''Louise, Louise! Who?''

''Only Nora and Jan and Mary. They phoned; I had to tell them. But I also told them it was no go.'' She sighed. ''There's one thing that would keep me safe.''

''What?''

''Another dog.'' She smiled up at him.

He rolled his eyes. ''Oh, no, not another long-term commitment to a *pooch.* Dogs are like babies, but worse: They never grow up so you can have a decent conversation with them.''

''Bill,'' she pleaded.

''But maybe a dog would be good. We could get a great big monster with a scary bark.''

Louise hugged him. ''Oh, thank you! You know I've wanted

a new one ever since Scruffy died! We'll get one *you* like. He doesn't have to be as wiggly and obsequious as Scruffy was."

He picked up his hat off the top of his neat pile and twirled it around his forefinger. "Now, Louise, since I'm yielding on the dog question, how would you like to do me a big favor?"

"What?"

"A dinner party for about thirty people . . . and soon."

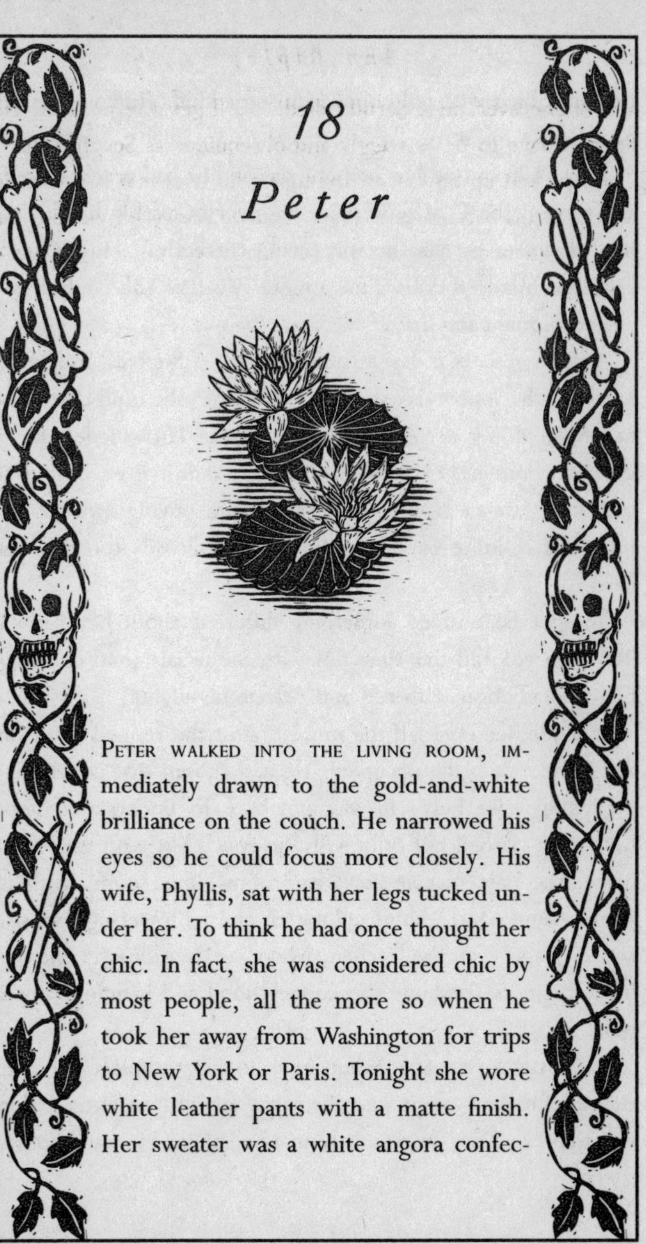

18

Peter

PETER WALKED INTO THE LIVING ROOM, immediately drawn to the gold-and-white brilliance on the couch. He narrowed his eyes so he could focus more closely. His wife, Phyllis, sat with her legs tucked under her. To think he had once thought her chic. In fact, she was considered chic by most people, all the more so when he took her away from Washington for trips to New York or Paris. Tonight she wore white leather pants with a matte finish. Her sweater was a white angora confection sprinkled with gold objects of some kind. He knew he had paid dearly for it.

It had lain out on her bed one day and he had reached down and flipped the I. Magnin price tag over in his big hand, then bent down to be sure he was seeing correctly. "Holy Christ. Eighteen hundred dollars for a mere sweater? You could buy a designer gown for that."

"Darling, it is a designer *sweater*. It's a Sophie. You know how much Sophies cost." At the time she said this, she had been doing aerobic exercises on the Ultrasuede mat in the bathroom next to the Jacuzzi. She didn't even bother to escalate it to an argument, just kept on sawing away at her imagined cellulite excesses with muscles already too thin and hard.

Tonight he noticed something different about her hair. It had been colored this time not with the usual blond coloring, but a concoction with red and orange highlights.

It made her clash all the more against the refined Mies van der Rohe couch she occupied. He had chosen that couch, and everything else here. It was a tribute to understated good taste. She clashed not only with the couch but with the whole place, the pale marble-lined bathrooms, this room, with its white, taupe, and walnut coloration and its towering two stories of glass, even the kitchen, where, extraordinarily enough, her brassiness outshone the copper hood and hanging copper pots.

Just over a year ago, when he'd bought the place, he considered Phyllis gave it just the right amount of extra color, extra spark. They were newly married then. He had thought this marriage might be different. But it had gone sour, just like the other two.

As he stared at Phyllis, he realized she was sitting just the way Kristina had been sitting the night he had strangled her. Two women more different had never been born. One, gentle and loving—the one he had killed. Why hadn't he . . .

"What's the matter with you now, Peter?" Phyllis's shrill words broke in, and he started. "You're just standing there, staring at me." She glowered at him. "You are so strange lately. What's with you?"

"Sorry, Phyllis." He had better be careful or he'd lose it. This was no time to lose it. "My thoughts were a million miles away." No, he had to do better than that. Phyllis was a suspicious sort with a woman's hypersensitive antennae; he used to admire her for that; he didn't want it turned against him now. With a nonchalant stride he crossed the room and joined her on the couch.

"As a matter of fact," he said, "I was thinking about our invitation."

"To the Eldridges."

"Yes. Did you know he's with the State Department, EUR?"

"And EUR means exactly what?" She reached out a well-manicured hand to him, friendlier now that he was sharing the couch with her. He took it and absentmindedly examined it while they talked, then focused in on it closely. Examined its carefully tanned skin, its absence of freckles, its absence of *innocence.* He caught himself, dropped her hand, and felt a sudden sweat. His thoughts were out of control. Some fucking psychiatrist would probably tell him he was suffering from the Macbeth syndrome.

He'd had a couple of lapses like this lately, and he needed to do something about them. This was no time for lapses. There were lots of parties where he had to show himself off, a meeting with the president, two or three appointments where he was supposed to kiss ass with congressmen on the Hill. And then of course he had to manage all the little details necessary to keep the murder hidden, including Kristina's mail, which was a hell of a lot more voluminous than he'd expected. Here he thought she had been a loner, and instead she had friends writing to her from all over the world. Handling a dead woman's mail was a shitty job, and every time he laboriously answered a letter, it depressed him a little—and scared him, too, for any time he could make a misstep.

It all took its toll.

Right now, it was keeping Phyllis happy that mattered. He had taken so long to answer her again that she looked at him with suspicion.

He tried to make his voice steady and ordinary. "EUR stands very simply for the Bureau of European Affairs." To gain time, he sat back, took off his thick glasses, and wiped under each eye with his forefingers. He peered at her myopically. "He's one of that precious crew of foreign service officers who get stationed in London, Paris, or Rome—livin' the high life while *we* American taxpayers foot the bill." He was interesting her; she'd forgotten his strangeness. "Yeah, the State Department crowd: a bunch of incompetents. They do second best what others like the NSC do best. They ought to be out of business.'' His tone turned conspiratorial: ''You know what this Eldridge really wants?''

''What, darling?'' She looked interested.

''He wants to look me over.'' Peter sat back, relaxed now, confident, over the rough spot. ''He wants to see me close up, one of the bad boys of international arms but good at inventing war toys. He could be a spook.''

''A spook?'' asked Phyllis, her eyes wide. She loved spy thrillers and mysteries; he would play to her strong suit. ''You mean a spy?'' She sat up straighter and wriggled a little with excitement.

''We're talking *The Third Man* here.'' He gave her a quick smile. ''Maybe more like George Smiley without the paunch, or one of the sexier guys out of a Ross Thomas novel.'' He looked into his wife's face. ''Dead giveaway: There's no reason for him to invite me over to dinner. Nobody from the State Department ever holds a dinner party that isn't job related. So he's probably not State Department.''

He could tell she wanted more. He gave her more. ''I hear Eldridge's very attractive: You'll probably get all hot over him.''

''Really, Peter.'' She shoved him away in mock anger but could not repress a pleased smile. ''Am I that transparent? But I've met his wife at two swim club meetings—you were at one of them, you remember. Tall. Perhaps a little ungainly. She isn't *that* bad-looking, but she ought to know women over forty shouldn't wear such long hair.''

Peter remembered meeting the wife there, too—Louise, or some such name. The hair fantastic. Big hazel eyes, terrific legs, soft-looking breasts, a concave belly. And with that freshness that Kristina possessed: a perennial innocence. It always blew his mind.

At the thought he felt himself hardening. He reached over and thrust a hand under Phyllis's fuzzy sweater to surround a thin, exercised breast with his large hand. He put the other hand between her muscular thighs. Not a soft body like Kristina's. . . . No, he had to forget that.

"Darling, I didn't know you still cared," said Phyllis. She smiled her little coy smile. Playing games with him. Never sincere.

He leaned near her, playing with her breast, feeling the nipple harden despite herself. He said, "What I want us to do at this party of theirs is play the part well. The acceptable candidate and his faithful wife. This bastard Eldridge has something to do with Paschen; you can bet your life on that."

With scant attention she murmured, "You mean the president's in on this?" Her breathing was shallow and she was intent now on Peter's caresses, directing his hand to where she wanted it to go between her thighs.

"Only indirectly. Fairchild doesn't give a damn about anything but my military expertise. Tom Paschen's the one—he hates my guts. He's using this argument that I'm some sort of a barbarian who isn't even acceptable with the Washington power elite."

"Darling, since I've known you, you've never bothered to even try to be acceptable."

He rubbed his nose against hers and growled suggestively. "Maybe it's time your Peter grew up and learned how to act like a little gentleman. Shit, I could charm the pants off the Congress, the joint chiefs of staff, Sally Quinn, Ben Bradlee, or anyone else in Washington they have that needs impressing—and most certainly, the esteemed Bill Eldridge.''

''But don't start just now,'' she said breathlessly, and wrenched her sweater over her iridescent hairdo to give him more room to work.

19
Mary

Louise collected the mail at the curb, and wandered back to the house. Armed with a fallen branch, she poked and prodded among the leaves but knew well she would find no green in late November— no little magical rosettes of emerging plants to cheer her sober heart. She quit her futile search, and scanned the woods. All was beautifully in place—the trio of robust rhododendron, waiting for spring to belt out their beauty, like three Italian tenors. The two free-growing amelanchier for balance. The carefully placed camellia, and the new little cluster of plants near the path. The craggy witch hazel, waiting to give forth its spidery yellow flowers. Scores of bulbs hiding beneath the ground, waiting to come up. Only the Concord grapes had not worked out, so the pergola was still bare.

Despite this perfection, her yard seemed neglected. Truth to tell, she hadn't been out here, not even to shoulder up the oak leaf mulch around the plants, hadn't had the heart to do a thing outdoors since that Sunday a month ago when they unbagged the leaves. Humps of leaves dotted the back corner, left whatever way the police had left them. She hoped they did not smother the skunk cabbage, but did not have the will to go and look. Anyway, she had an inkling that skunk cabbage was as tough, underneath, as she was.

Somehow the murder had spoiled this place for her. Working outdoors gave her bad vibrations. But she had no time for that kind of self-introspection right now: She had a writing job to finish, and finish soon.

As she turned to walk back in the house, she saw a bright figure across the cul-de-sac. Walking a little closer, she saw it was Mary Mougey standing at the curb. When Mary beckoned her, she welcomed the excuse to stay outdoors a moment longer.

They met in the middle of the cul-de-sac, and Louise did a double take.

"Why, Mary . . ." She stopped, not wanting to offend her neighbor. From being a rather colorless person with graying blond hair, Mary appeared to be almost a new person.

The smile was the same, or was the smile different, too?

"Ah," Mary said with satisfaction, "you noticed. I've gone and done it—had my hair colored—as well as a few other, uh, *amenities.* Face-lift, actually."

"It looks—very nice." Combined with her stylish winter white sports outfit and shrugged-on car coat, her neighbor suddenly had become high fashion.

Mary shook her head, as if regretting the whole thing. "You don't have to approve. I didn't want to do it, myself. I have always deplored bottle blondes and face-lifts, but fifty comes and goes, and then *sixty* looms ahead." She stepped closer to Louise as if sharing a confidence. "If you want to know the truth, I did it for the children."

"The children?" said Louise. "You mean . . ."

"I mean, my dear, the big donors are a funny bunch. They live lives wrapped in cotton—you know, only going to certain places, clubs, stores, vacation spots, to their fourteenth-floor offices in the district, or their fortieth-floor offices in the suburbs. Most mingle with—and are used to looking at—people who have gone to a great deal of trouble about their appearances.

"So," she added briskly, "I decided an upgrade of my image as graying earth mother was in order. And here I am. Same person underneath, just shinier on the surface. Now—are you up for lunch? How about going with the new me for barbecue at the Dixie Pig?"

"I've seen it while driving by, but must admit I've never been there."

"Then you know it's only a couple miles from here—one of the wondrous attractions of Route One." Mary's eyes twinkled. "Route One also includes high-rises, brothel motels, fortune-tellers, and those ghastly new condos that eventually will elbow out all the good old stuff like the Pig."

She told Louise she needn't change out of her garden clothes, and when they arrived at the restaurant, Louise could see this was true. Its welcome sign featured a porky pig and would have discouraged anyone wanting to keep their figure, she decided. Sure enough, entering the restaurant just ahead of them was a vastly overweight family, father, mother, and son, mouths obviously watering for the barbecue. The sunny booths were filled mostly with men in work clothes who had not bothered to remove their billed caps.

"Richard and I come here sometimes on Saturdays," Mary told her. "We love their barbecue sandwiches. Barbecue brings out the South in me." It turned out she was from North Carolina, but living in many different parts of the world had subsumed her Southern accent and left her speech with simply an anonymous softness.

Mary had clout here, and Louise had a suspicion that was true of the finest Washington restaurants as well. To the cheery waitress behind the counter, she said, "Can we please sit in the bar? We're having—a sort of *meeting.*" The waitress hesitated a moment, then responded to the golden smile, and took them and two plastic-protected menus into a tiny bar room at the front of the place. She flipped on a set of dim lights, and said, "Sit anywhere. Want your special, Mary?"

"Yes, please." Mary smiled, looked at Louise, and said, "Trust me?"

Louise nodded, and Mary said, "Make it two."

When the waitress left, her neighbor folded her arms in front of her on the wood table, and said, "I have important matters to talk to you about. I've been home for two weeks, recovering from the effects of my face-lift.'' Her hand went out and gently touched her cheek near the hairline. ''It's given me time to organize things around my house, which heaven knows gets very little attention, except when the cleaning woman comes, bless her heart. *Two* things, Louise, involve you.'' She smiled, with her face and her eyes. ''One is just fun: I'm thinking of getting fish and a pond to put them in, come spring, and I need your input. But I wonder if Richard and I are really fish people.'' She cocked her well-coiffed head. ''Do you know anything about fish—and will it be as much trouble as having a dog, for instance, or a kitty? For, you know, we travel quite a bit, and it isn't as if one can drop them off at a vet—or can one?''

''You know, Mary, I don't know very much about them. Do you mean koi, those Japanese kind?''

''Exactly,'' said Mary enthusiastically, and then put out a hand in a stop gesture. ''But that's all right—I'll research the fish. Richard and I talked about it, because we saw some at a friend's this summer, and they were so *tranquil* and *beautiful*; they quite captivated us. But it was a big party, and we never had a chance to talk *pescatore* with our hosts.''

Louise chuckled. ''If you like them, I'd go for it. I could baby-sit them when you go away. I can't believe they would be any bother.''

Mary's face changed, the smile gone, the focused look restored. Her voice was quieter, no longer laced with the delight that it was when she was talking about fish. ''The other matter is the mulch murder. Louise, the police just have not solved it, have they?''

"No."

"I saw you, Louise—" She broke off her sentence as the waitress brought in their drinks; both had ordered tea. When she left, Mary resumed. "Staying home gives one time to observe one's neighbors. When you got out of Bill's car the other day, you were all dressed up in boots and things, but you looked so unhappy. If you'd had a dog, you would have kicked it. Then, a couple of nights later, I saw Bill come home, all flustered, and storm up the walk. From then on, I have done nothing but worry about the two of you. This is the first day I have been out since my operation—otherwise my swollen face would have scared people—and I was just on my way over to visit when I saw you in your yard."

Louise well remembered the day she failed hypnotism and then fruitlessly retraced the trail to houses where she'd picked up leaf bags. "All I can say is, I'm glad I have a writing job to distract me." She told Mary about her assignment from the garden editor. "It helps balance out those bad days."

Her neighbor frowned. "Do you have lots of bad days like that? Why is this all falling on you two? It is outrageous that the police can't do any better. Surely, *someone* is missing!"

Louise looked at Mary, and a small epiphany sounded in her head. She leaned forward eagerly. "Yes, *yes,* that's the whole point. Someone is missing, and why can't they find out who it is? I told you the last time we talked that I was being hypnotized. I think they thought I was going to solve the crime. Well, I failed to go under, and the police were very disappointed in me, according to what they told Bill: He's the only one who has talked to them recently. Detective Geraghty told him, quote, 'Otherwise, the trail is cold.' "

Mary looked at her intently. "I'm fascinated. Why weren't you hypnotized?"

Louise hadn't known for sure until this moment why. "Because the man was a fraud, and I didn't trust him."

Mary looked up, to see the waitress arriving with two large platters, each holding two barbecue sandwiches bulging with meat, a paper cup filled with coleslaw, a rash of french fries, and half of a dill pickle.

"*Won*derful," exclaimed Mary, and the woman left them alone. She gracefully gathered up one of the sloppy sandwiches, and said, "Pork: You'll love it," took a bite, and chewed happily. Then she said, "Now, Louise, tell me some details. Exactly what did those, uh, pieces of the body look like?"

Louise looked down at the barbecue extravaganzas on her plate and could barely restrain herself from gagging. "Uh . . ."

Mary smiled apologetically. "I'm so sorry. Let's eat first."

When they had finished most of their food, Louise reluctantly continued. "I saw—the arm, and a piece of the leg." This was what she had avoided: putting a whole body together from the parts she had seen. First, Nora, and now Mary, was forcing her to bring the dead woman to some sort of reality as a person.

"It must have been ghastly," said Mary. "What did they look like, these sections of the body—lots of tannin in the skin, or light, like me?"

Louise stared off into the gloom of the tiny bar and tried to remember. "Actually, there were freckles on the arm—sort of pink-looking freckles against pale skin. It was a small, shapely forearm, minus the hand.'' Pictures of that bloody body part flashed through her mind. ''And the leg—it was very—finely turned, you might say.''

Mary leaned forward, cradling the heavy teacup in her hands. Her eyes were broody. ''Too bad you didn't see the torso. Did they find any of the torso?''

''Part of it.'' She sucked her breath in, remembering that gruesome talk. ''Geraghty told Bill it was a, quote, 'well-formed' female.''

''That means good breasts, knowing men. Ah, just *so.*'' Mary sat back in satisfaction. ''I am beginning to develop a theory.'' She leaned forward again toward Louise. ''Finely turned leg. Petite arm. Pink freckles, but not obtrusive freckles. Well-formed breasts, most likely. What does that say to us?''

''Good-looking woman,'' Louise offered. ''Maybe a redhead.''

Mary pointed a graceful finger at her. ''More than that: It says *mistress.* After all, no wives are missing, are they, or the police would have found out by now. But 'mistress'—the woman the man keeps in the background, in a secret apartment in SoHo . . .''

''All right. Hidden mistress. But where does that get us? When I drove around the other day to all the houses where I got the leaves, it was lunchtime, and I saw a surprising number of people home, or coming home. And believe me, Mary, they all looked as innocent as lambs.''

She told her of the elderly couple, of the children entering another house, and then they laughed about the suburban mom who might actually have been a murderess.

"There's nothing much we can do about those outlying mulch bag addresses," said Mary. "That's up to the police. But closer to home, why, I can think of at least six men who live in Sylvan Valley who could have had a mistress."

"No, really?"

Mary nodded. "I've lived there for almost twenty years, and it is surprising: You would have picked up these same vibes if you knew them as long as I had."

"Gosh. Who, for instance?"

"This is strictly between the two of us, and I'm not accusing anyone of murder, mind you. But Eric VandeVen, for one. Mort Swanson, that wonderful Sarah's husband, for another. Frank Stern, maybe—simply because he is such an unknowable quantity and has been ever since I first met him. Do you know him?"

"I just met him once—he's away a lot overseas with his electronics business. But I've known Sandy since we moved here. We started playing tennis together at the club. I like Sandy."

Mary stretched out a hand and squeezed Louise's. "My dear, let's try to separate the personal from the practical. I'm just talking husbands." Then she went on to mention three more Sylvan Valley men.

Louise came to a realization that made her skin tingle. "Do you realize Eric and Mort are in the poker club with Bill?"

"How interesting, and how handy."

"You've not mentioned Roger Kendricks. Or Sam Rosen."

"Clean, I'd say," declared Mary with a hard look in her eye that seemed out of character; but she had obviously stepped into the detecting business with relish. "Of course we can't be certain about anybody. I'd even mistrust that Peter Hoffman over on the edge of the neighborhood, but he's freshly married and so new around here that I doubt he's had time or inclination to get a mistress." She looked at Louise, and almost broke into a giggle. "Aren't we the snoops?"

Louise couldn't help smiling. "So what do you think we should do?"

"Unfortunately, I'm packing up for another trip, this time to the West Coast, but I'll be home for your dinner party." She gestured toward Louise. "That party, for instance, will be a splendid opportunity to do background work. And while I'm gone, you can do a little casual surveillance—I believe that's what they call it. . . ."

Louise sighed. Surveillance. If Mary only knew that she wasn't as naive about all this as she thought she was. She had sat with her husband Bill and done surveillance on at least half a dozen occasions, in various parts of the world. It was no fun—getting hungry, uncomfortable, struggling to keep one's eyes open, having to urinate, but not being able to do anything about it.

Mary smiled. "Do you have birding glasses? You could check things out from the comfort of your own home, especially Eric." Then she looked troubled. "I confess I don't like this whole thing, Louise, thinking that my good friend Jan has a husband who is cheating on her. But, in fact, I somehow feel that's the case. Whether we can pin anything down, I don't know. I do know Eric has been very circumspect since the murder, and I don't have a clue as to what that means."

"We didn't talk about Nora's husband. What about Ron Radebaugh?"

Mary's smile was rather like Mona Lisa's. "I do not think the beautiful Nora has a husband who is unfaithful. Actually, the reverse has sometimes been true in the past."

Louise's eyes widened at this disclosure. Here she was just developing a friendship with Nora, and it turned out her first impression—that she was a home wrecker—was the correct one after all!

Mary looked concerned, and reached over and touched Louise's hand again, as if this would give her colleague strength. "My dear, I am really telling you too much. But it's just what everyone knows or senses about the neighbors, and I don't mean to be too modern, but one must deal with realities, especially if one is ferreting out a secret murderer who is threatening the peace and quiet of one's family."

"Mary, how do you know about Nora?"

"Unfortunately, it became common knowledge." Louise thought back to the story of the Sylvan Valley wife-swapping. Could that have involved Nora? No—Nora was much too private for that, though not private enough to keep the affair a secret.

Mary went on: "And she told me herself. Since I see you two are becoming friends, she will tell you eventually, too, since Nora isn't as . . . hung up on sex as the rest of us. It was before she became active in writing and teaching—I think that's helped her feel more fulfilled."

Louise let her glance go to the sunny windows beyond the dim little room. She was anxious to get back out into the sunlight. "I think I'm learning more than I want about everybody." She looked over at her lunch companion. "Nora is very—strange about this murder. Has she ever talked to you about it?''

''Oh, yes. Dear Nora is terribly sensitive. Poets, of course, are. But don't minimize Nora: She can be very right about things.'' She opened her purse to get out money to pay the bill, since she'd said the lunch would be on her. ''Louise, regarding our little spy efforts, try the Gallic approach—keeping the personal feelings carefully separated from our professional efforts. I know you have it in you, from all your experience in the—foreign service.'' She looked up slyly. ''In fact, I bet you know better than I do all the little investigative tricks we could use. . . .''

Louise knew immediately that Mary knew Bill was undercover. She must have learned it from her husband, Richard. Not too unusual, in the Foreign Service.

Mary went on. ''This is serious, Louise: Someone killed that woman, and now all the burden is falling on your house, by horrible mischance. It's time for you to act. You have every right to do all the snooping you want. I promise to help you investigate as soon as I get home from my trip.'' She smiled encouragingly. ''Don't go too far—don't *follow* anyone, or dangerous things like that. Listen. Listen in on the poker club if you can.''

''Actually, I've done that already, inadvertently, when I was reading on the couch in the next room. There's nothing to learn except a few mild dirty jokes and all the procedural details about how to play things like 'Follow the Virgin Queen,' or 'Anaconda,' or 'Shit or Git.' The game envelops them and reduces them to giggling schoolboys. Believe me, we'll never learn anything from listening in on a poker game.''

"How interesting," murmured Mary. "Maybe Richard could play with them sometime. Poor dear, with his nose always in a book, or running off for State business to Vienna, he doesn't seem to have much fun. So. We'll scratch poker club from our list. But we'll take every other opportunity to observe, and listen. I have no doubt that you and I might uncover something the police could use. After all, my dear, women are intuitive, they are excellent listeners, and, to paraphrase that old radio program from my childhood, they can *read the hearts of men*!"

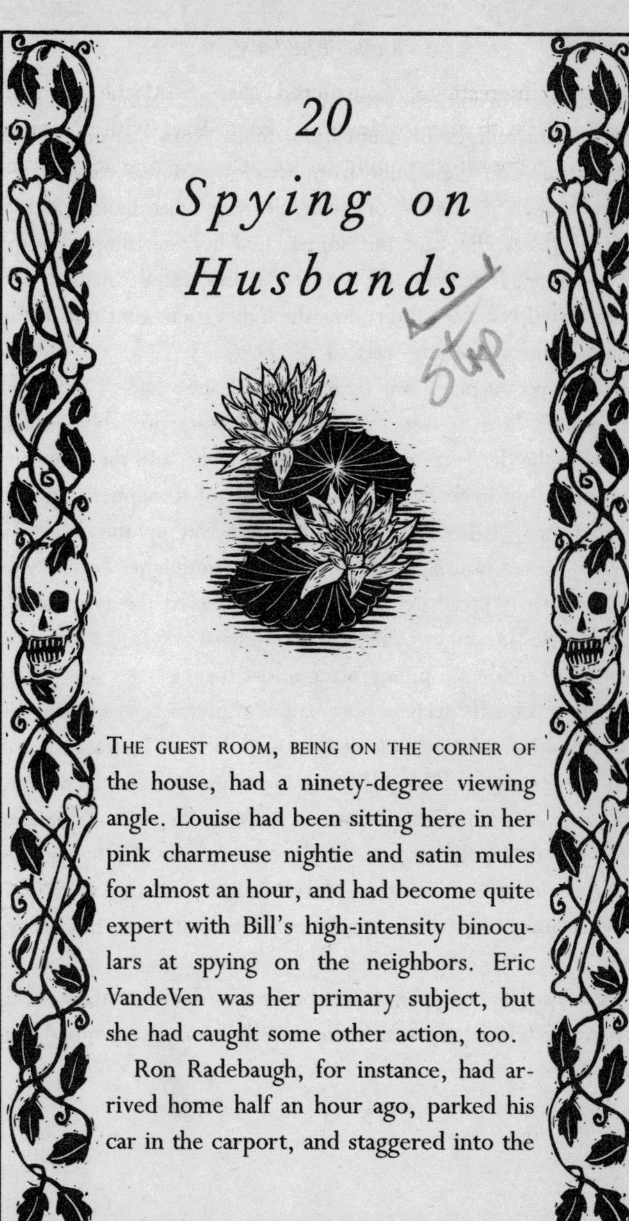

20
Spying on Husbands

THE GUEST ROOM, BEING ON THE CORNER OF the house, had a ninety-degree viewing angle. Louise had been sitting here in her pink charmeuse nightie and satin mules for almost an hour, and had become quite expert with Bill's high-intensity binoculars at spying on the neighbors. Eric VandeVen was her primary subject, but she had caught some other action, too.

Ron Radebaugh, for instance, had arrived home half an hour ago, parked his car in the carport, and staggered into the house. Dead drunk, she was fairly sure. Celebrating some new Pacific Rim merger or acquisition? Since Nora had not pulled the curtains on their huge front windows, it was easy to see what happened next. Nora was wearing what looked like a bunchy robe. Her husband approached her, seeming to want an embrace, but Nora did not appear interested. Instead, she moved swiftly across the room; the lights soon went out in the living room and in the rest of the house.

The next surprise was Sam Rosen. Louise hadn't intended to include him in her surveillance. A car, probably Sam's, went up the driveway out of her line of sight, and then another car pulled up in front of his place. Out of it stepped a petite woman in high heels, who swished her way up the driveway toward Sam's house. Female visitors at midnight? Louise was amazed; their jovial neighbor had not seemed the type at all. In fact, she'd thought of him as a somewhat arrested-schoolboy type who might be pining after a lost love.

Eric had finally arrived home a few minutes ago, so now she had done her job and was ready to go to bed. Eric's behavior was the strangest. He put the car in the garage, and then came out and stood on the front lawn. Was the metro planner brooding under the stars about the fate of cities? Or had something changed him lately, as Mary Mougey had suggested, into a more introspective human being? Was that something murder?

She had just slipped Bill's binoculars back in their case, when she felt a light touch on her shoulder. She jumped and cried out.

"Honey, whatcha doing?"

It was Bill.

"You could have called my name first," she said lightly. "As it is, you've scared me. I might even have turned gray."

"Sorry. So, what are you doing? What's that in your hands?" He took the glasses from her, and knew immediately. "Spying. What's the matter—I thought you'd had enough of that, for both you and me."

"I . . . just couldn't sleep. There's nothing wrong with just looking out your own window."

He sat on the edge of the guest bed, binoculars in his lap, and ran his fingers through his hair. "This is just the kind of thing that leads you into trouble, Louise, the kind of thing I asked you not to do. Who the hell are you interested in, anyway?" Being wakened at one in the morning had not produced a happy husband.

Her chin jutted out. "As a matter of fact, Eric, maybe Ron, Mort Swanson, maybe Sam Rosen."

"*Sam?* Come on, not Sam." Suddenly, he was wide awake. "And those other guys—you know who they are? They're in my poker club. What do you think, that one of them murdered that woman?"

"Bill," she said with growing impatience, "how did you happen to come in here, anyway?"

"Had to go to the bathroom. Drank too much liquid before I went to bed. And the heat's too high. Didn't *expect* to find my wife spying on my new poker buddies. But go ahead. *I'm* going to bed. There are easier ways to solve this murder than what you're doing there—for instance, cooperating with the police. But, no, you couldn't do that, because the guy trying to hypnotize you didn't speak proper English—admit it—and you're a snob about proper English."

Taking the binoculars with him, he went back to their bedroom and their warm, comfy bed.

A tear rolled down her cheek. She wondered if she could forgive him for that.

Then, lights shone in the cul-de-sac, and here she sat without the binoculars. Parking lights only, on an automobile that drove slowly around the perimeter of Dogwood Court and then disappeared.

Suddenly, Louise's body felt ice-cold. She was overcome with a sense of danger. As fast as she could without tripping in the mules, she made her way back to their bedroom and climbed in bed with Bill.

He was lying on his side facing away from her. She faced the same way, and put a trembling hand lightly on his waist, for comfort. She pressed a little, hoping he would wake and she could tell him about the car. Then she pressed harder.

This caused him to emit a gobbly little snore, and she knew he was fast asleep.

21
The Party's Ready

THE PARTY WAS READY. LOUISE WAS ALMOST ashamed that she felt so self-satisfied. Her long brown hair swung clean on her shoulders and the legs of her yellow nylon running outfit whispered as she walked from room to room through the house. She checked the surfaces, touched a bouquet here or there to ensure that it fell gracefully. There were freesias, alstroemeria, and other pale flowers, the fragrant stock that she loved so well, as well as bowls full of holly and eucalyptus.

She admired the glisten of her enormous living room windows, heard but didn't absorb the caterers' low chatter as they set up the buffet table. She had no worry that the food at this party would be less than perfect. From the moment the gold-decorated purple Ridgebrook's truck pulled up an hour ago, she felt a sense of security she wished every hostess could feel. The back hall was filled with refrigerated and heated steel cases containing goodies of all kinds for thirty guests. Now it was 4:30. Countdown in one hour. And everything was perfect.

The physical stage for this party was perfect. But this morning over breakfast she had discovered she and her husband had different agendas about what the party would accomplish. She had been surprised when Bill suggested catering the affair, since she had done parties of this size on her own. She thought it was because of the short lead time. Then he came out with the real reason for a caterer. "I want you to do some role-playing tonight. I want you free to observe."

"Observe what, pray tell?" she had demanded. "What do you want me to keep my eye on—possible trysts? Shall we wire the bedrooms?"

Bill, who seemed nervous today, had not been amused. "Nothing heavy," he replied grimly. "I'd just like you to tell me what you think about Peter Hoffman. And his wife—let me know what you think of his wife."

She was silent a moment. Then, in a quiet voice she said, "This party has become more complicated, hasn't it? You're doing it again . . . but this time it's not legal, is it?"

"I'm doing . . . what do you think I'm doing?" He looked at her innocently, his blue eyes feigning surprise.

"Bill, don't give me that crap," she'd snapped and she'd walked angrily from the room. He followed her, so she let him have it. Her voice was dangerously low. "You're spying, and you're on domestic ground. That's about the craziest thing I ever heard. What do you want, to get hauled before Congress? Sent to jail in disgrace?" Her eyes brimmed with angry tears.

It was one thing for her and Mary Mougey to spy on the husbands in order to try and ferret out the mulch murderer. It was quite another for her undercover husband to be vetting a deputy secretary of defense. She looked straight in his eyes. "Who put you up to this?"

Bill had come over and taken her in his arms. She dropped her head and refused to look at him, but he pulled her chin up with an insistent hand. "Honey," he said, "I didn't think you'd mind. Truthfully"—his blue eyes shone with truth—"I am not doing any more than inviting a neighbor to dinner. After all, you said you'd met these people at some meeting or other. Tonight is just . . . checking out a man up for confirmation to an important job. Tom Paschen—you remember him. He asked me—so what could I say?"

Then he had led her to the couch and they sat down together. He continued his reassurances. "What I am doing is not illegal; it is not surveillance. The FBI is doing surveillance on Hoffman, probably right as we speak. Please stop fretting."

She searched his face. It was thin and pale, with deep forehead lines clearly showing. "You're worried too, I can tell. No wonder: Paschen's entrapped you. No way to say no to a man in his position."

Then Bill had hugged her tight and rocked her gently back and forth in his arms. "Ah, but I won't go a step further. This party's the end of it, period." He held her away from him so he could see her tearstained face. "And just you see. This will be a great party. It'll be like a new start in this neighborhood. We'll forget all this bad stuff that's been happening to us, and our old friends can meet our new friends."

She gave him a wan look. "Okay, honey."

As the day wore on, she got into the party mood, and now it was all in place. Despite their ulterior motives—Bill's now revealed, hers still secret—this could be fun, for people from every part of their lives would be there: friends from Washington, friends from the Bethesda neighborhood, a few "famous" people they had become acquainted with along the way—people who made parties interesting—key State Department associates, and people from their new neighborhood. Flowers, ready. CDs, ready. A little Mozart chamber music during cocktails. Beethoven's fifth piano concerto during dinner. Later, Mahler and Strauss and Purcell. She had some pop favorites in the wings in case it became one of those memorable Eldridge parties where everyone grew shiny with alcohol and ended up singing together.

The nicest thing about parties was that you could never tell for sure how they were going to turn out.

Louise, ready except for slipping into her hostess dress. Bill, bathed and dressed, picking up a few esoteric items at the liquor store.

Janie, not ready. Put off by the presence of caterers, she had loped off with Chris an hour ago. Louise hoped that boy didn't have a sexual interest in Janie. Although Janie certainly knew the facts of life, Louise wasn't sure she would *act* on the facts of life. The girl was totally unequipped, and she wasn't about to get her equipped, the way some of her friends had done with their daughters. Or maybe she should. . . .

"Quit fussing," she advised herself out loud.

"Ma'am?" A squat Scandinavian woman with flour on her florid cheeks stuck her head out of the kitchen to inquire.

"Oh, nothing," said Louise, tossing her head and laughing. "I guess I was talking to myself again."

"Yes, always a reliable listener," said the woman, smiling. "Don't let me interrupt."

Louise wandered to the front door, wiped a small smudge off an expanse of glass next to the door, and looked across at the hut. The flow of her writing had been interrupted by arrangements for the party. She would have to make up time next week, since she had fallen far behind on the second assignment her editor had sent her. It was on bromeliads.

Her eyes glazed over, and her mind wandered down a tropical garden path filled with the plants, thinking of the myriad species she would have a chance to describe—from the big, strappy-leaved kinds right down to the tiny ones, and each capable of producing a complicated, long-lived bloom. A Washington florist had somehow obtained five hard-to-find varieties for her and would deliver them Monday. Having them nearby when she wrote about them was going to give her real inspiration.

The door opened alongside her. Janie and Chris bounced into the front hall. "Mom!" cried Janie. "Are you all right? Why are you just standing here, staring?"

"Oh, hi, Chris. Hi, Janie." Louise pulled herself back into the present. "I was just standing here, thinking about writing."

Her daughter's face turned bright red.

Chris ducked his head, not quite looking at Louise. "Aw, it's okay, Janie, don't be embarrassed. My mom does the same thing. She gets her head in the clouds when she writes. It's best not to talk to them then." With that they ran down the hall toward the kitchen, attracted by the good food smells.

Louise stood perfectly still in her yellow running outfit. Suddenly she felt tired. She'd have a little sip of wine. Then maybe she would lie down and rest for a minute. She was sure the competent floury lady in the kitchen could handle those two teenagers better than she could.

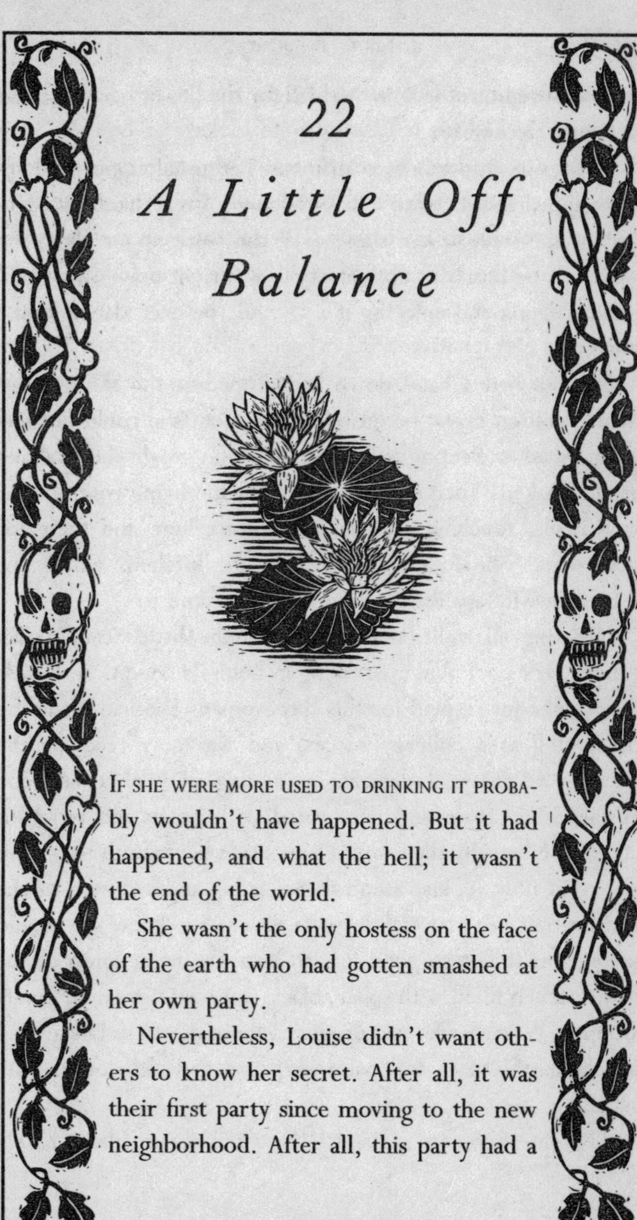

22
A Little Off Balance

IF SHE WERE MORE USED TO DRINKING IT PROBABLY wouldn't have happened. But it had happened, and what the hell; it wasn't the end of the world.

She wasn't the only hostess on the face of the earth who had gotten smashed at her own party.

Nevertheless, Louise didn't want others to know her secret. After all, it was their first party since moving to the new neighborhood. After all, this party had a couple of reasons for being, which for the life of her she could not quite remember.

So it was important to maintain her usual upper-middle-class appearances, wasn't it? Suddenly a great truth came to her: If she were lower class, or if she were upper class, she wouldn't be nearly as uptight as she was right now! She would just be drunk and enjoying it . . . maybe even dancing on a table.

She reached a hand down and groped at the skirt of her mauve chiffon dress, because for a moment she could not feel it and had a fleeting sensation that she might be walking around naked. Then she minced across the living room in her high heels, touching a piece of furniture here and there for good luck. She found sanctuary in the kitchen, where she leaned heavily against the first wall she came to.

"Feeling all right, ma'am?" asked the little Scandinavian caterer, her cool blue eyes taking in Louise's condition. Louise had enormous respect for this tiny woman. She had made the party sing as a culinary success and was now readying the encore: an array of desserts swimming with chocolate and custard and cream and punctuated with green and red fruit accents. Normally they would have made her mouth water but not right now. Louise stood there, as big and awkward as she had been at her first eighth-grade dance. She knew she should move, but it felt so good just to lean, in the warmth of the busy kitchen filled with sober, black-and-white-dressed, kindly women. Women who had produced those meats and fishes and artichoke mixtures and pasta surprises and deliriously tasty salads.

The caterer raised a hand. "One minute, madam. I have

just the thing for you.'' She went to Louise's refrigerator and poured a glass of tomato juice. Then from a case she had brought with her she took an envelope of something and stirred it into the juice.

She came up close to Louise and handed it to her conspiratorially. ''This won't do everything, but it will do some to set you to rights.''

''Oh, thank you,'' sighed Louise, willing to drink almost anything, but knowing she should drink no more of that divine wine that Bill had brought into the house. Allure, he had called it. What a wonderful name!

She drank the tomato juice, tasting its special flavor, which she realized was yeast. Maybe this woman should just carry liquid vitamin B-12 in syringes, the stuff they gave alcoholics in hospitals. At Washington parties, there surely would be plenty of customers.

She wasn't sure, but she thought the juice helped her stand straighter. ''Thank you,'' she murmured, looking down at her benefactor. ''Mrs. Wickstrom, is it?''

The woman smiled and nodded dismissal. Louise realized she had been standing in the way of progress in setting out desserts.

Now, if she just went to the bathroom and relieved her strained bladder, she would be back to normal. Then Bill would stop giving her those concerned glances from across the room, where he was talking nonstop to her friend Nora. When she saw them talking that way, heads together, like two lovers, she wanted to rip Nora away and shove her right out of her house, right across the cul-de-sac into her own damned house. What a fatiguing prospect, to say the least. And anyway, she liked Nora, didn't she?

To keep out of the traffic pattern, Louise made her way toward the master bathroom. She was still sober enough to know she and Mary were supposed to be doing something at this party. Mary, lovely in pale blue silk, was moving through the party like a bluebird gliding through a summer garden. She was conversing with each and every man present. Spying on the husbands, of course! Louise, too, would do her part, but first, the bathroom.

When she reached the dim master bedroom, she found the farthest corner occupied. Sandy and Frank Stern were in ecstatic embrace, and in imminent danger, Louise felt, of falling onto the bed, in which case she wasn't sure what would happen next.

"Oops!" cried Louise, before she could stop herself and back out again. The couple broke apart. Frank grinned. Sandy smiled and said, "Just a little private hello—he just blew back into town after a business trip. You, of all people, understand how it feels to have your spouse away for a month."

So, one man down. Surely a guy who smooched his wife like that wasn't fooling around. Pleased with herself, Louise entered the bathroom. Sweeping aside chiffon skirts that seemed to have multiplied during the evening, she sat down on the toilet and held her head in her hands and closed her eyes. The whole world went around in wild circles. In alarm she opened her eyes. She cautiously sat back, enjoying the feel of cold porcelain through the thin fabric of her dress. Hail to the British who had invented this splendid thing! She tried reclosing her eyes. This time things didn't swim around so much.

Sitting here, she could actually think and remember. There was not only her and Mary's caper to handle. There was something Bill wanted to accomplish out of this party, too. Ah, Peter Hoffman. She was supposed to talk to him, and she hadn't. She was supposed to find out . . . she couldn't remember what. She noticed this Peter had talked to only the best-looking women at the party. He had captured Nora on the couch for his dinner partner until Bill somehow took over. Hmmm, that Nora.

So. To review: She knew it was a good party. No one except Bill had noticed she was a little drunk. That made her suspect others also might be pie-eyed. The woman novelist wasn't; she had glommed on to their psychoanalyst friend, Ian, and was draining him dry of the dark juices of his clinical experiences. Louise was reminded of a sucked-dry bug caught in a spiderweb, although Ian was a little large to imagine literally sucked dry. Louise now knew where this woman got the material for her books.

Her old Bethesda friends were out there in the living room and the family room, even pouring out into her studio, happily meshing with the new ones here in Virginia and with the State Department types.

Of course, some had met before somewhere or other in Washington. They were all from the same cloth. All poised. All ready to either talk or keep their mouths shut, depending on whom they were thrown with. Most with some kind of expertise, and all knowing the same inside-the-Beltway gossip. That meant they could at least fake their way through any kind of conversation, no matter how shallow or how deep.

Even behind closed lids, the bright lights of the bathroom

were beginning to make her feel like a prisoner undergoing interrogation. She got up from the toilet as gracefully as possible, to prove to herself that she was not a staggering drunk. She did it without a misstep. Standing up, the world became dizzier. Although that concoction of Mrs. What's-her-name had been helpful, she wasn't out of the woods yet.

Louise went back to the party, determined to get done whatever it was that attractive husband of hers on the couch talking to her too-beautiful neighbor wanted her to do.

Everything had now changed. Even the music. From classical, it had become Sinatra favorites.

Mort and Sarah Swanson were dancing to "A Foggy Day in London Town." He was a thin stick; she, in her yellow and black chiffon gown, was the rounded and beautiful attached chrysalis. They swayed to the music in a little space near the fireplace. Hmm . . . could she cross Mort off her list, too?

Bill was now captured by—or had captured, who knows?—Peter Hoffman's wife, Phyllis. Louise had tried a conversation with her and come up empty, although the woman was well read, she would give her *that.* She had read all the latest books, even the nonfiction.

It was as if Peter Hoffman had been waiting for her. All of a sudden he was next to her, looming over her. "I was looking for you," he said. He was very tall—six-six, she guessed. She liked very tall men.

She smiled up at him. "I've wanted to talk to you, too."

"You're pretty tanked up, I see."

Louise's mouth fell open and she stared at him. Should she laugh or cry? She giggled. "My secret is out."

He moved in close to her. "You're a cool one. I'm glad I

didn't upset you by observing the obvious.'' His voice was soft but penetrating. Rather pleasant, she thought. ''What I think we should do is this: I'll get two desserts with *coffee*.'' He whispered ''coffee'' as if it were the magic word. ''Then we'll go into a bedroom—with the door open, of course—and eat and drink. Then you'll feel better. And we can talk, too.''

She looked up at him and grinned. ''Great idea,'' she purred. ''I'll just stand here and be social while you do that. People might have missed me.''

Several passed her on the way to the dessert table, telling her what a lovely party it was, how delightful the food, the wine, the flowers. . . .

''Ridgebrook—yes, lovely caterers.''

''The red is Allure. Yes, it's a lovely wine.''

''David Travers did the bouquets. Yes, they are lovely, aren't they?''

She was gracious but tried above all to not smile like a fool. Smiling too much was a dead giveaway.

Peter came back, a plate with a cup on it in either hand. ''You lead the way,'' he said. She had to think a minute, then led him to Janie's room. It was unoccupied by either coats or humans.

They sat at Janie's desk in two black lacquered student chairs.

''Nice room. This your daughter's?''

''Yes. Janie's—or Jane's. I guess we'll have to call her that soon. This is her room.''

''Saw her tonight,'' said Peter. He cut into his pastry with a fork that was dwarfed by his large hand. ''All dressed up for the occasion. I think I've seen her before somewhere.'' He looked over at Louise. ''She's a beauty, you know. I hope you're prepared for it.''

Louise chipped away at her napoleon, taking small bites. It wasn't sitting well down there in the old stomach. The coffee tasted better.

''Oh, yes, Janie. She's a very attractive girl.''

''That her boyfriend with her, that tall young guy?''

''Oh, Chris. No . . . I mean, I don't know. I have the feeling they're just . . . good friends. He lives in the cul-de-sac.''

A few more swallows of coffee. Wonderful coffee. Peter was still talking . . . about what? Still Janie? Treating Louise so well, thinking she was sodden with drink.

Suddenly, from barely hanging on to his remarks, she came back a little. It felt like the dawning of the age of Aquarius. Back from the brink. Back to sobriety. Gentility. Probity. Clear analysis.

She was ready to take command again.

She cleared her throat. ''Now tell me, Peter, about your background.'' Her voice sounded natural enough. ''I'm so happy to hear you're being considered for such a . . . a . . . high post.'' Where were her adjectives when she needed them? She looked at him with wide eyes. ''It is a very, uh . . . high job, is it not?''

''High? High?'' he mimicked, laughing. But his voice was harsh. ''It's a damned important job. You bet it's, as you call it, 'high.' '' He looked at her through his gold-rimmed aviator glasses, and she saw how good-looking he was. He seemed to exude energy; maybe it came out in his sweat glands. She also sensed that in spite of her tongue-tiedness, he knew she was no longer completely drunk. She felt almost, but not completely, equal to this man Peter.

"What exactly will you be doing as deputy secretary of defense?" Now her voice sounded prissy. "Do you know in advance what your responsibilities—"

He bit off the end of her sentence. "Not completely, of course not. It depends on the players. What they want me for is my expertise on artillery." He looked at her again, as if deciding something. "Are you really interested or"—he chuckled a little—"are you just toying with me?"

She sat back and relaxed and smiled. "I truly am interested," she said in a lilting voice. Bill had assigned her some vague, informational mission; she was sure he didn't mean it to be Mata Hari, but what the hell, it was kind of fun.

He put his fork down and sat back. It was working. "Well, I could tell you all about tactical arms, the kind of arms that will be our future—the small but very lethal arms—they're my specialty." He sighed. "But when you smile like that, with that figure of yours and those great legs"—he waved a hand in a wide gesture that ended up with his fingertips just touching her upper arm—"well, let's just say if I were your husband, I wouldn't be making out with that neighborhood poet."

She flinched as if she had been lashed in the face.

"Oh, please, no . . . she's my friend . . . she's our friend. She wouldn't . . . he wouldn't . . ."

Peter leaned over, took her hand in his warm hands, and said cajolingly, chuckling a little as he did, "It's all right, my pretty Louise. I'm putting you on; you're so innocent." He looked straight into her eyes. "You're like a breath of spring." He shook his head as if in disbelief. "They just don't often make women like you. Of *course* your husband is innocent—doing his party duties. Right now he's talking to *my* lovely wife.'' His voice had developed a little sneer. ''And I'm sure no woman will be bereft of a conversation with Bill Eldridge before the night is over.''

Louise's voice was very low. ''He's a lovely man. You don't know him, do you?'' She looked down at her hand, which at last she noticed was still in his possession. ''I . . . I didn't mean lovely man.'' She made a pushing move with her free hand. ''Strike 'lovely.' I mean, he is a fine man—they don't make them any better than Bill.''

Peter started nodding assent even before she finished. Then he said, ''He has to be pretty damned fine to have a wife like you.'' He caressed her fingers, rather like a doctor, as if he were exploring their narrow bone structure. Although it was pleasant, she wished he would give her hand back to her.

''Now,'' he said, ''let's change the subject and talk about your little, uh, misfortune here with the police. Have they found anything at all?''

She was telling him what she knew when she heard a lilting voice. ''Oh, excuse me.''

Janie, with faithful Chris. ''Hi, Ma. I don't mean to break in, but the caterer wants you for something.'' The teenagers stood in the doorway, embarrassed, as if they had interrupted a tryst.

''Yes.'' Louise jumped up from the chair, amazed at her agility. ''I'll come right away. Janie, Chris, I don't think you've met Peter Hoffman.''

Peter languidly got to his feet, as if he had all the time in the world, and approached the young pair. ''We invaded your bedroom, Janie. It was crowded out there." He stood looking down at Louise's daughter, whose hair tonight was twisted and pinned up, with just a few blond curls falling artlessly down the sides and back. She wore what she called her Victorian dress, soft pink printed silk in an old-fashioned style with a square lace collar low enough to show the tops of her young breasts.

First he stared at her face. Janie stared back, as if in thrall. Then he raised a big hand and gently caressed a curl that had fallen on her right cheek. He moved the hand and raised her chin for an instant. Finally he took both of her hands and drew them up for closer inspection. "Beautiful face, beautiful hands. Like your mother." That intimate, steely voice.

For an instant they all stood as if frozen. Chris looked embarrassed, his eyes seeking something to look at other than the tall man. Janie flushed, only increasing her luminosity.

Louise felt every alarm in her body activate.

"Excuse me while I go to the kitchen," she said breathlessly. She clasped Janie's arm and said, "Come with me, dear. They may need some help from us." She pulled her gently away.

"Ma," said Janie in a low growl, as they went down the hall. "Why did I have to come? I don't think they need our help—I just think they need to talk to *you.*"

Louise tried to keep her voice light, under control. "I'd prefer you don't continue to stay in your bedroom while the party is going on out here."

Janie looked curiously at Louise. "Oh. All right for you, not all right for me. Another double standard." Her voice softened. "But it's okay. It's something about that man—something you didn't like, right?"

Louise looked into her blue eyes, innocent eyes, but painted tonight with the skill of Cleopatra.

"My love," said Louise, and paused and touched the sleeve of her darling daughter's gown. "Some other time I'll try to explain it."

Janie patted her mother on the shoulder. "Well, anyway, Ma, it sure sobered you up in a hurry. For a while there I didn't think you were going to make it till the end of the party."

Louise heaved a long sigh. "Oh, Janie. Sometimes I wish . . ."

"What?"

Louise smiled weakly. "Never mind. It's just that you are such a truth teller."

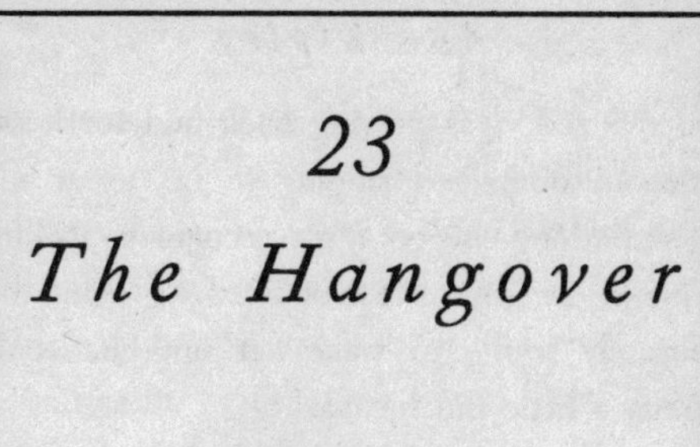

23
The Hangover

THE FIRST THING THAT CAME INTO HER CONSCIOUSNESS was the singing. She opened an eye and focused in on the white knobs on the antique dry sink across the bedroom. The white sheet and coverlet covered practically her whole head and face, and she felt like a bear coming out of hibernation.

But much worse, probably. A bear would not have a head that felt like this. A head with a round ball of pain in it that needed excision.

Bill, she realized, was passing back and forth outside the closed bedroom door and singing in his usual adventurous monotone something she couldn't recognize. Rolling Stones? Yes. "I'll Never Be Your Beast of Burden." Out there in the hall, deliberately trying to wake her up. She couldn't help smiling. What a little pill he was!

She stirred her head and moved her shoulders and decided maybe she could get up after all. She swung weak legs down to the floor and sat there, trapped by her twisted silk nightie. Then she waggled her toes until she found her waiting mules and decided to rest for a moment.

The door opened. Fresh and dressed, he smiled at her. "At last! She lives. She sits up. Will she take nourishment?" He came over and started to sit down beside her on the bed.

"Be careful," she warned. "Don't rock the bed."

"Bad head, huh?" He sat down and held her head in both hands as an archaeologist might hold an ancient skull. Then he gently massaged.

"Oh," she moaned, leaning toward him. "Keep it up; I'll follow you forever."

"The reason I want you up is I have this great breakfast for you—a little sausage, a little scrambled egg with mushrooms."

"Oh, no, I can't eat that."

"Of course you can eat. Come on, just try it. Besides, I have no one to talk to when you're asleep; Janie went to church, to represent the family and keep us okay with the big guy upstairs."

She looked at Bill, buoyant and cheery, carrying her again. What would she do without him?

He jumped up and brought her two aspirins, a glass of water, and her robe. Clad now in its comfy fleece, she walked with him into the living room. No one would have known they had had a big party last night. Between Bill and the caterers—no thanks to her—the place was perfect, the bouquets giving extra elegance. Bill had drawn closed the wide gauze curtains across the broad expanses of windows.

"It looks so nice and peaceful here, with the curtains closed," murmured Louise. "Very womblike; just what I need."

"I thought you wouldn't be able to stand the light for a while. Now you sit down and we'll eat." He served the breakfast at the dining room table, complete with orange slices on each plate.

She picked at the eggs and situated her feet at the ready, in case she needed to rush to the bathroom.

Surprisingly the eggs slid right down and tasted delicious. She sipped a glass of milk he had brought her, then sampled the coffee. "You've saved me again."

He smiled a little. "I knew you weren't going to be a total loss." He looked at his watch. "Although I didn't figure you'd sleep this long—eleven-thirty."

She looked at him quickly and then looked back at her plate. "I didn't really get *that* drunk, did I? I mean, I don't remember drinking that much."

"You didn't," Bill assured her. "But somehow you didn't eat anything, so everything you drank went to your head." He sat back and wiped his mouth with his napkin. "I'd say, on a scale of one to ten, ten being stinkin' drunk, you were seven and a half—maybe eight.'' He grinned. ''You were actually kind of funny, and not too gross.''

''Oh, indeed,'' she said, looking at him closely as if for the first time. Sometimes Bill thought he was so funny. ''Tell me more.''

''You know: You kind of minced around, trying not to collide with large objects, and from what I heard, trying to make sense even though your head was probably spinning all to hell-and-gone.'' He chuckled.

''Bill Eldridge, you're just mean.'' She drank her coffee and wouldn't look at him.

He reached a hand over and put it on hers. ''Okay, honey, I won't tease you any more. The only one who even mentioned your condition was Eric. Said you were asking him nosy questions that implied he might be the mulch murderer—but I can't believe you did that—or did you?''

She looked up at him silently, like a kid who'd been caught. ''Can't remember; I guess I must have.''

''Aw, Louise—''

''I know, he's in your poker club. But last night, Mary and I were trying to check the men out. I won't believe in anyone's innocence until someone is proven guilty.''

''Hmm. I guess you have a point. Hope we have some men friends left afterward. Now, let me get you some more coffee, and then I want you to tell me what you and Peter Hoffman talked about.''

''Oh, him.'' Through the mists of alcohol and dreamless sleep came the memory of Peter. The man she was supposed to analyze. ''Since I was a little bombed, I was laboring under somewhat of a disadvantage.'' She turned her mouth down sardonically. ''I guess I wasn't in my top form as an observer.''

''You guys spent a lot of time eating dessert together in Janie's bedroom, didn't you? You must have talked about something.''

She looked at him. ''I'll tell you what I remember, if you'll tell me what you and Nora were talking about during dinner.''

Bill looked pleased. ''Oh, Nora and me? We had a great talk. She is *some* woman.''

Louise brushed a stray clump of hair out of her eyes. ''I know she's some woman. That's what all you men think. I just want to know what you were talking about.'' She cast an angled glance at her husband. ''You looked like you were thick as thieves, and planning something . . . like a love tryst or something.''

''Oh, did we?'' His slightly hooded eyes with their devilish glint belied his innocent mien. He grabbed Louise and pulled her up. ''Let's go sit on the couch and relax. First, you tell me what Peter had to say. Then I'll reveal all about Nora.''

They settled on the couch. Louise began. ''Let's see, first, he seemed really interested in Janie, and wanted to know who Chris was. Then, let's see, what *did* we talk about? Oh, I asked him about his appointment. And he told me he was very sharp about weaponry—invented them, et cetera.''

''Was he interesting? Did you like him? Would you trust him?''

Louise shook her head a little, as if remembering. ''Oh, he was very kind, and actually kind of charming.'' She looked at him without smiling. ''There was one thing that bothered me

. . . oh, and he asked a couple of questions about finding the body in the yard."

"Oh?" he said. "What did he ask?"

"Nothing much. Had it bothered us to be pestered by the police and the press; was there anything new that the detectives had found lately that I knew about . . ."

"Hmmm," said Bill.

Louise grabbed Bill's arm. "But there's something I really didn't like about him." Her eyes widened. "There's something about that man with Janie. He looked at her as if he wanted to devour her. And she was—what would you say, *captivated* by him, too. It really scared me."

"What did he do?" He frowned with concern.

Louise shook her head. "Nothing you could put your finger on. It was just the way he looked at her, and touched her hair. Then he took his hand and tilted her chin up. It was very intrusive. You can bet I dragged her away in a hurry."

Bill stared into space. "Interesting. But the guy charmed most everybody else. A number of our friends thought he was brilliant."

She shivered. "I just wouldn't want our daughters anywhere around him."

"And I thought it was you he was coming on to."

She looked at him and frowned. "You don't think I can tell that? I know he was flirting with me, too. I know how to take care of myself, don't think I don't."

He smiled and reached over and rubbed her back. "This is a new Louise Eldridge I seem to be living with. I like her. And now I suppose you want to hear about Nora and me."

"It's your turn."

24
No One Listens

JANIE HAD FIRST FELT THE CRAMPS IN CHURCH. She hoped the minister wouldn't talk too long, and miraculously he didn't. Now, walking home, the pains were getting sharper. She told herself she was not nauseated. Still three blocks to go. She made her steps into a glide so her lower stomach would not be jarred.

Last winter, just before she turned fifteen, was the first time it had happened. She thought she had appendicitis. But then the blood came, her first "period."

A moment of mixed feelings, including pride in becoming a woman at last. Her mother told her that the first periods sometimes brought cramps but that later her body would adjust. Now, two blocks from home and feeling the pain increase, she slowed her step and thought wanly about a whole lifetime of months of bloody periods and sickening cramps.

When she got home her mother would give her a golden pill that worked like magic.

"Hey, you sure got up early!" Chris bounded across a woodsy yard, wearing jeans and jacket and clasping his basketball with expert long fingers, tossing it up in little spinning twists, then beating it rapid-fire a few times on the sidewalk. As if to say, here I am with my signature basketball. I know you like me.

She smiled but did not otherwise respond. He fell in step with her and looked at her curiously. "You look pale. What's the matter? You don't look nearly as good as you did last night. Maybe you should have slept in like I did."

She looked at him obliquely. "Chris, it's not exactly polite to tell girls how bad they look. As a matter of fact, I don't feel very well."

"Oh. What is it, that time of month?"

She felt herself blushing. "Oh, boy, I can't keep any secrets from *you,* can I?" She shook her head. "As a matter of fact, it is. I only admit this because you're my friend." She walked with her head down; her face was hot. Since last night Janie knew Chris was more than a friend. They thought alike. They had fun together. He had even offered to study math with her to bring her along faster. It made her whole body feel feverish. Or maybe it was her period. Whatever. Her life had changed, and she was becoming very committed to this boy, who was almost a man.

"So. Guess what I did this morning?"

"I don't know," she said, her thoughts softening her tone toward him.

"I called up Tracey."

Janie's heart lurched. Her voice was lower. "Tracey, what's her name?" She knew her last name as well as her own. "Burton, is it?"

"Yeah, you know. Tracey Burton." The ball in his flying fingers was now going up as high as he could pitch it without moving his arms upward. Up and down to his waiting palms.

"Why did you call her?"

"I invited her to the winter dance." His voice had a slight mocking quality, as if she should already know why he called this fellow classmate of his.

"Oh." A hollow "oh."

"It was really cool." He threw the ball far, far up to show how cool it was. "I'm 'Hi, Tracey, this is your chemistry partner. Whaddaya know?'

"She's, 'Oh, it's you, Chris'—real girlish, like girls are when they know someone's called them up probably to invite them somewhere—'how are yuh anyway?'

"I'm, 'You know the dance is coming up. I bet you're going, right?'

"She's totally silenced. She's, 'I was *going* to go with someone, but then . . .'

"So I don't want her to suffer from embarrassment or anything so I'm, 'How about going with me? We've proved we can do scientific experiments together; maybe we can show them how on the dance floor.' Actually,'' and he turned to Janie with an uncertain look, ''I'm a terrible faker on the dance floor.''

She looked at him briefly and then turned frostily away.

He held the ball still for a moment and looked over at her. ''Well, anyway, she's, 'I'd love to go with you, Chris.' ''

He was silent for an instant. ''You didn't think I was going to ask *you,* did you?''

She held her chin high and tried to keep a tremble out of her voice. ''Of course not. Why would you ask me?'' She felt like she was falling down a hole.

The ball ended its time out and was now busily traveling up in the air again. ''Well, because we're pals. Of course, you're only fifteen. So I couldn't exactly ask *you,* since I'm almost eighteen.'' He looked enthusiastically at her, as if they might both enjoy a change of subject. ''I'll be eighteen in July; want to help me celebrate?''

Janie reached back into what she thought of as her private reservoir of strength. She had needed it a lot this year, leaving old friends behind when they moved, enduring a certain aloofness from her fellow sophomores at the new high school. She knew she could either be brave or burst into tears and drive him away. She knew her mother sometimes cried, and her father didn't mind it; in fact, sometimes it made him very tender.

Somehow she didn't think Chris could handle a girl crying. More important, she didn't want to cry—not over this. She remembered how much fun she and Chris had had last night, and she knew she would win him in the end.

Provided, that is, that she wanted him.

She smiled at him. The bad moment was gone. "I would love to celebrate your eighteenth with you."

"Okay, kid." He slung an arm around her shoulders and they walked in step, slower because of Janie's dress shoes. "Now let's talk about that Peter guy I met last night. Remember him? What did *you* think?" Chris's brow was knotted in a seldom-used frown.

"How could I forget him! He was scary. I think Mom thought he was trying to pick me up or something."

He squeezed her shoulder. "She was right. I think he likes nymphets."

Her eyes blazed. "I am *not* a nymphet!"

"You were last night," he said matter-of-factly. "You're not today. But sometimes you are, more often than not these days."

She blushed again and sighed. "Oh, Chris, I don't even know what a nymphet *is*. It makes me sound like a . . . a slut, or something."

" 'Nymphet' implies neither positive nor negative values; it only means a pretty, young girl. Haven't you read *Lolita*? Never mind, I'll explain it later. Anyway, back to that guy. There's something about that guy I didn't like. It made me feel like I had to protect you against him."

She looked over at him and smiled. "Thanks, Chris."

He gave her a short peck on the cheek. They had reached the turn into the cul-de-sac; he dropped his arm from her shoulder.

He began bouncing his basketball vigorously on the sidewalk. "Why don't you go get those fancy clothes off and we'll do a little investigating, okay?"

"Okay." She hurried up the sidewalk toward her house. She felt better; after taking a golden pill, she'd be ready for anything.

Geraghty tilted far back in his old chair, and then snapped up straight. He fastened his bright blue eyes on the pair of them. "So, to sum it up so far, you say you were at a party given by *your*"—he pointed his pencil at Janie—"parents, and you, Chris"—now the pencil was pointed at Chris's heart—"*eavesdropped* at a bedroom door—"

Janie interrupted in a quiet voice. "We were both there, but we weren't eavesdropping, Detective Geraghty." She knew Chris beside her was awestruck by this big policeman, but he had been to her house so many times to question her family that she was used to him. "We were trying to find my mother, and we were just being polite and waiting for the conversation to finish."

Geraghty waved the hand with the pencil in dismissal and leaned comfortably back. "Whatever you want to call it. You heard a conversation not meant for your ears, right?"

"Right, sir," said Chris. "Was that wrong or something?"

Geraghty sat forward again, his chair screeching in complaint. "Not at all, son." He gave the two a smile. It was the first friendly sign since they walked in to tell their story. Janie thought he looked like a big honey bear at home in his messy nest.

"Good thing you caught me here when you phoned," said Geraghty. He sighed. "It's not my habit to work on Sunday. The wife doesn't like it. But this mulch case was naggin' at me.'' He frowned and looked down at an open file on the littered desk. Then he looked up at Chris and Janie and nodded. ''So I'm willing to listen to this conversation you unintentionally heard.'' He waggled his hand at them. ''Just sit back, the two of you, and relax. Then you tell me everything you heard. Either one of you chime in when you want to.''

''What I first noticed,'' said Janie, ''was he was, oh, coaxing, as if he wanted information or something.''

''Wait a minute,'' said Geraghty. ''Whoa. What were they doing in the bedroom, Janie? Was he getting his coat?''

Chris answered for her. ''It's one of those really big parties some people throw—you know, when there's not enough room for everyone, and they're eating their dinner in their laps, and catering ladies are running around—you know, buffet style.''

Janie slid a glance at him. ''I suppose your mother only gives intimate little dinners.''

''Yah,'' said Chris, grinning and tossing his blond hair back. ''That's her style, I guess: little dinners where they sit around the table really late and drink out of little glasses.''

''Liqueur,'' she said dismissively, in an accent that reflected her skill in conversational French. Then she looked over at Geraghty. ''This was a different kind of a party than the usual in our house. It was business. My dad invited his business friends, and then they invited some of the neighborhood people, including this Peter Hoffman and his''—she rolled her eyes upward—''wife.''

Geraghty said, ''What's your impression of his wife?''

''Very flashy,'' said Janie, leaning forward. She put out both thin hands and splayed her fingers. ''Big diamonds on both of her hands.'' She swooped her hands over her breasts and down her body. ''A tight fuzzy sweater with big gold dangles on it, and a long, tight skirt.''

Chris looked at her. ''Janie, he doesn't want to hear about that.'' He looked at Geraghty. ''Do you?''

Geraghty almost smiled. ''You can't tell what little details might help. But you were talking about their conversation in the bedroom. Janie, you thought he was prying information from your mother?''

Janie thought for a moment. ''Yes, that's what it was like. And she, well, she wasn't herself that night.'' She looked down at her hands in her lap. ''She isn't a drinker at all, but she must have had a couple of drinks.''

Chris chimed in. ''She was a little drunk—quite a little drunk.'' He paused. ''But maybe not that bad; staggering a little when she walked, but she could still walk.'' Janie felt her face burn. Then Chris added enthusiastically, ''And it might have loosened her tongue; alcohol loosens your tongue.''

Geraghty looked at Chris. ''You're almost eighteen, and you're not a drinker, eh?''

''No, sir,'' said Chris, smiling, ''not yet. I may be. Some of my best friends are.''

Geraghty stared in the distance, as if remembering a lost youth. ''Drinking isn't all it's cracked up to be. You're smart if you can . . .'' He shook his head. ''Never mind. Tell me, Janie, what did this man ask your mom?''

''Obviously they were talking about the mulch murder. And she was just finishing up telling him something—''

Chris leaned forward in his chair and interrupted. ''And he said, 'How can you be sure of that since almost two months have passed?' and Janie's mom—Louise, that is—she says, 'They *thought* I might remember some important detail, but I didn't get hypnotized.' " Chris looked at Janie. "I didn't know they tried to hypnotize your mother."

Geraghty said, "The police don't publicize those things in a murder investigation. Mrs. Eldridge—Louise—is right." He smiled. Janie had seen men smile before when they talked about her mother. It was very annoying. "She wasn't a good subject for hypnotism," Geraghty recollected, "in spite of having one of the best hypnotists in the nation." He had regained his serious look. "Now, this is important. Try to tell me exactly what came next."

Janie and Chris looked at each other. Janie continued. "Mom said, 'So tonight I've finally remembered something—about a car—that could be important in solving the crime.' He sat back and looked at her and said, really casual, 'If you think that might be important, aren't you going to tell the police?' And she said, what did she say then, Chris?"

"She's, 'Yes, I'll probably give them a call on Monday. Even though those headlights may not be as important as I think.' "

Janie said, "And then he said, like a real know-it-all, 'Headlights are fairly . . .' uh, what was it he said, Chris?"

" 'Generic,' " supplied Chris. "Although anyone who knows cars knows headlights are a way to tell one car from another. But then this guy looks up as if he wants to be sure there was no one else around, and there we are in the doorway, about eight feet away. And then he stands up and he's all over Janie, like an old lecher." Chris made his voice low and hollow: " 'How do you do, Little Goldilocks?' Boy, what a wolf."

Geraghty said, "Did he touch you, Janie?"

"Only with his eyes," said Chris, blue eyes blazing. "No, I take that back. He touched her hair, and her chin, and her hands."

Janie blushed and looked down. Geraghty leaned back again and wearily lifted one large leg on top of his extended lower drawer. He tapped his pencil a few times on the open file and thought.

Then he looked at Chris and Jane. "Okay, what else have you got in *your* file?"

"Our file?" Chris's face turned red. "We don't have a file."

"But you've been around, haven't you?"

"Yeah," said Chris, sitting very straight on the edge of his chair. "We did do a little investigating."

"What'd you find, if anything?"

Chris told him about prowling around what looked like an abandoned house on Martha's Lane.

Geraghty waved a hand. "No problem there. The woman is abroad and has been heard from. That place's not involved . . . though it's close to where this Peter Hoffman lives, isn't it?"

"It's just over one hill," said Janie.

"Janie," said Geraghty, "have you ever met this Peter before last night?"

"Only one night when I was walking, and I happened to walk in his backyard and see him working in his workshop."

"Workshop?"

"He has a workshop on the back of his property."

"A lot of people in your neighborhood have garage workshops—complete with saws."

Janie's eyes widened. "Oh. He has a saw. That's what he was doing when I came by. He was sawing some wood. And he was angry at me for coming in his yard."

"When was this?"

"Oh, maybe in September. A long time ago."

"Before—"

"Oh, way before that."

Geraghty said, "Hold on a minute." Then he was silent for a long while before he pulled himself up straight again. He looked at them sternly. "I appreciate you two coming in. But I want you to keep our conversation confidential, okay?"

"Okay," they said, in unison.

"And harder than that, I want you to keep your imaginations in check. The police already knew about this guy's workshop. We're talking here about a man who is being checked out at the highest levels of government. You're aware, I'm sure, that he's up for an important government post; you both know that, right?"

"Right," they said, in unison.

"Then"—and Geraghty turned his palms out as if in submission—"I don't think we can make much of this conversation you heard. And your mother undoubtedly will call me if she's concerned. Did you find out specifically what she remembered about the car's headlights?"

Janie felt helpless. They were both looking at her. "I asked her this afternoon before we came. She couldn't remember what she'd remembered—and anyway, she was writing like fury, because she has a job now.''

Chris nodded. ''Alcohol can do that to you.''

Geraghty said, ''We'll give her a little time. It'll come back to her again.''

Janie and Chris were silenced.

Geraghty struggled loose of his complaining chair, which sounded as if it didn't want to give him up. He stood and reached over a large hand and shook each of their hands across the worn desk. ''And you two, you be careful. Keep your eyes open but don't go tearing off on something you hear. You bring it to me.''

''Yessir,'' they said in unison.

They left the little office and went out the door of the police station and started the walk home in silence. The sky was gray and dismal, and the wind was picking up.

''You know, Janie,'' said Chris.

''Yes, Chris.''

''We both know there's something fishy about that Peter. But who'll believe it? Nobody. So it's all on us.''

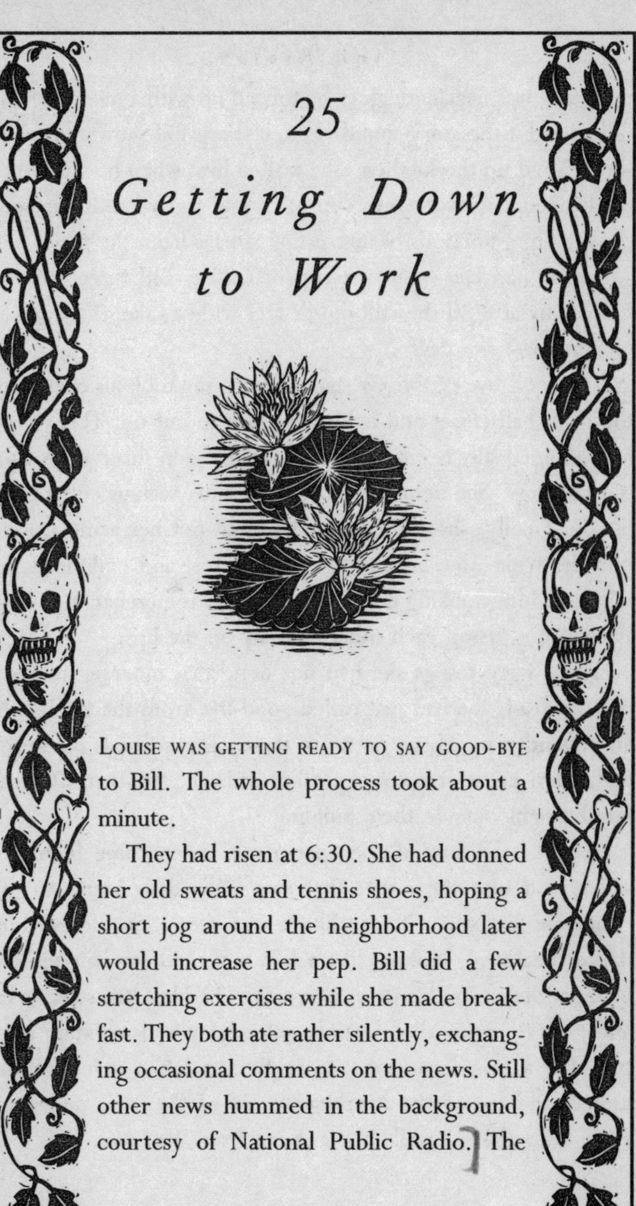

25
Getting Down to Work

LOUISE WAS GETTING READY TO SAY GOOD-BYE to Bill. The whole process took about a minute.

They had risen at 6:30. She had donned her old sweats and tennis shoes, hoping a short jog around the neighborhood later would increase her pep. Bill did a few stretching exercises while she made breakfast. They both ate rather silently, exchanging occasional comments on the news. Still other news hummed in the background, courtesy of National Public Radio. The radio dial was near enough to be turned up with a movement of Bill's hand if the story sounded interesting. Bill showered while she cleaned up the kitchen. She trailed him when he went into the bedroom with a bonus cup of coffee, and while he dressed she read him portions of interesting stories from the paper.

Louise had had only one cup of coffee, Bill three. Maybe that's why at 8:30 she still didn't feel wide awake. A hangover couldn't last *two* days.

The good-bye ceremony started when she took his coat from the front hall closet and held it for him to put on. This would have seemed silly *before* the incident in London three years ago, but not now. She helped him straighten his various collars and his tie. Finally, she came up to him and put her arms around him the wide way, around his upper arms, and embraced the whole of him, looking at his face, so as to remember it always. Finally they kissed each other soundly on the lips.

These were things she had not done that morning in London. Instead, she had just called good-bye from the kitchen in an offhand way. Then, no more than a few seconds later, she had heard an enormous explosion outside. Another IRA car bomb, right outside their building.

She had run out of the apartment, down three flights of stairs, and into the street that was Bill's daily route to the American Embassy. It was like a war scene. She found him dazed, deafened, looking like a lost boy, with his hair disheveled and debris on his dress overcoat. The blast had sent metal and glass flying in all directions, bloodying and maiming people only a few yards away from Bill. It left a crater in the asphalt and tossed the burning carcass of the car's undercarriage onto the sidewalk like a scene from *Mad Max*.

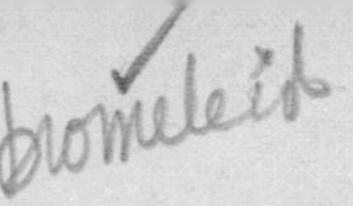

She had hugged him then, and could hardly be persuaded to let him loose. And since then she had always bid him a careful good-bye, a good-luck ritual.

This morning she gave him a kiss that lingered and promised more that night. As soon as she let him go, though, her thoughts turned to her own life without Bill in her arms.

He went out the door, and she followed him onto the front porch. "Better go in, darling. It's cold out here—storm coming in. Take care now, and I'll call you later, so don't forget the portable phone in the hut."

She made a mental list of the things she had to do today. Writing came first. Her editor had called Sunday noon and speeded up the deadline on her bromeliad article, which meant she had dressed and gone straight to the hut to work despite her hangover. It made her feel rather macho, like a recovering drunk out of *The Front Page*. But she still had a couple of hours of writing left to do.

She also had to call Geraghty and tell him she remembered something from her leaf-collecting trips: There had been a set of distinctive parking lights on a car that was following her. She needed to tell Bill that, too. "Bill . . ." Then they saw the frantic deliveryman coming up the walk, pushing an overloaded dolly filled with florists' packages.

"Oh, my gosh—they're here already!" she cried.

"You asked for an early delivery," snapped the man, "and you got one. Lend a hand, why don't you?"

Bill leaned down and grabbed hold of a couple of unbalanced packages.

"Careful, now," cautioned the deliveryman, "these things are worth a bundle."

"I bet they are," said her husband, wryly.

"And handle 'em by their bottoms," the man directed sternly.

"Yessir."

Louise went quickly across the walk and unlocked the door to the chilly addition. "We're going to put them in here."

The man sniffed the cold air. "Then you better heat it up quick; these are tropical plants, you know."

"I know," she said, smiling, fished in her pants pocket for a stray couple of dollars for a tip, and found a five-dollar bill.

With the plants safely positioned on the floor of the hut, the deliveryman snarled, "Sign here, lady," and she did and slipped him the fiver. More sweetly, he said, "Thanks, folks—have a wonderful day."

Bill leaned on the door and looked at the scene, deadpan. "Did you buy one of every plant you're writing about?" He shook his head slowly. "I can see what's going to happen: another addition on the house. The bromeliad bower."

Louise was on her knees ripping open a package. "There's not that many." As if showing off a baby or a puppy, she held out for Bill to see the large, cumbersome plant with soaring pink and blue flowers: "Look, Bill, at this darling billbergia—in *full bloom.*" She tore into the other packages. "I only ordered five—and these are five that you don't *see* every day but are coming into greater cultivation, they assure me." She freed the rest of the plants from their packaging. "Although there are literally dozens of species, you know."

"Good-bye, Louise," said Bill, exaggerated patience in his voice.

" 'Bye," she said distractedly.

After he closed the door of the hut, she hugged herself and grinned. Then she shivered. The maintenance electric heat unit was on, but low. She would build a fire in the stove to supplement it and get started writing.

Using the careful piling of wood that her husband had taught her, she built a fire inside the black Swedish stove that pleased her soul by roaring up at the touch of a match. Everything was going so well for her today.

She arranged the five bromeliads on the table so they were close enough to send her good vibrations. Writing about them was going to be so much easier.

She sat down in front of her computer and took a deep intake of breath. The air was filled with the robust smell of healthy plants, laced with the subtle scent of flowers she had never smelled before.

"Aah." She half smiled, leaned her head back, and slowly breathed in the air. These plants were perfect specimens, their exotic colors evoking the jungles of Brazil and Africa. Her eyes rested on "Snowflake," big pale green leaves speckled like a snake. Bold yellow flowers. She touched a leaf; it was cool and waxy. "Heart's Blood," with its leaves that looked as if they were drenched with dried blood, and its flowers brilliant bloodred. *Aechmea recurvata* x *Aechmea pimenti-vilosoi,* probably the rarest one of all, with its unreal cylindrical blooms in yellow, black, and orange. And then the delicate *Tillandsia cyanea* from Ecuador, not quite as fierce as the others. And, of course, the billbergia.

She rubbed her upper arms. It was warming up already.

Computer, ready. Notes, ready. Reference books, ready. Specimens on hand for close scrutiny.

What she didn't have, and what would be nice, was a pot of coffee. She went out of the hut and across to the front door of the house to the kitchen. She brewed the coffee in her old aluminum pot, and hoped once again it wasn't giving her Alzheimer's disease. On a tray she put the pot, a mug Janie had bought her that read, "Go, Girl!", an apple, and four Fig Newtons. This should last her indefinitely.

She picked up the tray and suddenly remembered she hadn't called Detective Geraghty. Setting the tray back down, she quickly dialed his number. He was out of the office, but would get back to her as soon as possible.

Why, when she might actually have a clue to the case, did the bloody man have to be unavailable? It stirred a little element of discomfort in her. She now possessed some information of value, that had only shaken out of her consciousness this morning. And now there was no one at the police station, not even that obnoxious Morton, to tell it to. Yet the matter had waited this long; it surely could wait a little longer.

She went to the hut and positioned the pot on top of the stove, now too hot to touch. The room was comfortable—no, more than that: as cozy as her European down comforter.

She looked out once through the long glass doors at the end of the room to the woods beyond—the skeletal trees with hardly any leaves left, the ground brown, the sky dark gray.

Then she turned on the computer and began her work. And the outside world fell away.

Between reading the references and writing and examining the blossoms through a magnifying glass, Louise forgot everything, including her coffee.

26
Calling for Help

ONLY THE PALE LIME-COLORED RAYS FROM THE Art Deco light bathed the work area of Bill's desk. But he rejected its comfort and swiveled around in his chair to stare out the window. A barrage of wet snow fell from the sky. This morning, as he drove into the city along with the other gray ghost cars, the radio had excitedly talked about the storm that was coming. He had been so distracted he had paid little attention to details. Now it had arrived; it caught his attention for an instant because of one dreary realization. Going home would be a time-consuming drag. In Washington, where only a dusting of snow made folks nervous, a real storm sent them into orbit and slowed them to a virtual stop. Then he rested his elbow on the leather arm of his chair and propped his chin in his hand, and his thoughts retreated inside again.

The question was, was he happy, and was Louise happy? For years he had made a daily examination of conscience, a habit left over from his Catholic childhood. An examination that required him to put into perspective the reasons for living a secret life and telling a mountain of lies over the years.

Lately he found himself sliding over this daily moment of introspection. Was he growing numb and uncaring about the purpose of his job? As for Louise, he had never wondered before whether she was happy. He always took for granted the answer was yes. But she was so feisty lately. Were those brief freelance writing jobs going to be enough for her? She needed more, and deserved it. Pretty soon Janie would be leaving for college, and then she would be even more dissatisfied, prowling around that house in the woods, improving the gardens—or the woods, in this case—until they were perfection. Not nearly enough.

She had always been the model foreign service wife, close to him, never asking questions when none were appropriate. Helping him when he needed her. She made their life a perfect cover, mixing well with whatever international community they were living in.

His job had changed a lot in the past few years. Not only was his life adrift, no longer clearly defined; his wife was drifting away from him, too, not physically but in some other important way. Something to do with what Nora said Saturday night: ''Your wife is not the same woman you married. She is changing.'' So simple, almost corny, although not when coming from a woman like Nora. But frightening. He frowned and stared out unseeing at the snow falling on Foggy Bottom.

''Changing,'' he said out loud. The word sounded ominous in the quiet room. What was she doing that he didn't know about?

If the truth were told, he felt a little guilty about Nora. He had had a great time with her Saturday night, forgot his host duties for quite a while as they shared dinner balancing their plates on their laps. It was that feeling he'd had in his teens or early twenties when he'd come upon some young woman who was truly sophisticated, who made him feel totally comfortable, not afraid of saying the wrong thing. As if every word of his were poetic and every gesture admirable. A woman who made him feel as if he could say or do nothing wrong. That was the true essence of Nora. And intellectually challenging as well. That was another thing: Louise's apparent jealousy. Not because of her attraction for him but almost because he was interfering with the friendship the two of them had developed. Unusual. *He* was the one who usually had to deal with quirks of jealousy. That was because Louise had a way about her that led less sophisticated men to misunderstand. He'd witnessed it many times. There she'd be, warm, accepting, listening—actually, quite a bit like Nora—and the male was sure she was coming on to him. When, in fact, she was merely curious. Her curiosity about people could be damned annoying. Annoying and dangerous. What a wife! He shook his head. Somehow he couldn't corral his thoughts. All this worrying about Louise when he should be thinking about Peter Hoffman. That reminded him; he looked down at his list of things to do. "Tom." The cryptic note at the top of the list was the thing he wanted to do least.

He was put through right away at the White House.

"I was waiting to hear from you," said Paschen, abruptly. "How was the party?" Bill could picture Paschen in his White House office, in the pose he remembered best: standing, staring out a window, rocking back and forth on expensive Italian shoes, demanding all phone callers be brief and to the point.

"Very successful. Everybody ate a lot, drank a lot, mingled successfully. A good time was had by all."

"All? Including Hoffman?"

"He's a party animal. Hardly made a wrong move."

"Charmed the populace?"

He and Paschen had had some old joke about that years ago, about how politicians had to "charm the populace" to be able to bull through any meaningful legislation that would matter to the country.

"Charmed the populace. Except Louise. She, as far as I know, registered the only nay vote."

"That's interesting. Tell me about it. Just a second." Paschen went off the line. While he waited, Bill turned his chair and stared, as if unseeing, at the snowstorm outside his window.

Paschen came back on the line. "I have plenty of time now to listen, with no interruptions. I'm even sitting down. Tell me every little thing."

"About thirty were there. Dick Elkins and wife, just home from London; four or five more couples from State; Maria

Doren, the novelist—know her? Some friends from Bethesda from the last time we lived here. Some of the neighbors, including Roger Kendricks of the *Post.* A couple of doctors, one shrink."

"And they all liked him?"

"Yep. Hoffman is very brash but skilled in Washington small talk. Charmed the ladies. And earned the admiration of the men. Eyes dart about a lot, but so do lots of people's. His wife is an intelligent woman, although somewhat hard—maybe mercenary's the word."

Paschen chuckled maliciously on the other end of the phone line. "That makes two mercenaries in the family."

Bill laughed briefly. "So, as I said, it was only Louise who put her finger on something."

"What's that?"

"She and Hoffman were eating dessert in Janie's bedroom at a table."

"Janie—that's gotta be your daughter, right?"

"Right."

"Why were they taking their crème brûlée in the bedroom?" he asked snappily.

Bill was annoyed. He knew full well that Paschen lived on an estate in the horse country near Middleburg. He might have a tough time understanding that Bill and Louise, for whatever reason, could not afford a mansion.

"The place was crowded," said Bill, no apology in his voice. "No other place to roost. They were talking about a variety of things. First, he asked her some questions about the body parts found in the yard."

"Is that unusual?" said Paschen. "I would think everybody would ask that kind of question."

"They do. Everybody who meets us or knows us wants an update on the situation. We constantly answer people's questions about how the investigation is going: 'Don't they know whose body that was?' et cetera. It's not that; it's how the guy acted when he met our Janie."

"So what'd he do?"

Bill shifted in his seat. "I don't even like to talk about it. When he met her, he came on like Don Juan. Very noticeable to Louise. All her alarm bells went off. Now, Louise wouldn't feel like that unless there was a reason."

He wasn't going to tell Paschen that Louise was also a little drunk, the first time she'd been drunk since the time years ago in Florence. Suddenly his tired mind went back to that sunny vacation, filled with footsore, wonderful walks on the cobblestone streets, dinners with too much wine, lovemaking each night in their rooms in an ancient castle-cum-hotel.

"All right. So back to my question, Bill: What exactly did he do?"

Bill tried to focus back on his story. "Janie and a neighbor boy were popping in and out of the party. And Hoffman hadn't had a chance to meet her until this particular moment. Apparently he tilted her chin up and gazed in her eyes . . . and he touched her hair. . . ." All of a sudden, Bill's stomach felt queasy. "It doesn't *sound* so serious. But Louise said he acted as if he would have thrown Janie on the bed and . . . taken her if he'd had the chance. What's strange is that most people there saw a completely different man."

At the other end of the line, in Chief of Staff Paschen's

White House office, there was a long silence. Finally, one word: ''Lecher.''

''Lecher,'' repeated Bill. ''But that's not necessarily illegal. Depends on where you go with it.'' He sighed. ''Look, Tom, you have the proper agencies to run this guy to ground. You decide what you do next; it's your baby. That's all I have.''

Off the hook. What a relief. But a sense of decency made him say more. ''One more thing. As a father I don't like to say this, but maybe this isn't fair to the guy. I mean, to a man, everybody was noticing Janie the other night.'' He paused.

''Yeh. Why?''

''Look, Janie's almost sixteen. An innocent, well-behaved girl. It was only yesterday''—his voice broke. This was his baby he was talking about—''she was a skinny kid. But Saturday night she was a knockout. All of a sudden here's this beautiful young creature just coming into womanhood. Peter Hoffman wasn't the only man who was caught in her spell. As a father, the whole thing made me damned nervous. But I said to myself, remember, that's what happens with daughters. So I don't know what to say, Tom. Maybe he's just normal. Or maybe somewhere down the line he'll get into woman trouble.''

There was another long pause on Paschen's end of the line. ''The FBI tail's been pulled for a couple of months; he's been leading such a dull life lately. . . .'' Another pause. Bill could imagine Paschen on his feet again, impatient for action, like an animal ready to stalk its prey.

The president's chief of staff said, ''I'm standing here thinking hard, Bill. What you told me—not much to go on. But I'm going to resume surveillance on him anyway. Just on general principles. I'll send someone down to his offices in Alexandria today.''

''Yeah,'' said Bill. ''He works near us; he lives near us. I don't like it.''

Paschen's voice was dreamy. ''I wish I could get that bastard on something.''

Bill leaned forward and clutched the phone and his hands around his head as if shielding himself from a blow. ''Tom, let's backtrack. When did you pull the tail on this guy?''

''Oh, I don't know . . . sometime in September.''

''I don't know why, but I'm damned glad to hear you're resuming the tail. The guy just doesn't—''

''Track. That's it exactly, Bill. He doesn't track. And thank you. And thank Louise for me. I'll keep you posted.''

After he hung up the phone, Bill stared for a long moment at the pool of soft green light. Interesting, beautiful. Like Louise, who had given it to him. He couldn't unlink Louise from his thoughts about Peter Hoffman. This guy had been right on hand all the time, in Alexandria and Sylvan Valley, and Bill hadn't been sensitive to it until now.

The neighborhood with the mulch murder. The questions about the police investigation. Coming on to young girls. Stories of missing women. Couldn't be . . . or could it?

He grabbed the phone and punched out his home number. Then he sat very still and prayed with every ring that she would answer. She was home; he knew that. She had a deadline she had to meet today.

''Damn it, answer!'' he yelled.

Someone knocked on his door. Ed from the next office. ''Everything okay in there?'' Bill ignored him.

Louise's recorded voice said, "We can't come to the phone right now . . ." Bill slammed down the receiver.

He sat for a minute quietly. He had to keep his head. He was probably being silly: too little sleep lately. He punched in Information and asked for the Fairfax Police number. At last he had an out-of-breath Detective Geraghty on the line.

"Mike Geraghty? Bill Eldridge here. Now, you may think this is totally off the wall—"

"No, I don't," Geraghty curtly interrupted.

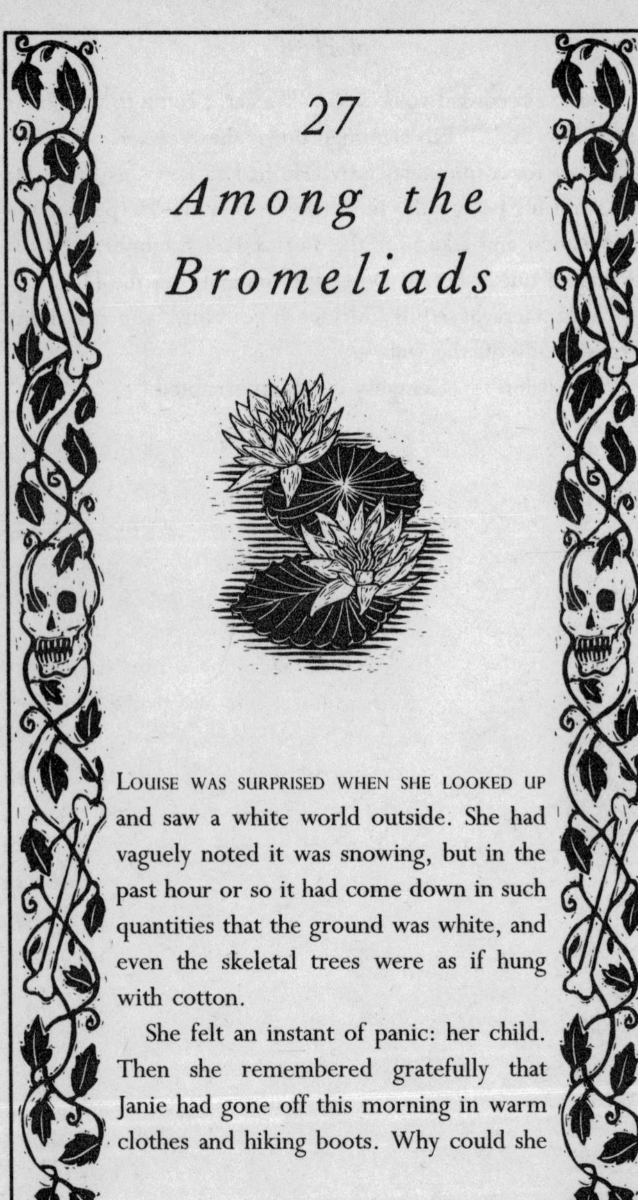

27

Among the Bromeliads

LOUISE WAS SURPRISED WHEN SHE LOOKED UP and saw a white world outside. She had vaguely noted it was snowing, but in the past hour or so it had come down in such quantities that the ground was white, and even the skeletal trees were as if hung with cotton.

She felt an instant of panic: her child. Then she remembered gratefully that Janie had gone off this morning in warm clothes and hiking boots. Why could she never relinquish this motherly concern about the children getting their feet wet?

She shivered. The stove had died down, and the temperature had dropped. She opened the stove's small door. Only a little bed of embers—orange, squirmy worms—remained. She put in more kindling, and a piece of paper for good luck, then the bulk of her wood in the prescribed fashion. Once lit, she clamped the door shut, keeping the damper open just a crack. "C'mon, baby," she urged, "do it again for me."

She sat down and slouched back in her chair. Like a cat waking from a sleep, she stretched out her legs and her arms and yawned. She looked at the apple on the tray and considered eating it, but chewing a Granny Smith seemed too large an effort right now. Yet it must be lunchtime, or was it later? She had no watch on. And she had forgotten to bring the phone out. Bill probably had called and gotten no answer.

She picked up a Fig Newton and took a bite through its gentle protective exterior. As usual, it tasted ordinary until she got to the fig part, exotic as Morocco.

With her free hand, she cursored through her story and felt better than she had in a long time. It was a good piece of writing, and she was almost finished with it. As if thanking it for providing good vibrations, she touched the plant nearest to her, the billbergia. She ran her finger carefully along one of its swordlike leaves. They were ratcheted like devilish daggers. Its graceful, looping pink and blue blossoms were traced with purple accents. She liked it the best; it was the roughest and at the same time the most beautiful.

Then she looked over at the glass doors. The bulk of the snow surprised her; it had accumulated to what looked like three or four inches. The now-white woods would have been picture-perfect if it weren't for the threatening sky. She thought she saw a flicker of movement in the backyard. A bird, perhaps, not used to winter yet.

Then came the series of knocks.

She realized her little joke about the protection provided by the sound of crunching leaves was moot. Whoever was here had traveled here soundlessly. The leaves were covered with a snowy blanket and gave no warning. And in spite of Bill's admonitions, the door to the hut was unlocked.

These realizations didn't worry her, because she was almost certain it was Nora. She sat up straight and, with some reluctance, came out of her writing daze.

Another rat-a-tat-tat of knocks. Suddenly she went cold. It couldn't be Nora. Too demanding and impolite. Every nerve in her body came alive.

Suddenly the door flew open and a thin burst of snow flew in, as if attracted by her or the fire. There stood a big man in mirrored ski goggles and white hooded Goretex ski outfit. A stranger from an alien planet. Louise immediately conjured up a memory of spooky-looking white-clad Finnish soldiers in World War II, fighting Russians, on skis with rifles strapped across their backs.

With one hand the man threw back his hood, lifted his goggles onto his forehead, and pulled down the scarf that covered his lower face. His other hand was bunched in his deep coat pocket.

It was Peter Hoffman, with blue eyes glittering, blond hair in disarray, and what looked like two days' worth of gray-blond beard.

He stamped in, unbidden, the snow that hung on him cascading onto the flagstone floor.

Louise remained seated, both hands over her heart. "Oh, it's only you. You about scared me to death! What are you *doing* here?"

He smiled down at her. Again using only one hand, he unsnapped his jacket, removed the goggles, and stuffed them in a pocket. From the same pocket he extricated a pair of bifocals and slipped them in place on his nose. He looked around the room as if to memorize its furniture plan. "Louise. It's a helluva day, isn't it? I'm sorry—didn't mean to scare you." He looked at the rapidly melting snow he had dragged in. "Didn't mean to mess up this place, either. But it won't hurt these flagstones, will it?"

Louise, who was beginning to recover her composure, reflected that she had just waxed those flagstones. She said, "No, don't worry about it." She looked at him with her forehead furrowed. "What on earth brought you over here? You really scared me, you know."

He looked at a nearby chair. "Can I sit down?"

Her solitude was gone, and Louise could hardly conceal her impatience at the loss. "Of course. I'm sorry I'm so short; I'm working. I don't have a lot of time. But do sit down. Although I think I might have to go soon. The weather looks so bad that I may have to pick Janie up at school."

"You're going to have trouble driving. Roads are a mess. Very slippery."

"Then I wonder how—oh, I suppose the school buses—or maybe they'll just . . ." She stopped.

"They'll just what? They won't walk all the way home, will they?"

"I doubt it," she lied. She would love to see the teenagers walk in right now. With an effort, she sought a cordial tone: "So, you walked here, from your house?"

"Yes. You know good and well that my house is less than a mile from here."

"How did you know I'd be home?"

Hoffman sat back comfortably. "You told me Saturday night. Don't you remember? You told me lots of things Saturday night."

Louise quietly pulled herself up in her chair. "Mr. Hoffman . . ."

"Peter," he said, cajolingly.

"Well, Peter, then. I may have been a bit tipsy, but I *can* remember our conversation in Janie's bedroom." A flash of anger came over her. She glared at him. "Do you think I'm some fool?"

"To the contrary, my dear." His voice had become low and sexy. "I think you are smart. You are also a very hot woman. And I think your pantywaist State Department husband doesn't realize just how hot you are."

She got out of her chair and walked toward him, her teeth clenched with anger. She stood over him, her arms akimbo. "You are so . . . *inappropriate* I can't find words for it. Who do you think I am? You have a dirty mind, mister. And I guess it's because you're such a macho guy that you don't even know the difference between a 'pantywaist,' as you call it, and a real man. Which is what *my husband* is, and which *you* obviously are not. So please leave. Neighbor or no neighbor, big shot or no big shot, I don't want you here.'' As she strode past him toward the door he jumped up from his chair and grabbed her arm as if it were tinder. Pain ran through her body, a rank intruder. She couldn't move without hurting herself.

''How dare you!'' she cried. ''*Goddamn* you! This is my house!''

She looked down when she felt the gun barrel in her stomach. A large black pistol. She felt dizzy and knew she would fall. He maneuvered her backward with an iron hand and pushed her awkwardly into her chair. Mouth agape, she breathed in little, short gasps. As if warning her too late of danger, her heart started to palpitate, so hard she was sure that her adversary could see the motion. She lowered her head and willed it to stop. How could she handle all this and a palpitating heart as well! As if the prayer were answered, the irregular, nervous rhythm stopped, then was followed a millisecond later with one familiar, dull pain in her chest. She sighed with relief.

He looked down at her. ''Is something wrong with you?'' he asked crossly.

She shook her head. In a quiet voice she said, ''No, I'm just . . . surprised.''

''Can I trust you now not to do anything foolish?'' he pursued, as if talking to a misbehaving child.

Louise's voice was low. ''What on earth are you doing this for? What do you want from me?''

Watching her, he walked to the end of the room and pulled the draperies across the glass doors that looked into the woods. As he came back to his chair, he gave her a smile and said, "It's so damned cold and wet out there. I like the feeling of this place, all closed in, just the two of us."

She stared at him. She felt as if every synapse were at the ready. Did this bastard want to do something to Janie? If so, he had *her* to take care of first.

"Let's get down to it, Louise. I didn't come here to rape you . . . or Janie . . . Janie, that's who you're afraid for now, isn't it? Just because I admired her the other night. You're such a clucking mother. Don't you know every man at that party wanted to fuck her? She's a little old to be a virgin—how old is she, fifteen? She cried out, in that basal way young females do, 'I'm ready to be taken, take me.' "

"You bastard," Louise whispered.

"And you, baby. You have the same quality; you're just a little better at covering it up. But I know you'd love it."

She put her hands over her ears and stared at the now prosaic-looking plants that sat in front of her on the table.

He snarled it: "Louise!"

She snapped her head toward him, frightened again, and a whimper escaped her. Her heart threatened to resume its irregular beat, and again she tried to fool it, to pull a veil of calm over her body. Again the palpitations receded.

"Baby, I'll lay that aside for a bit," he said, smiling. His tone, she noticed, had softened. "Maybe later we'll get better acquainted. Not enough time right now. I'm here on serious business." His tone turned nasal, matter-of-fact.

"You have the key to the little mystery that turned up in your backyard. A mystery that hasn't been too pleasant, has it? Newspapers, police. Neighbors always asking you about it. You didn't expect to be the center of such a, shall we say, disjointed affair.'' He laughed uncontrollably at his joke, putting one hand on his belly as if to control its movement, rocking back and forth a little with enjoyment. The other hand attempted to keep the gun level with her head.

She looked at him, her mouth curled down. Her hands were clutched to the inside of either thigh as if to give her some inner support.

''Lighten up, Louise,'' he snapped. ''I'm telling you a story. I'm *honoring* you by telling you *my* story.''

Suddenly it fell into place. She realized she had only one weapon. This man was attracted to her. Liked to *teach* her things. Like a Svengali. With an effort she let the sneer melt from her face. She crossed her legs, slowly relaxed her hands, and turned them up in her lap. Her survival could depend on how well she did this.

''Ah, better. You were so angry I'd thought you'd burst. Well, to move along . . . there's not much time. We have to get outta here.''

''You're telling me I know something about the body in the bags?''

''Yes. You know what kind of a car was pulling out of Martha's Lane the night you were there.''

''No. I just remember the headlights.''

''But if you'd gone to the police—I was afraid you might go first thing this morning. I discredited the information, but I still couldn't count on you. They could have helped you identify *my* Porsche 911 Carrera II, the one with the distinctive lights.''

''Your car,'' she said dully.

''Fortunately, Geraghty was out chasing me this morning.

And because you're so goddamned polite—one side of you is an uptight Presbyterian, isn't it? The side opposite the sexy, hot, adventuresome side—you wouldn't have bothered anyone else with it, would you?'' His eyes glittered at her. ''You get the hots for Geraghty, Louise? You like stocky, middle-aged detectives with bright blue eyes? Can you imagine being in *bed* with that great big law enforcer crushin' down on you?''

''How do you know he wasn't there?'' She felt the fool. She had even forgotten that she was going to call the detective.

A smile crept about his lips. ''I found out through an exploratory phone call. It was easy. I obviously am more interested in this case than *you* are, although right now it's *your* ass that's on the line.'' His voice rose. ''Reason I'm more interested's because I'm the one who put the *body* there. Can you believe that, or are you still in denial?''

Louise shuddered a little, fighting to keep it from being obvious to her tormentor. She had known he was the murderer, known since he had pulled out his gun. But the reality of his confession, the certifying of the deed in words, was a shock. She was in the presence of some kind of monster. And she wouldn't be facing him alone except for her hubris—her refusal to take seriously the warnings of others: her husband, even her neighbor Nora—and her witless capacity to be sidetracked by the delivery of a bunch of houseplants. Now she had no weapons, no phone, and she had even left the door open for the monster to walk through!

She held her body carefully, as if it were one of those delicate blown-glass figures that would break on slightest impact. She brought her breathing under control. She kept her lips relaxed and her gaze steady upon him. She had been a good actress in high school but had left it totally behind; if ever there was a time to call it back, it was now.

She spoke slowly. "So you're the killer. And who is it that you killed, for us to gather up in the mulch?"

She realized immediately that this was a misstep on this high, dangerous trail. His face grew hard. He was angry.

"Listen, suburban slut," he snarled, and she wouldn't have been surprised if saliva had dropped from his mouth. He leaned forward for emphasis, gun steady. "If your little life-style were more interesting—if you'd order mulch from the garden center like *my* wife would do, instead of mopping up after homeowners, picking up other people's trash like a fuckin' homeless person or something . . . if you hadn't been so *weird,* woman, I wouldn't have to be taking all this trouble to remove you from the neighborhood and from my life!"

She flinched involuntarily, then steadied. Her voice was even. "You still haven't told me who it was you . . . killed."

He sat back, slightly deflated. The gun hand rested on his right thigh but was still pointing at her. "*That* was a woman. You would have thought so, too. *That* was a woman. Not some suburban breed like you and the others. Worldly, romantic, smart, very smart." Like an afterthought that explained all that came before, he said, "Austrian."

"The woman who's supposed to be in Hong Kong—the one who lives on Martha's Lane?"

"*Lived,* stupid! She's dead." His eyes were wide and staring. "I killed her. But that wasn't the worst part. It was the getting rid of her . . . the blood in the laundry basins, from the saw . . ." He sat and stared beyond her, as if seeing something she couldn't see.

"So you put her in those leaf bags. But what did you do with the rest?"

He looked at her admiringly. "Ah, you mean the head and the hands? You're smart: You realize the importance of that. First I thought I'd weight that package and throw it in the Potomac. Then, I decided to, shall we say, keep it nearer at hand." He smiled a terrible smile. "That's the beauty of architect-designed houses."

Then, incredibly, she saw tears come to his eyes.

"You loved her, didn't you?" For a minute she forgot to be scared. She was intensely curious about this story. If she were to be kidnapped, or raped, or worse, the very least she could expect was to know why.

"Of course I loved her. Want to know why? Because she was loyal. She never criticized me. She loved me for whatever I was—I know I'm a bit of a shit sometimes—and whatever I did, she liked it."

"You . . . knew her for a long time, then."

"Not long enough. Just spring until fall. Then they put the screws in me."

"They? The . . . government?"

As if he'd forgotten where he was, he focused back in on her. "People like your goddamn lily-livered, undercover secret spy husband, in his secret State Department spy cubbyhole."

The polite charade she and Bill had conducted all these years was shattered. They had been hiding their secret, while the whole world knew anyway, even this horrid man! The explanations she gave of what Bill did for the government. Bill's glossed-over accounts to one and all about his long absences and strange habits. Here she was with this gross creature, Peter Hoffman, who knew the truth all along. Was he going to kill her because of her husband's spying?

"My husband, he has had nothing to do with you."

"Shit, lady, why do you think we were invited to your house Saturday? He was called into play along with the others. They're observing Hoffman at another Washington party to see if he has any warts showing. I've been to lots of parties lately, I'll tell you that." His voice was rising again. "Analysis: no fuckin' warts showing. So what will we do to him *next*? Do you know they followed me and Kristina for months, except Kristina, because she was so discreet, kept her identity from the whole bunch of them."

"Kristina." Louise said the name slowly, knowing this was his soft spot. She needed to buy time. But now her stomach was churning, as if filled with green acid. She could hear it gurgle; would he hear and discover how frightened she was?

"Kristina." She rolled the word out of her mouth slowly, sensually, so that it sounded like an invitation to the Casbah. Then she whispered, "What a beautiful name."

Hoffman deflated like a punctured beach ball, seeming to shrink into his crumpled white parka. "It hasn't been the same without her." He muttered this, then fell silent, his chin pressed down on his chest, his mouth drawn down in sadness.

She hated to disturb the quiet. But she had to know the answer. "So . . . why did you think you had to *kill* her?"

He looked at Louise as if for the first time. "Lady, you are *so* naive, here in your leafy bower in the suburban woods.

Only a provincial person like you could live in the social structure of the most important capital in the world and not know what you don't know. Do you know who I am? Let me tell you: I am an arms dealer. I have my own company, right in friendly downtown Alexandria, near the Potomac River, and, incidentally, a lock on some armaments that this country desperately needs. Long before that, I was with Army intelligence, where I just happened to meet the guy who is now president. He has a few old warts of his own from Vietnam. I am a killer. I have killed, not just gooks famous and not so famous, but an occasional American who got in the line of fire.'' His voice had taken on a conspiratorial ring, as if Louise had passed a security test and could be told anything. ''I have *had* to kill. A woman once, in Europe. That's the one they wonder about at the FBI. Then there was the man who didn't know the meaning of paying his debts. He just had an accident. And then, regrettably''—he bowed his head—''Kristina.''

He sighed a deep sigh. ''That goddamned Paschen made me do it. And Kristina. She was so goddamned emotional about my leaving her, she wouldn't *let* me leave her. But I had to. We've got this president who says he has known no woman except his wife—if you can believe that you can believe anything—a president who's forced to play to the right-wing assholes in our fucked-up society. Can't afford more scandals . . . 'safraid he won't get reelected next year. So,'' and his voice trailed off, ''that's why I had to get rid of her—to get the job. She wouldn't go quietly.'' His head dropped to his chest.

Louise frowned. She knew they were approaching closure. Something had to happen soon. She was torn between a concern for her own safety and the need to tie up a couple of loose ends. "Ah, could I just ask—you mean Tom Paschen, the president's chief of staff?"

"Yeah. Tom Paschen. World-class bastard. You may think *I'm* evil, but this guy runs circles around me. He destroys people just for the fun of it."

"And the letters. Kristina, the woman in the house on Martha's Lane . . . she was *heard* from, that's what Mike Geraghty told me."

Hoffman shook his head in disgust. "You are so unbelievably naive. Here's a clue for you: I have connections in Hong Kong. Now, how much trouble do you think it is to send some letters that you want mailed back to the States? I bet you think everybody in the world is *innocent.* Have you ever heard of faking a letter, faking evidence in court, faking a bill of sale for a million dollars in arms?" His voice was rising with irritation. "What the hell do you think your neighborhood cops do? They frame suspects all the time—dropped guns, dope planted on them during a body search. *Stealing* dope, cops steal *millions* of dollars' worth of evidence. Lawyers, fuckin' lawyers, ninety-eight percent of 'em are crooks. I bought my own lawyer so he doesn't dare fuck me over. But see, I *own* him; most people can't afford to *own* their lawyer."

She listened to him carefully. She was satisfied now that she knew the story. She also knew that this man was right on the edge. And he wanted her dead. If his mood changed again, she might get raped first, but eventually she would be dead.

"And judges," he was saying, "on almost any level below federal, and a few at the federal level, can be bought, for Chrissake." She looked straight at him, while in her peripheral vision she collected the scene around her, her eyes searching for weapons. Of course. To the left of her left hand by just two feet: The coffee. She needed to get him closer, without arousing suspicion. Her heart thumped, but she told it to be quiet.

She threaded her fingers through her long brown hair and pushed it slowly back from her face, a gesture that was a come-on, at least for Bill. "Peter," she said in a low voice, "I feel . . . sorry for you. What can I do for you? I know you want me to do something. Just what is it?" She gave him a smoldering look; she hoped he didn't see through her and hit her in the face with the gun.

He bit. He smiled, and a light came into his tired eyes. Never say die to sex, thought Louise. He struggled up out of the chair, where he had become comfortable in the hot room.

"It's funny," he said lightly. "You've sensed it; all this is a turn-on for me. Now I find it's a turn-on for you, too." He was about three feet away, probably planning on using the daybed against the wall.

With her strong backhand she reached and grabbed the hot coffeepot and with a crushing forehand flung the steaming liquid into his face.

"Jeee-sus!" he bellowed, dropping the gun to cover his face with his hands. In an instant he made toward Louise like an angry giant, grabbing her around the neck, shoving her against the stove. Her head crashed against the yielding stovepipe, and its sections broke apart, releasing black smoke into the small room. She screamed. The backs of her legs were burning.

He shook her like a rag doll. In a moment she would be too weak to resist. Through the swirling soot she sensed rather than saw another weapon. She reached far back and grabbed a plant, the billbergia, knowing it was the billbergia by the pain in her hands where its sharp edges cut into her flesh. Lifting the plant and shoving it pell-mell into Peter's face, eyes, nose. Pink and blue blossoms torn and falling, black dirt splayed about, falling in her eyes, her mouth. Grunting and shoving it deep into his face.

He screamed and let her go and his hands went up like claws. "My eye, my eyes!" he yelled. "You incredible bitch!" With horror, she saw him swoop down and grab for the gun. His face was scored with heavy scratches and gouges, and one eye was spurting blood, but he was like the unstoppable monster in a Saturday-night movie.

"Oh, *God,* don't *shoot* me!" she yelled, jittering around like a frightened animal.

She had never felt so alone. She would either beat him at his own game, or he would kill her. Desperately she looked around and spied her only remaining weapon: the poker stand. It was a heavy, black wrought-iron thing, but she picked it up as if it were weightless and slammed it into the side of Peter's head.

Screaming in pain from his new wound, he stumbled back against the chair and fell to the floor. Not completely out, she saw with dismay, just momentarily disabled. She raised the black stand above her head. The door opened.

"Ma!" It was Janie, carrying her book bag, and Chris, basketball in hand.

Louise held her second strike. "Kids, get away!" she warned.

"Chris," yelled Janie, "do something!"

The prone man swept his arm back and forth on the flagstones until he found the gun. "No!" she yelled. Before she could strike again, Chris raised the basketball in both hands, swung it far back of his head, and then flung it at Hoffman, with all the force and accuracy accumulated in a seventeen-year lifetime. The gun clattered away. "And take that too, you jerk!" cried Janie. She slung her book bag into his bloody face, knowing, as fighters do, that injuring your opponent's face can be decisive.

Hoffman lay back and moaned. But one hand still groped feebly for the weapon, looking to a horrified Louise like the involuntary twitching of a slain animal. At that moment, Detective Geraghty's large presence filled the door of the hut. Uniformed men hovered behind him. "Peter Hoffman," Geraghty warned needlessly, "just leave that gun right where she lays."

28
I Know!

"There you are, all tucked in, like a bug in a rug. Getting a little warmer?"

"Yes, darling. Thank you."

"The doctor wants you to take a pain pill. Otherwise, he doesn't think you'll be able to sleep. Here's a glass of water to swallow it down with."

"Thank you, sweetie."

Her husband had arrived home soon after the police, although not in time to see Peter handcuffed and taken away. Just as well: Bill's eyes were filled with rage when he saw her cuts and burns. She had never seen him so upset. He had shoved the questioning detectives aside and rushed her to the hospital to get her wounds dressed.

She shuddered under the white comforter.

"Still cold, huh? Uh . . . Geraghty wants to ask just a few questions. Do you feel up to it?"

She shivered again. "Sure. If it will help."

He invited the detective to step in for a minute, then sat on the bed beside his wife.

Geraghty lowered himself cautiously into the only available seat, the apricot boudoir chair. He looked at Louise and Bill uncertainly, as if he had interrupted something intimate. "First, I want to tell you how sorry I am that you were attacked. I have been laboring on this case since early this morning, trying to get hold of Hoffman, and it hasn't been easy. People like him are harder to track, and he was out of his house yesterday."

"Why were you going to question him?" Louise asked.

"On the basis of what your daughter and her friend Chris reported to me yesterday afternoon."

"*Janie's* in on this?"

"Oh, yes, ma'am. Jane and Chris. They got real suspicious of the guy at your party. I'll be happy to tell you all about it when you're feeling better. But now I need a few details that will help nail this guy—then I'll be gone. Do you remember what time Hoffman showed up?" He held his usual notebook on his wide thigh, pencil poised to record her answer.

"I . . . wasn't wearing my watch, and there's no clock in the hut." Silence. A silence that condemned someone who didn't care enough about time either to wear a wristwatch or to have a clock handy. ''I don't know. I worked for a long time, and I looked up and it had snowed a lot . . . let's see . . .''

The detective scratched his short-cropped white hair. ''Let's look at it from another angle: How long was he there before we arrived?''

''About half an hour.''

Bill, who was perched on the bed beside her, turned to her. ''Half an hour—I didn't know he was there *that* long! What the hell did he do for half an hour, besides choke you and throw you against a hot stove? For Chrissake . . . Louise, have you told me everything?''

Geraghty watched with his cool, marble blue eyes. It was as if he were doing research again on the behavior of couples.

She put a placating hand out to him. ''Believe me, Bill. Nothing . . . like that happened. First—did I tell you this? I threw a pot of hot coffee in his face. He must be badly burned. I *hated* throwing it at him, but it was all there was. . . .''

Bill patted her. ''Good for you!''

''And I jammed him in the face with the billbergia.'' She grimaced as she imagined the pain she had inflicted.

''Mmm,'' said Geraghty. ''Is that the plant we found in pieces on the floor?''

''I think so,'' said Bill. ''The one with leaves like swords.''

Geraghty's big fingers riffled back through the pages of his notebook. ''Uh . . . billbergia? I thought she said something about bromeliads—that the same thing?''

Louise smiled faintly. ''All in the family.''

''So that's what blinded his eye.''

''Oh, my God, *blinded,*'' moaned Louise and put her hand

to her own eye. "I *knew* I hurt it! It was spurting blood. But then I had to hit him in the head with the poker stand. He finally fell down. I was *sure* I was killing him." She began to sob.

Bill gripped her shoulder. "Honey . . ."

Geraghty's harsh voice interrupted. "Mrs. Eldridge, get a grip! Stop doing that to yourself. Hoffman's a murderer, not a choirboy. He was trying to *kill* you. You did right laying into him like that. Think of it—*you* caught a killer. And you're alive to tell about it. You should be proud of what you did, not lying there crying about it."

"He's right, Louise," said Bill. Then he chuckled. "You realize what happened? You vanquished the arms dealer, the master of modern weaponry. With nothing but ancient techniques of warfare: scalding, jabbing, clubbing . . ."

She smiled, then sobered. "It's funny; we keep talking about the violence, but the violence only took a minute. And then Janie and Chris came in. They were really brave. *Most* of the time Peter was just talking, sitting there in the big chair. He had that gun pointed at me the whole time. God, I was so *afraid.* And he told me those terrible things about killing Kristina—and the other woman three years ago—and people in jungles . . . but I guess that was part of the war. . . ." She shook her head as if to rid herself of the memory. "What a terrible man." She looked at Geraghty. "And then Bill called you and you came. Thank goodness you came quickly."

The detective gave them a sheepish look. "I was on my way to your house when he phoned and the station patched the call through. Y'know, when Chris and Jane came over on Sunday to tell me about Hoffman, I brushed it off—figured it was totally off the wall. The government would do a full background check on a guy like him, so I just thought, 'the kids are overexcited.' And his workshop was clean—we checked out all the workshops in Sylvan Valley and even beyond. But it bugged me last night, so I woke up this morning and called a friend in the FBI, to try and find out what the Bureau was doing with Mr. Hoffman. He was able to tell me a few procedural things, which were just the things I needed to know—about how they actually tailed the guy, for some reason he didn't divulge, from May through August. But then they quit."

He was getting into his story, raising his big hand to emphasize his point: "Now, that really got me going. At least the guy would have had the opportunity to do this murder, without anyone hovering around, checking his movements. We went to his home: nobody there. Then, we went to his plant in Alexandria, and got stonewalled—in a real high-class way, of course. Actually, Hoffman had to have been holed up back in his house and they may or may not have known it. Then I was certain you could be in danger." Geraghty looked at her with remorseful eyes, and she knew he would regret forever not getting here sooner to save her from Hoffman's attack. "But this damned snow came along—slowed us up just those crucial minutes. . . ."

Louise tried but could not help yawning. She was fighting sleep now. But she had to know. "Bill, why did you call Detective Geraghty?"

"It was only four weeks ago that I learned about some of Hoffman's background, including the Rhine River incident. But, like Mike here, I didn't even think of the guy in relation to the woman's body we found. Until his unusual interest in our family. Even then it was just a sense of unease. Then I remembered something we'd not related to this: Remember, Louise, when Sam Rosen heard someone out in the woods? It was the same night you and Janie went around *our* neighborhood gathering leaves. I thought, it could have been Hoffman, frantic that someone came along and picked up the bags that he had just put out to be hauled away. Then the other details: Hoffman has a house in the area. Not only a house, but also his *office and plant*—they're only a few miles away. Here's an entrepreneur with freedom of movement. The government's off his tail—I just discovered that today. I thought, so what if I'm wrong? If I'm right, he could hurt you, and by God, I was right. The son of a bitch nearly . . ." He shook his head in disbelief. "But you did him one better, Louise, damn it: You not only drew the whole story out of him, you *took him out.*" He reached down and gave her a hug.

Geraghty looked at her, and she thought his eyes looked misty. "We might never have known the real story. Hoffman had, practically speaking, 'disposed' of Kristina Weeren through his phony letters from Hong Kong."

"Has he confessed to you?" asked Louise.

Geraghty shook his head. "He's not in too good shape to talk right now."

"Oh." She was silent a moment, trying not to feel guilty. "Then I'm the only one he's told."

"Your word against his, I'm afraid," said Geraghty. "We may or may not get him for those crimes, but we'll sure nail him for attempted murder." He struggled up out of the low chair. "Physical evidence: that's what we need on the mulch murder. And speaking of physical evidence, I have to check in. Thanks, Mrs. Eldridge. I may have a few more questions for you tomorrow. Just remember, you did great."

Before she drifted off to sleep, she needed to take inventory. What had she accomplished? She had finished her assignments on deadline. She had taken charge in a crisis—in fact, caught a murderer—and emerged with her life intact. Although bruised and burned, she felt stronger than she had in years.

One idle last thought—she wondered where Janie and Chris had disappeared, they who had done so much to save her. Probably out telling the neighbors the whole story. They would be bosom friends after this experience. And maybe more.

A phone rang. Later, she heard Geraghty, his voice filled with regret. "They haven't found anything yet, but they're still looking."

She closed her eyes. Sleep was just a moment away. The head and the hands. Peter had mentioned them . . . said they would unmistakably tie you to a crime. They were somewhere, quietly rotting, the smell confined inside double or triple plastic wrappings.

The smell. It made her think of the rank odor in the closet when they moved in, that dead air coming up from under their slab house.

She sat straight up, wide awake. "I know!"

29
Defenseless

PRESIDENT FAIRCHILD OPENED THE DOOR OF the private living quarters and admitted Tom Paschen, his chief of staff. The commander in chief was in pajamas and robe, and barefoot. His hair was uncombed and he needed a shave. In his left hand he grasped the front section of *The Washington Post*. In the background was the chatter of a TV news show.

He looked disbelievingly at Paschen. "Can't anybody do anything right? Why do I have to hear this on TV and read it in the paper?'' He flailed the paper back and forth in front of Paschen's face. ''Do you know what this *means*?''

Paschen, dapper in his navy Italian suit, strutted past the president and sat in a flowered chintz chair. His voice was quiet and steady. ''Chief, this was inevitable. I warned you about that bastard from the first.''

The president walked to the chair and stood over it for a moment, then retreated to the nearby matching sofa, where more newspaper sections were strewn about. ''I know you did,'' he said, ''but I also told you to run checks. *Checks.* You didn't do enough checkin'!'' His voice had escalated, his blue eyes widened in anger.

Paschen took the liberty of pouring himself a cup of coffee from the tray sitting on a table in front of the couch. He sipped it calmly.

President Jack Fairchild slumped over, his elbows on his knees. ''You know what this means? This means I'm fucked.''

''You mean just because your deputy secretary of defense nominee killed his lover, sawed her body into parts, buried them in leaf bags, and tucked her head and hands in a secret compartment under his house?''

''Don't be funny, Tom. You know why he did it, don't you?''

''Not exactly. Do you?''

The president glared at his chief of staff, who was really a very small man. ''Because you gave him that big lecture about cleaning up his act, and he took you literally.''

Paschen jauntily crossed his legs. ''Just proves what an asshole he is.''

The president trembled, as if about to explode. ''That asshole, as you call it, was going to be *my* asshole—*my* expert on arms, *my* defense against the secretary of defense! Without him I am totally—''

''Fucked?''

''Yes!''

Paschen took a final sip of his coffee and got up from his chair. ''Mr. President, I agree it's going to be a blot on you. I mean, presidents have selected folks with many problems, drug problems, even fraud problems. This is the first time I've heard of choosing a guy who's a cold-blooded murderer.''

The president held his head in his hands. ''You're no comfort at all, Paschen.'' Then he raised his head, squinted up at the other man. ''You know, you professionals bug the hell out of me. You think just because you've been around through four or five administrations, pulling wires behind the scenes, that you're so smart, so . . . *indestructible.* While we pols sweat and bust our asses to win the approval of the fickle American public every four years. Not only that, but we take responsibility for every fuckin' thing that goes wrong, while you *professionals*''—he sneered out the word—''stand around in your elevator shoes and second-guess us. But I'm fuckin' good. I can make a good case with the public.'' He sat back against the chintz flowers and smiled maliciously up at Paschen. ''*You and you alone* dealt with this guy from the start. I had only that one meeting with him—upstairs, in private. I hadn't seen him before that in twenty-five, thirty years. Who knows what happens if I can play it right? I may get renominated after all. But for that to happen, I know whose head has to roll, my friend.''

Hands in pockets, Paschen raised and lowered his heels

several times as he stared down at the disheveled commander in chief. In a cool voice he said, "I'll clean out my desk today, if that's what you want, Jack. But it remains to be seen who can achieve the greatest deniability. As you say, I'm the professional with the smarts: I'm betting *I* can."

With that he gave his chief a little mock salute, executed an about-face, and left the quarters.

ABOUT THE AUTHOR

A former newspaperwoman, ANN RIPLEY now spends her time organic gardening and writing novels. *Mulch* was the winner of the Top Hand Award, given by the Colorado Author's League, and she is the author of two other Louise Eldridge gardening mysteries. She lives with her husband, Tony, in Lyons, Colorado.

If you enjoyed MULCH, the first book in Ann Ripley's marvelous gardening mystery series, you'll love DEATH OF A GARDEN PEST, now available in paperback from Bantam Books—and you won't want to miss Ann's hair-raising new Bantam hardcover, DEATH OF A POLITICAL PLANT, coming in March 1998.

Look for all of Ann Ripley's gardening mysteries at your favorite bookstore—and please turn the page for an exciting preview of DEATH OF A POLITICAL PLANT.

DEATH OF A POLITICAL PLANT

A Gardening Mystery

Ann Ripley

IT WAS AT THE END OF A LONG DAY. THEY HAD BEEN ON LOCATION IN Manassas, Virginia, doing a show on the restoration of an Early American garden near the Occoquan River. Their attire was an echo of colonial life: Louise in a flowing mauve skirt and lace-edged blouse; and John Batchelder, her co-host, in a loose-fitting poetic shirt that emphasized his dashing looks. When they were finished there, Marty Corbin had insisted they return to the station to discuss program ideas for *Gardening with Nature.*

The producer was large, with dark, curly hair, shaggy eyebrows, and big brown eyes that most of the time were filled with life, fire, and kindliness. They sat in Marty's office for one of his typical "pow-wows," and he outlined an ambitious travel schedule that threw Louise into a profound, thoughtful silence.

Marty described his ideas with dramatic gestures of his big hands: "We're not gonna be one of these garden programs that think the East Coast, with its rich, acidic soil, is all there is. We're gonna travel, Louise, and we're not going to leave out one growing zone. We're even going to Hawaii and

Alaska, how'dja like that? We want all fifty states to watch your program, not just the thirteen original.''

John Batchelder, slouched in a chair opposite hers, smiled and nodded approval. ''It's high time we did it, Marty.''

She didn't know what to say. The Eldridge home life had already been seriously impinged upon by her full-time job and her extra voice-over job with Atlas Mowers. She wondered how much more away-time her family could handle?

Marty read her expression. ''Think of it this way, Louise: at least it will discourage houseguests.'' He grinned at her, anxious to have her happy.

It seemed a propitious time to ask *him* a favor in return. She laid out her proposal for a two-part program on the president's environmental bill, making it sound as if the idea came from her.

''You're kiddin'.'' His eyebrows skidded down over his skeptical eyes.

''Why would I be kidding? I am quite serious, Marty. The bill just got through Congress. It's timely, and the topic merits it.''

He hooted. ''Timely, all right: just in time for the November vote. Hey, I know you have a pipeline to the president. Don't tell me *this* show is going to save his ass: that man's down the tubes, Louise; hate to tell you.''

She saw he was hungry and impatient, ready to go home to one of his wife Steffi's fabulous meals. ''Okay, but can we talk about it again?''

''Sure we can, when my stomach isn't protesting.'' They left Marty's office, and the staff drifted off.

When she gathered her things and walked to the lobby exit,

a stranger was waiting, smiling at her. It took her a moment to recognize the man, and when she did, her heart began to pound. For an instant, she was swept back to her college days and a romantic interlude in Washington, D.C.

"It couldn't be. Not Jay McCormick."

"Oh, yes, it could be," said the voice, a familiar, jesting baritone.

Tall and slightly stoop-shouldered, he approached her slowly. He came right up and took both her hands in his and gave her one of his crooked, Irish smiles. He planted the faintest of kisses on her lips, and it made her tingle.

"Louise, you dear thing, you haven't changed at all."

Standing before her was her former boyfriend from that brief summer more than two decades ago when they were both graduate students at Georgetown University. His face was unremarkable, with an anonymity that made you wonder what he really looked like once he was out of your presence. No high cheekbones or other defining features; sandy, nondescript hair that tended to fall in his face. Pale blue eyes: again, unremarkable. And yet, a man with an inner light, who could make her heart beat faster simply because he cared more about other human beings than he cared about himself.

That quality had nearly persuaded her to commit herself to Jay McCormick, to go forward into life like a team of missionaries and try to make the world better for suffering people. Then, through a fluke, along came Bill Eldridge from Harvard to the same campus to substitute for another lecturer at Georgetown's International Institute; she turned onto another path with a man who soon became a spy for his country.

"Outside of the glasses, you haven't changed, either, Jay."

But even as she spoke, she saw the worry lines in his face: what kind of disappointments had he suffered during the past two decades? He looked to be on hard times: his dress shirt and pants were scruffy.

"Look a little closer, Louise. I'm having one hell of a hard time right now. I came here today because I sort of need a friend. You may not have heard of what I've been doing."

"Oh, I heard a couple of things, that you were speech writing—or was it reporting—out in California."

"I've done both. I live in Sacramento. But I've been in Washington for a little while now, five months, actually. I've heard about your show and how well you're doing. I've even seen you on that TV ad promoting some mower."

"Yeah," she said sheepishly, "on-air spokesman for the Atlas mulching mower. It helps us make ends meet at the Eldridge house."

"And I also got wind of your detecting." There came that smile again. "Pretty cool of you, Louise, solving two crimes."

"All of a sudden, I have a career of my own, Jay. But what kind of a problem are you having? How can I help you?"

He looked around, as if to be sure no one was listening. No fear of that. Channel Five's crew had gone home; only a couple of engineers were left, busy at their control panels. "Let's just say I'm in a bit of, uh, hot water, and I need a safe place to stay until I finish some writing. Do you know anywhere I can hole up? I'm trying to avoid hotels and motels. Checked out of one yesterday morning and ended up sleeping in my car."

As always, she decided quickly. "Come to our place. Bill and I live eight miles from here; it's just south of Alexandria.

We have empty bedrooms, because both of our girls are away."

"Where are your girls?"

"Martha goes to Northwestern, but this summer she's involved in a self-help project in Detroit. Janie, our sixteen-year-old, is in Mexico City for three weeks, helping build houses for people."

Jay raised his eyebrows. "You and Bill have done something right with those kids. As for your offer of a room, that would be perfect, Louise. I won't bother you. I'll eat out; if I could just stay for a week or so, it would be a lifesaver."

A week! The warmth of this reunion suddenly evaporated, and cold reality set in. There went that window of opportunity, that interlude alone with Bill, without kids, without company, maybe making mad love on the living room floor. It dissolved instantly in the name of an old and once very torrid friendship.

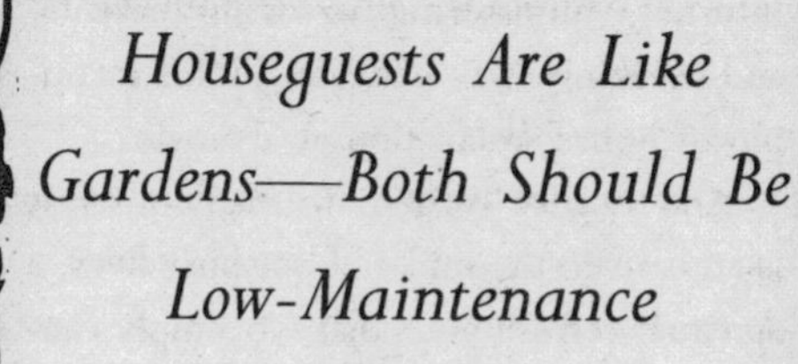

Houseguests Are Like Gardens—Both Should Be Low-Maintenance

Big bluegrass lawns and fussy flowers such as black-spot-prone tea roses are habits we can give up, just like smoking. They don't fit into the American gardening scene as they used to, for leisure is ephemeral. Few of us live the life of the Victorian lady who had the time to walk up and down the borders with a basket on her arm, dallying with the flowers and picking off diseased leaves by hand. Instead, we are a nation of frenetic, fast-moving people, balancing our time between jobs, shopping, errands, taking kids to game practice, plugging into the

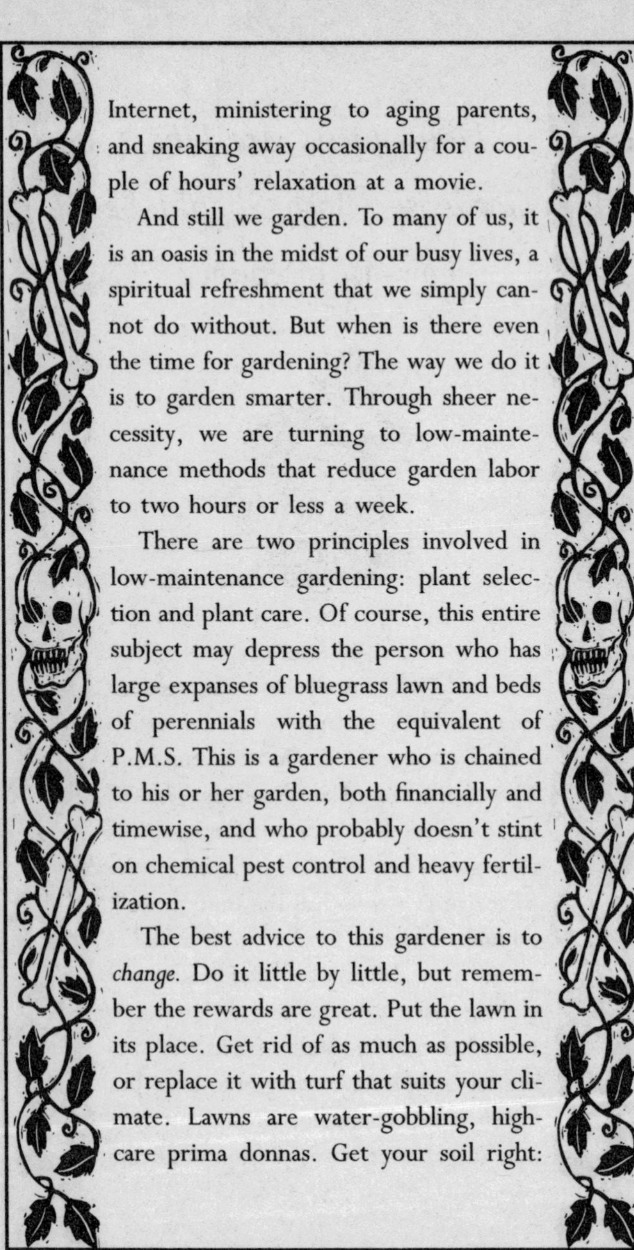

Internet, ministering to aging parents, and sneaking away occasionally for a couple of hours' relaxation at a movie.

And still we garden. To many of us, it is an oasis in the midst of our busy lives, a spiritual refreshment that we simply cannot do without. But when is there even the time for gardening? The way we do it is to garden smarter. Through sheer necessity, we are turning to low-maintenance methods that reduce garden labor to two hours or less a week.

There are two principles involved in low-maintenance gardening: plant selection and plant care. Of course, this entire subject may depress the person who has large expanses of bluegrass lawn and beds of perennials with the equivalent of P.M.S. This is a gardener who is chained to his or her garden, both financially and timewise, and who probably doesn't stint on chemical pest control and heavy fertilization.

The best advice to this gardener is to *change.* Do it little by little, but remember the rewards are great. Put the lawn in its place. Get rid of as much as possible, or replace it with turf that suits your climate. Lawns are water-gobbling, high-care prima donnas. Get your soil right:

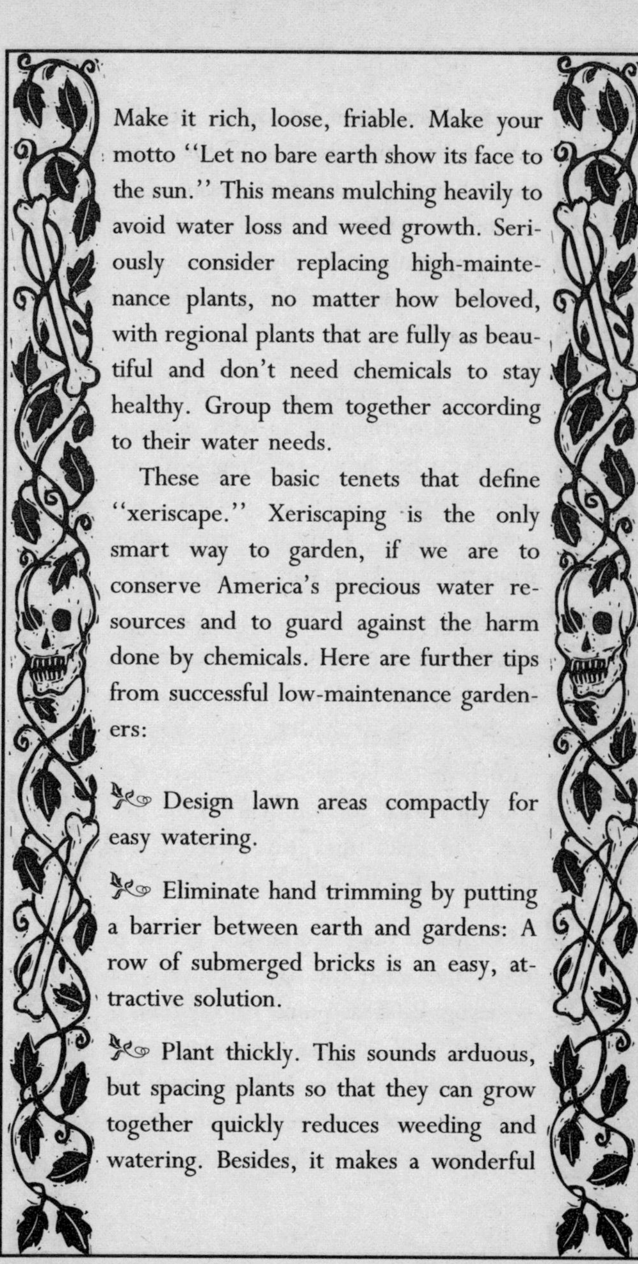

Make it rich, loose, friable. Make your motto "Let no bare earth show its face to the sun." This means mulching heavily to avoid water loss and weed growth. Seriously consider replacing high-maintenance plants, no matter how beloved, with regional plants that are fully as beautiful and don't need chemicals to stay healthy. Group them together according to their water needs.

These are basic tenets that define "xeriscape." Xeriscaping is the only smart way to garden, if we are to conserve America's precious water resources and to guard against the harm done by chemicals. Here are further tips from successful low-maintenance gardeners:

- Design lawn areas compactly for easy watering.
- Eliminate hand trimming by putting a barrier between earth and gardens: A row of submerged bricks is an easy, attractive solution.
- Plant thickly. This sounds arduous, but spacing plants so that they can grow together quickly reduces weeding and watering. Besides, it makes a wonderful

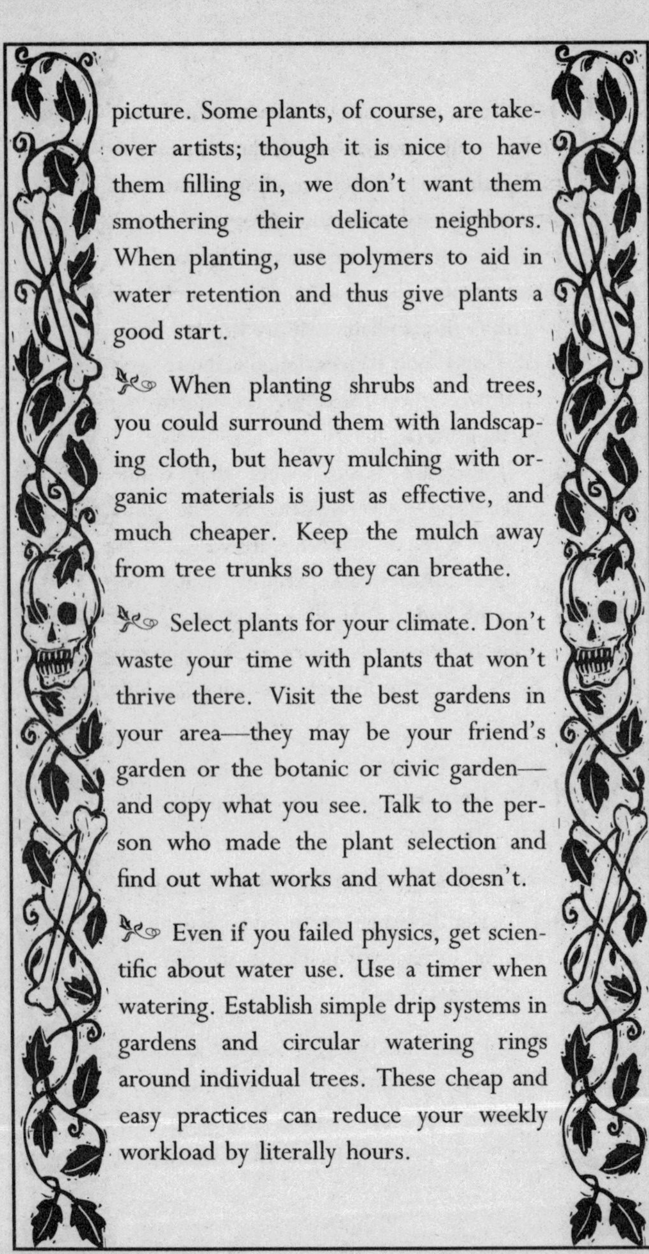

picture. Some plants, of course, are take-over artists; though it is nice to have them filling in, we don't want them smothering their delicate neighbors. When planting, use polymers to aid in water retention and thus give plants a good start.

When planting shrubs and trees, you could surround them with landscaping cloth, but heavy mulching with organic materials is just as effective, and much cheaper. Keep the mulch away from tree trunks so they can breathe.

Select plants for your climate. Don't waste your time with plants that won't thrive there. Visit the best gardens in your area—they may be your friend's garden or the botanic or civic garden—and copy what you see. Talk to the person who made the plant selection and find out what works and what doesn't.

Even if you failed physics, get scientific about water use. Use a timer when watering. Establish simple drip systems in gardens and circular watering rings around individual trees. These cheap and easy practices can reduce your weekly workload by literally hours.

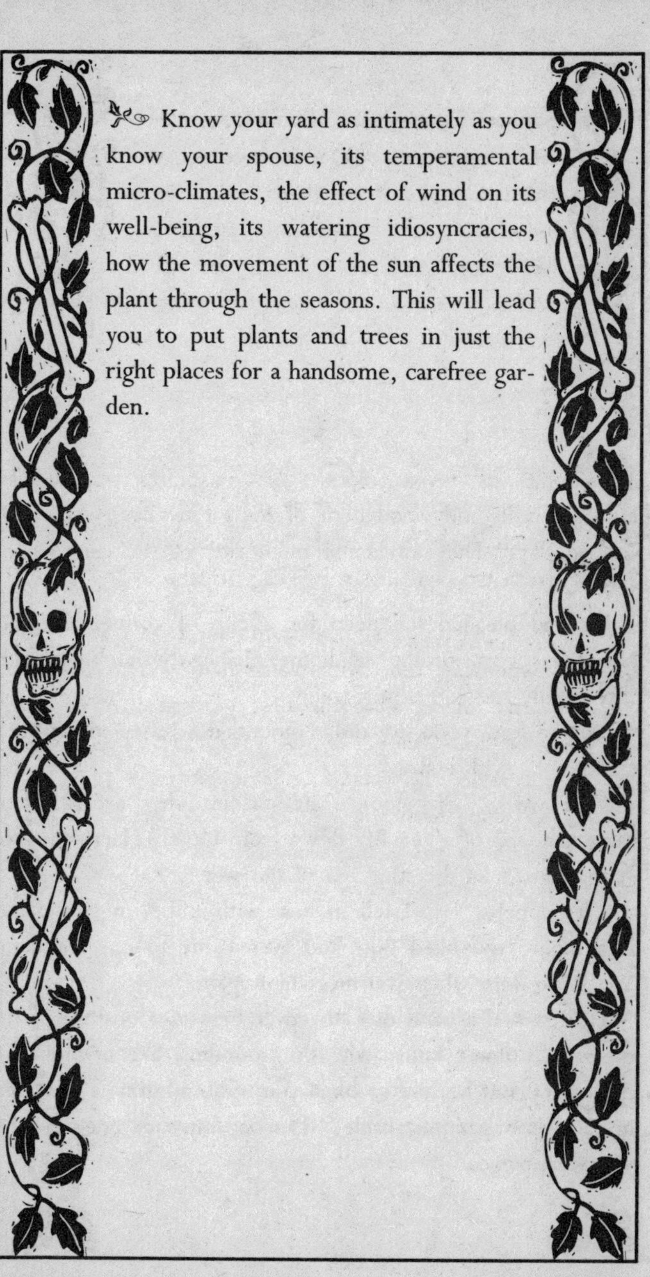

Know your yard as intimately as you know your spouse, its temperamental micro-climates, the effect of wind on its well-being, its watering idiosyncracies, how the movement of the sun affects the plant through the seasons. This will lead you to put plants and trees in just the right places for a handsome, carefree garden.

THE ODORS OF FRYING ONIONS AND DRAUGHT BEER, SOAKED into the walls and wood floor of Joe's Raw Bar, went with college days. They awakened memories of the summer of 1975.

Jay had pleaded the need for a cup of coffee, and this nostalgic bar was on the way home. He slowly shook his head. "We really had something going."

"For a few weeks we did," amended Louise, stirring her cream soda with a straw.

"Six weeks." Jay looked straight into her eyes. "Then came that son-of-a-gun Bill down from bloody Harvard." He grinned, to take the sting out of the words.

"It happens, Jay. I fell in love with Bill. I'm sorry, but remember, you liked Bill. You even came to our wedding. You'll like him when you meet him again."

He reached a hand over to cover hers as a gesture of remorse. "I don't know why I'm sounding like a vindictive spoilsport. But he sure grabbed you up in a hurry." The pain in his eyes was unmistakable. "I turned my back one day, and you were gone."

She realized how selfish it was to reminisce about those days. To her, it was romantic, but to Jay, it was painful. Back then, she had found him to be a man for all occasions: They went to foreign films and art events, explored Virginia waterfalls, and hiked the Shenandoah trail, Jay adroitly leading the way over rocks and ridges. She remembered best the simple walks along the C & O Canal at twilight and the canoe trips on the Potomac. Jay would beach the boat and hide their packed lunches so cleverly no animal could find them, while they skinny-dipped in the river.

Her face flushed at the memory. When she looked over at Jay, his pale eyes were shining with the same devotion that she had seen there twenty years ago. "Louise, we would have been great together. Maybe I would have done better if only you'd been with me."

"Jay, we both know this is useless. Let's just remember those lovely days, and not regret anything. You married, didn't you? I thought I heard that." She stopped, wishing she hadn't brought up his marriage. Who knows what happened to it?

His eyes changed, grew wary. "I married a wonderful woman named Lannie Gordon; she was in law school at Georgetown. We settled in Sacramento after Lannie got a job out there. She was very successful—became the youngest partner in her law firm. Meantime, I got into investigative reporting at the *Sacramento Union*. Specialized in Death Row cases that were faulty and got a number of people freed, too. If anything in life was satisfying, that was."

"Was?"

"Lannie had a baby, and that meant getting a house, and Lannie wanted a pretty fancy house. I sure wasn't able to carry my part of the financial load on a reporter's salary, so I ended up joining a p.r. firm to make some bucks." He attempted a smile that was more of a grimace. "I became expert at writing speeches for candidates; I'd write speeches for anybody, as long as they were a paying client."

"So you felt like a sellout."

The faded eyes looked at her from underneath the unruly brows. "Yeah. I was no different from Lannie." Then he frowned down at the bar-finish tabletop. "Even with those concessions, I haven't made the marriage work; that left our daughter, Melissa, squarely in the middle."

"And Lannie . . ."

"She's a big-time lawyer now. She's here in D.C., a top litigator and lobbyist for the tobacco industry."

"I think I've seen her on television, speaking up for the tobacco companies. Shoulder-length red hair, very serious?"

"Yes, that's Lannie. We divorced five years ago, and a year after that, she moved to Washington for this new job and took Melissa with her. Like a dope, I went along with the idea, and that caused all the trouble. Melissa was nine then, thirteen now. She and I missed each other so much that I went to court to change things, and I succeeded beyond my wildest hopes. Lannie was upset, of course: She loves the girl just as much as I do. Melissa is wonderful and beautiful."

He strained for an image special enough for his daughter. "Just about as beautiful as that first day of spring. Loves to read and write, loves animals. She has a canny nature, and I like that because she reminds me of *me,* but maybe that comes from her mother, too."

"You were so idealistic. Was Lannie that way, too?"

He stared off into space, remembering. "Yes, like we all were in the seventies: idealistic, but with our old values undercut by the confusion of the sixties. She may still be idealistic way underneath; it was the job and the success that changed her. Maybe it's because she grew up on that pathetic little farm in southern Indiana, with so little in the way of material advantages, that she needs them so much now. Once her career got going out in California, it was as if we were two of the earth's plates that drifted apart."

He shook his head. "The funny thing is, I still love her, and if she ever asked me to come back, I'd do it. But she's heartbroken because of the judge's decision: He gave me custody for all of the school year. What really wrenched her was that our daughter got on the stand and told the judge she prefers to live with me."

"What a thing for a mother to hear!"

"I feel sorry for her, too, Louise, but what's going to happen is for the best. In a week, Melissa drives back with me to California, and then will stay with her mother in Great Falls at Christmas and for three months during the summer." His face clouded up again.

"Why are you concerned, Jay? It sounds like a great outcome for you."

"It's because my ex-wife's so darned disappointed, Louise. It's as if I've snatched her soul away. She firmly believes Melissa is better off with her: She gave her the best of everything and even took her to Europe a couple of times. I think the girl makes Lannie feel like a better *person.* So now, I'm hoping she doesn't do something desperate, like taking Melissa abroad to live. She has a house in Ireland, and God knows she has the money for the two of them to just emigrate.''

He leaned forward, elbows on the table, intent on his story. ''Right after the judge's decree in February, which takes effect next Friday, I flew here to D.C. to check things out. I was afraid Lannie might take off with our daughter then. I felt terrible spying on her, but I had to. Then, I came across a story that I first got wind of last fall in California. Got a deal going to stay in Washington, and I've been, well, working here ever since. And keeping an eye on Melissa, unbeknownst to my ex.''

He shook his head, as if he had dwelled enough on the matter, and then looked at the clock on the greasy tan wall. ''Louise, it's after six: Are you sure we aren't running overtime?''

She had called Bill from her office at Channel Five, telling him she was bringing Jay home. He sounded a little put out, but he remembered Jay. She told him they were going out to get coffee first. ''We'd better go, so I can dream up something for supper.''

Jay slid out of the booth, protesting. ''Louise, I don't need care and feeding—just a room where I can stay out of sight.''

''You're having dinner with us, don't be silly. Bill will be glad to see you again.''

As they walked to the door, Jay looked around the bar. He said, ''This place is just like our old college hangouts in Georgetown.''

She smiled up at him. ''That's why I brought you here.''

He followed her the eight miles home on the crowded highway in a dull-colored old Ford that looked like it wouldn't